Mystic Waters
Out of the Blue

By

Loretta Rose Didrikson

Copyright © 2015 Loretta Rose Didrikson

Mystic Waters Out of the Blue is a work of fiction. Characters and incidents either are the result of the author's imagination or are used fictitiously. Any resemblance to actual persons, living or dead is completely coincidental.

All rights reserved.

ISBN-10: 1517466768
ISBN-13: 978-1517466763

DEDICATION

I dedicate this novel to my mother, whose love and encouragement has never wavered. To my father, a tower of strength and wisdom. I love you both.

†

To my husband, whose love and support has been a beacon of light shining brightly through the densest of fogs.

†

My daughters, you are my heart and the roots of my courage. I was blessed the day you came into my life.

†

To my oldest granddaughter, Tajia, your beautiful soul shines through your smile every day, and your inner strength is astounding.

†

To my youngest granddaughter, Shae, whose imagination and enthusiasm changed our bedtime stories into settings for our dreams. You inspire me.

†

To my sister, my friend, and fellow author, our paths changed the day we met some thirty years ago. Thank you Jeanne Lahn, for the love, laughter, and tears we have shared.

†

I would like to send a special thanks to Teresa Johnson, Lorraine Smith, and friend Colleen, for taking on the gruesome job of proofreading and editing. You ladies rolled up your sleeves, dug in, and helped me move forward.

Prologue

During the years, (1958-1963), a Twins Cities ammunition plant dumped over fourteen hundred sealed barrels into Lake Superior. The reports claim, that the contents of the barrels are non-toxic consisting of dead ammunition and warhead parts presenting no threat to the environment.

Indirectly related to barrels, the Environmental Protections Agency (EPA), receives a small grant to collect data onboard a floating research lab to study the lake. It's anchored on the United States side of the Canadian and U.S. invisible border dividing Lake Superior.

Meranda Michaels, a young biologist, lands what she feels is her dream job at the Environmental Protection Agency. The pay is minimal, but the experience is priceless. She will remain onboard the lab for a 90 day period recording data from the lake. Her boss, insists she takes a tour of the lab, before she accepts the position.

As they leave the marina's channel, the wind is light, and the lake is calm. The clear blue sky mirrors the glass blue waters, a beautiful morning on the big lake.

Soon after, Meranda notices in the distant, a wall of dark swirling clouds sitting on the horizon, and her stomach tightened.

The marine radio started screaming that there are two fast approaching storms cells on a collision path. Unable to turn back to the marina or reach a safe harbor, they're forced to ride the storm out in open waters.

The cabin cruiser is well built, but proves no match for two super cells and sinks. Meranda quickly accepts her fate and stops fighting to survive. This lake has taken many lives and will now take hers.

Until she opens her eyes and finds herself in a cave.

1

The warm wind blew against her face and Meranda relaxed; she felt carefree for the moment. The gradual disappearing shoreline surrounds them in many shades of blue, as they head east toward the horizon.

Meranda blinked a few times, as she stared at the dense black wall of clouds that appeared out of nowhere. "Pete--is that fog?"

Pete's eyes narrowed at the storm front rolling straight at them, he had checked the marine forecast and all had been clear. However, on this big sea-like-lake the weather can change quickly.

He needed to go below and make sure the emergency radio was working. He turned to Meranda and asked her to take the wheel keeping a northeast heading.

Meranda jumped to her feet ready to meet the first mate's duties, and on cue the butterflies in her stomach released. She placed her hands at the ten and two o'clock position like her father had taught her when she first learned to drive, and firmly took the helm.

"I'll be right back!" Pete yelled before disappearing below deck.

No sooner had the small cabin door shut behind him, and the marine radio blared…beep, beep, beep…This is the NOAA weather service issuing a small craft advisory for Lake Superior and surrounding waters. A fast moving front, out of the northeast is approaching with winds gusting to 40 mph producing waves up to 15 feet. It will reach the Knife River Marina at 10:05 A.M. Friday, April 9th, 2011. Repeat…this is the NOAA weather service with a small craft advisory…take immediate shelter. This storm is fast moving and can produce waves in excess of 15 feet.

Meranda's muscles flooded with adrenaline as fear ripped through every fiber of her body and she wasn't sure what to do. Pete emerged from the kid-size door of the cabin. His eyes scanned the horizon and settled on the fast approaching wall of terror.

"Meranda," Pete yelled "We are not going to make it back to the marina, or the safe harbor, we're too far out."

Pete heard the alarm in his own voice and quickly regained his composure. He wanted to reassure Meranda that they were going to be okay. "It's going to get rough, but I have weathered worse situations." Pete glanced at the storm, trying to gauge how long it will take to reach them.

Meranda watched as the peaceful glass surface broke into rhythmic waves. In the next moment, the boat jerked sharply to the right and Meranda smashed into the steering wheel. The tossing and turning made the cabin cruiser feel like they were playing *London Bridges* between the now larger more violent waves.

"What do you need me to do?" Meranda offered sticking her chin out, shoulders back ready to take orders.

"There's nothing we can do, but ride it out. I'll drop the anchor for added stabilization. In the cabin, the seats have harness', it's the safest place. You might get seasick with waves this high." Pete tried to prepare her for what may be the ride of her life. "All the equipment down there is secured."

Pete radiated confidence. His eyes shined, and his hair danced in the wind. Meranda noticed his eyes had changed and were now a dark blue. Something was different about him as he anticipated the danger. He connected in some way to the approaching storm.

Without warning, the boat twisted, then swirled on the wave that had captured them. The organized mound of water began to lift the cruiser like a toy boat. They climbed higher and higher, until all Meranda could see was the sky. The wave spun the boat 180 degrees before it dissolved beneath them, dropping the boat on its side.

The boat corrected itself upright, and sent anything not nailed down slamming to the bow. With a death grip, Meranda locked her fingers around the railing, to keep from going overboard.

She tried to regain her balance by spreading her feet farther apart, it helped a little. Meranda turned around to see what side of the boat the storm was on, when a huge wall of water crashed over the side, drenching her. Another roller hit right behind the first, pushing her across the deck slamming her against the wall.

Pete reached her in a flash, "I think it is time for you to go below and buckled in." He looked slightly amused at Meranda's current state of wetness.

"I'm fine; it's been awhile since I've been on rough seas." Meranda replied.

"True enough, but there's nothing we can do out here, and I am responsible for your safety." Considerate of her feelings, Pete still wanted her safely buckled in.

He reached out his hand to steady her, as the next set of icy cold rollers hit, sending her soaking wet body smashing into his. He stood solid as if anchored to the floor. The next wave grabbed the cruiser and carry them straight to the top of the wave, as they teetered back and forth. Meranda couldn't see the lake anymore and braced herself for the drop, digging her fingers into Pete's arms.

Pete held Meranda tightly to prevent her from slipping away from him. Safely locked-in Pete's arms, Meranda looked over his shoulder and saw the swirling lake instead of the boats floor. She went weak behind the knees and her whole body shook with fear. The boat dropped. Then leveled out, at least to it normal rocking and twisting motion.

Pete gently suggested, "There's a warm blanket below."

Meranda let Pete keep hold of her, while he directed her toward the cabin door. Once below she did feel safer. Everything was spotless; the deep rich color of cherry wood encased most of the small cabin area. The polished wood glowed with warmth.

"Would you like a towel or a blanket?" Pete asked.

Meranda's teeth were starting to chatter. "Blanket, please. Are y-y-you sure there is n-n-nothing you need me to do?" Meranda quickly sat down in the chair letting Pete buckle her in, and tuck a warm blanket around her.

"I'm going back on deck to make sure everything's secure." Pete ducked out of the tight fitting door as it slammed behind him.

He faced the northeast and breathed in the turbulent wind. Pete dropped his shoulders and breathed out, letting go of the stress he had been feeling; now that Meranda was safely below.

He felt his scalp tingle as his muscles began to twitch; the electrical current in the air cracked and sizzled around him. He loved being in the middle of nature's fury. More lightening crackled and snapped, hitting the water ten feet from the boat creating a hiss of steam.

Pete tossed back his head and laughed. He felt alive, more alive than he had felt in a longtime. Pete knew he should go down below before he answered the powerful pull of the lake. He belonged out here, and not cooped up indoors shuffling papers.

Below, the marine radio warned of a second front coming from the southwest heading northeast.

With this new information, Meranda unbuckled her harness and tried to get to the door to warn Pete. As she reached the narrow stairs the boat whipedher backwards, and she cuts her arm on the harness' buckle.

Blood rushed to the surface and runs down her arm staining her white shirt red. Meranda then ripped off a piece of her shirt off with her teeth and wrapped it around the gash, all the while being tossed around like a rag doll. She had to warn Pete about the second front heading straight for them.

Shifting her body forward she banged on the door trying to get it open. The boat gave her a helping hand smashing her against the solid wood with unbelievable force. Pain ripped through her body and she instinctively tucked her arm into her side. She didn't think anything was broken, but possibly dislocated by the angle her arm hung at.

Using her uninjured side, she threw all her weight against the door. Coupled with the forward momentum of the next set of rollers; the door flew open. Meranda went sailing onto the deck. The boat twisted, tossing her across the wooden planks and landing her sprawled at Pete's feet.

From the floor, Meranda looked up, and all she saw was a huge mass of water swirling and gathering power before descending on the boat. She thought back to the pictures at the agency, of the powerful swells splitting ore boats in two. She felt small.

The wave unleashed its fury, but the sea worthy boat held together and started to climb up the side of the huge mountain of water. Once they reached the peak, everything went still, until it dissolved beneath them. The boat landed on its side, and where the floor had been, was now a vortex of black water.

Meranda didn't have the boat cradle her to safety this time. She dropped into the icy waters gasping as it engulfed her. She had instinctively filled her lungs with air before she went under, and began to fight for her life.

With her one good arm she tried to swim, keeping the injured arm tucked tightly under her breast. The frigid waters of Lake Superior numbed her pain as she tried to make her way to the surface; toward air, toward life.

Meranda had heard that before you die, your whole life flashed before your eyes. For her, it was her last night with Mitch, her high school sweetheart that played out before her. He seemed so real she felt she could reach out and touch him.

Meranda saw herself looking over at Mitch, mentally painting a picture of him in her mind. She was trying to record all the details she could about the man she loved and this memorable milestone.

It was a moonless night. They were driving on a two-lane road in rural Minnesota. Graduation night; *Class of 99*. With the formalities behind them, Meranda thought of all the parties they had been invited to. In a small community, everyone took turns going to everyone else's party. Same people, same food, different houses.

She dreamily eyed Mitch and smiled, noticing how his sandy brown hair was sculpted around his perfectly shaped ears. Even though his freshly cut hair was short, you could see a slight wave that promised a curl when it grew longer. He looked striking in his crisp white shirt stressed against his muscled shoulders. Muscles that a farm boy develops at an early age from chores.

In his stocking feet he was six inches taller than Meranda; add cowboy boots and he tower over her five foot six inch slender frame. Meranda imagined them in their golden years, looking back at this night as they sat on their porch swing. "What are you so dreamy eyed about, babe?" Mitch broke into her thoughts.

"I'm trying to remember everything about this day," and on cue her favorite song began to belt from the radio. *Crazy*, by Patsy Cline. Meranda couldn't help but sing along, even though she sang off-key. She and Mitch had dated since the seventh grade, and knew each other well, so not carrying a tune was no surprise to him.

Meranda had eyed Mitch suspiciously when he pulled the truck over to the side of the road. He shut the engine off and got out. He crossed over to her side and opened the door.

He dropped to one knee and Meranda's eyes filled with tears and her hands began to shake. She closed her eyes tight forcing the tears to stream down her face.

"For goodness sake woman, I haven't said anything yet. Meranda C. Michaels, would you do me the honor of marrying me? After college, that is." Mitch beamed up at her with a wide smile. "Well, will you marry me? He asked again.

"I will. I mean, yes." Meranda held out her left hand with her ring finger slightly raised and tried to stop her hand from shaking. Mitch fumbled, trying to get the ring out of the red velvety box and placed it on her finger. He let out a sigh not realizing he had forgotten to breathe.

"Mitch it's beautiful. How--I mean when?"

"I've had plenty of time to save up for it. We've been together forever. I love you babe." Mitch stood up and kissed her so tenderly she thought the wind had blown across her lips.

"I love you too." Meranda glowed as she wrapped her arms around him, returning that tender kiss.

"Well we better get going or Jena will never forgive me, or you, for not telling her immediately that we are now officially engaged." Mitch jumped up into his seat with a satisfied grin on his face, shoulders back, and chest out, feeling ten feet tall. Meranda wanted to scoot next to him, but her seat belt wouldn't allow it, so she slid her hand over his; she just needed to touch him.

Having saved the best party for last, Meranda couldn't wait to show her best friend her ring.

Jena's parents knew how to throw a party. In the barn, there'd be makeshift tables of plywood covered with red checkered tablecloths filled with crock pots of food. They'd have karaoke and dancing inside and a roaring bonfire outside that would light the sky, but leave plenty of dark places for a stolen kiss. Meranda knew this party would be full of memories.

"Mitch! Watch out!" Was all Meranda had time to say before the eighteen wheeler crossed into their lane, broadsiding Mitch's side of the truck. Mitch had cranked the steering wheel hard to the right, avoiding a head on collision that surely would have killed them both.

The driver woke up and swerved to the left, but not before crushing Mitch's side of the truck sending them rolling end over end. The pine trees finally stopped them as they settled into the ravine.

Meranda's shoulder strap on the seat belt had tightened at the first sign of trouble, yet her head still bounced off the windows.

Time stopped and her world was literally upside down. Meranda looked over at her fiancé and struggled to free herself from her confines as she shook uncontrollably.

Mitch's eyes were open, but lifeless, as he floated to the sway of the water that was rushing through the shattered window.

A red cloud was forming like a satin pillow from the gash on his head. She tried to reach out to him before her world went dark. The last thing she remembered was the sound of a door being pried open and arms reaching in to pull her from the wreck.

Loretta Rose Didrikson

2

"Meranda breathe! Breathe! Come on--you can do it. Breathe–harder. There's condensed levels of oxygen in the water. Meranda--you have to try harder! Meranda--I know you can hear me. Breathe--open your eyes and breathe."

Pete tried desperately to bring Meranda back to consciousness. He was sure he had gotten to her in time. He just had to get her brain to wake up and fight.

"Meranda, please...breathe." Pete squared his shoulders, he was not going to give up on her. Meranda, on the other hand, was ready to see her mother and father, and Mitch. She felt numb and peaceful ...now if Pete would only be quiet and quit yelling at her.

Pete started to fear Meranda was gone when her eyes popped open wild with fear. She immediately tried to claw her way to the surface.

"Meranda, calm down, I know it's hard, but you must stop fighting. You are using up precious oxygen."

Meranda stopped fighting and went still. She wondered if she was dead, because she could no longer feel her body. For some reason Pete's voice was calming… and in her head. She locked onto his eyes.

"I've put a film over your face that'll allow you to breathe in air, but not the water. There you go. It will get easier to breathe, and then I'll get you out of here."

Pete's non-voice was soothing, but she wondered how he could be talking to her without moving his mouth. She struggled to clear her head and sucked like a fish out of water. It did get easier to breathe as her lungs filled up with air, the unbearable pain began to subside. She didn't know how, but the water was not coming back into her opened mouth.

Clarity returned to her brain as it received the oxygen. She started questioning whether Pete's voice had been in her head or not. He hadn't moved his mouth and they were under the water. She searched for answers until she felt like she was going to lose control again, this was all so surreal.

Pete knew nothing would make sense to her right now, so he asked her to trust him. He had no clue that asking her to trust him was a tall order, but she didn't have a choice. Her limbs wouldn't move anymore, and she couldn't feel anything. She felt like a pair of eyeballs willing her lungs to move in and out.

Meranda shook her head yes, but her eyes looked like a trapped animal. With her injured arm tucked tightly between her body and his, she let him wrap his muscular arms around her and she gave in to him.

She buried her face into his chest, and in the next moment they were moving fast. She bravely peeked over his shoulder at the water that was streaming past them; it looked like a water tunnel. She relaxed. He was getting her out of here like he promised.

At that moment, she did trust him, and she hadn't trusted anyone since her high school sweetheart, Mitch. Meranda closed her eyes, she felt so tired and broken.

When she woke up she remembered being in the water and now she wasn't. She sat up and a fur blanket pooled in her lap. She winced from the pain that shot through her shoulder letting her know she was definitely alive. Her eyes darted around assessing her surroundings, she was in a cave.

The dim light reflected off the water making it dance off the smooth contoured walls. The beauty around her was mesmerizing and the sparkling lights were breathtaking.

Meranda eyed the layers of the cream colored walls, and it made her think of an orange ice cream bar. The carved walls had captured the motion of the wind and forever freezing it in time.

She was wrapped up in her stunning surroundings and hadn't realized she was alone, until she heard voices off in the distant. Her head felt foggy and her thoughts confused, but she was sure there were voices somewhere in the distances. When Pete had first talked to her and it was in her head his voice was clear, but these voices were muted.

She cocked her head to the right and listened hard. The muffled tones were external and coming from what looked like a tunnel off to her right. She was sure that was Pete's voice--was he calling for help?

Her flight or fight response kicked in and she started to rock back and forth taking in controlled deep breaths, trying to suppress a full-blown panic attack. She noticed that she was on a smooth bench like ledge behind some rocks. She peeked over and saw the cave's angular floor that led right back into the water like a funnel.

Meranda wanted nothing to do with that cold water. She felt scared and started to softly cry, the warm salty tears stung her face.

She hated feeling vulnerable, so she dried her tears and clenched her jaw together to absorb the pain and stood up. The pain in her shoulder was severe, and her head felt heavy, as if she was being pulled headfirst back into the water. She compensated the feeling by leaning towards the wall, and began to inch her way toward the voices.

She didn't get far before she stumbled and lost her balance, sending her sliding down that vortex shaped funnel and straight toward the water. She used her good hand as a rake trying to hook her fingers onto anything that would stop her fall.

Meranda came to a dead stop as her foot met with a small protrusion. Assuming it was a rock, she teetered back and forth trying to get her balance under control. Her leg was trembling so badly she wasn't sure it was going to support her. She had to locked her knee to stop the shaking.

Not daring to move a muscle, she molded herself to the wall. Her heart was pounding so hard she thought that alone was going to push her off her perch.

Pete? Hello…?" Meranda listened as it echoed off the walls before disappearing. "Hello?" She broke into a soft sob as she continued to yell for help.

Nothing came.

Thinking she was on her own, she bravely peeled her hand off the slick rock and inched it around feeling for something to grab onto. She found a rock off to the right but slightly out of her reach. She walked her fingers up getting as close to the rock as she could, then pushed onto her tiptoe, using her free leg to offset her balance.

With a slight push she was able to lock her fingertips into a small indent. Meranda felt dangerously stretched between the rock her toe still rested on and the ledge her fingertips had dug into.

She remained unmoving trying to give her limbs time to regain their strength. Meranda thought about the rock climbing class that high school had offered, but at the time felt it was a waste of time. A few tips would be useful now.

Her free foot searched for something to push against, and she connected with a rock higher up from the one she now stood on. Bending her knee at a forty five degree angle gave her the momentum she needed to push upward.

Meranda slowly inch her way to the flat ledge that led to safety. She hoisted herself onto the platform and clung to the rocks like a wet leaf on a window.

Knowing she couldn't lay there forever, she crawled over to the boulders and used them to help her stand up. She was going to find those voices one way or another.

Leaning harder into the wall, she braced her feet outward pushing against the slope. Pinching her lips together she took baby steps toward the tunnel. She had a few choice words for Pete when she saw him.

As she drew closer, she saw there were three tunnels. Deciding the middle tunnel was where the voices were coming from, she ducked inside its mouth. Meranda felt confident in her choice, despite the cavern's acoustics distorting the voices.

The walls had the same beautiful swirling orange and white coloring, only with added silver flecks that glittered like tiny stars. Despite feeling terrified she couldn't ignore the beauty. Little beams of light streamed through the cracks and allowed her to see details in otherwise dim light.

Keeping her hand connected to the wall she pressed her cheek against the cool silky stone and rested a moment. When she surged forward she noticed the floor had started a gradual descent, and the light was rapidly decreasing. Her stomach tightened sending out a warning.

Meranda continued to tap her foot out in front of her before taking the next step, making sure the ground was solid. The tunnel wound to the right and then the left. She recorded to memory the turns in case she needed to backtrack. It reminded her of the House of Horrors at the carnival; and this was horrifying.

The tunnel rounded off to the right and when she turned the corner the cave's floor disappeared from under her. She screamed louder than she ever thought possible, hurting her throat. Meranda grabbed at the air, free-falling through the blackness, not knowing if there's was even a bottom that would end her life.

Meranda splashed into the water that thankfully broke her fall. When she hit the bottom of the pool, pain shot through her body and jolted out the top of her head, before she popped back up to the surface.

She grabbed the ledge and hung on for dear life. Her head was spinning and she knew she had to get out of the water before she passed out. The pool wasn't that deep so she went back down pushing hard against the bottom. She sprang halfway out of the water and launched herself on the ledge like a dolphin.

Meranda rolled pressing herself tightly against the wall and passed out. When she came to, she was vomiting, but it tasted like bile not blood, which was a blessing, "Please somebody help me," she broke into tears as a new fear took over. Pain riveted throughout her body rendering her immobile. She crumbled into herself as the blackness surrounded her.

Meranda felt hopeless, but blinked repeatedly trying to adjust her vision to the darkness. Her stomach twisted in knots and her chest squeezed so tight from fear it felt like she was going to suffocate. Meranda knew she wasn't going to climb out of this rock tomb.

"Help--me--Pete--please," she softly asked the darkness. Her shoulders started shaking violently and pelting tears hit her hand. She laid her head against the cave's wall and closed her eyes surrendering to the darkness, and her obvious death.

Her breathing returned to normal and logic started to return to her fear soaked brain. She knew she couldn't go back; therefore, she had to go forward. Meranda struggled to bring herself upright when someone grabbed her. Her body went numb flooding with adrenalin and she almost lost control of her bladder.

"Meranda--you're okay. I've got you." Pete's voice was firm, but a welcome sound to her ears.

"Pete…" was all she could say before she started to cry sucking in restricted breaths of air between sobs. She was a mess.

"Hey, hey—it's going to be okay." Pete held her close trying to comfort her. "Just take some deep breaths."

"I-I heard some voices." Meranda tried to pull herself together but her shoulders continued to heave up and down with each sob.

"You're going to be okay. Can you walk?" Pete didn't wait for her to answer before whisking her up in his powerful arms and taking her out of that dark damp hole. "I'm sorry I left you alone. I was trying to arrange getting you home."

Meranda was barely conscious, but could feel they were climbing out of the hole she had fallen in. She didn't care about her pain or where she was, she was just happy to be alive.

Meranda felt the strength return to her limbs and told Pete she thought she could walk. He gently set her down keeping his arms around her waist making sure she could stand on her own. He took her by the hand, "We are almost there, just a few more steps," encouraging her along and she obeyed like she had when he told her to breathe under water.

Pete knew in a few moments they would be in the belly of the cave, and he would have some explaining to do. Meranda felt like they had climbed twice the length of how far she had fallen. They finally reached the mouth of the tunnel, and it opened into a huge cavern.

There were many adjacent tunnels, and she could see light coming from all the pathways. Her eyes began to adjust, and her mouth dropped open, as she look around the gigantic cave. The walls were more of the same beautiful flowing contours and colors, only with larger concentration of silver and gold streaks that stood out against a charcoal gray background of granite. Below where they stood were layers of slated ledges that spiraled down making a natural staircase.

Of course, at the bottom of this funneled shaped room, there was a pool of the clearest water she had ever seen, so clear that it was void of any color. Pete felt Meranda shiver at the mere sight of the water, and taking her good arm, he guided her to the left where the stairs led down to the next level.

Meranda was speechless and momentarily forgot the pain she was in. When she could finally form a coherent thought, the questions started to flood her head. "What is this place? Where are we? How do you know of this place? Where are we?" Her mind was racing back and forth with questions, but soon her only thought was, "It's beautiful, the veins of marble that paint the walls, go up as high as you can see. I feel like I'm inside the earth."

"I will explain what I can to you, but first you need to eat and rest." Pete tried to contain his urge to smile, which was hard because Meranda looked like a kid in a candy store; her eyes were glistening and capturing every inch of her surroundings.

"How are we going to eat and rest? Do you have food stashed somewhere or a packsack filled with army rations?" Meranda was weakened from the trauma, hunger, and pain. Her cheeks were sunken in making her eyes look too large on her face. They continued down the slate stairs, and she flinched from pain, but never once voiced a complaint.

"Well yes and no," Pete stammered. He didn't know how he was going to explain where they were. When they reached the lower level he motioned for her to turn left toward yet another opening.

Oh! My! How? Meranda could barely believe her eyes; she was looking at a completely furnished room—in a cave. She strained her eyes to focus on what looked like a dug out in the back of the cave that was made into a huge bed.

Next to it, was a fireplace with a fire in it, and a cast iron pot hanging over it with something that filled the room with a delicious aroma. "Pete how can all this be here, are you sure we're not dead?"

Pete chuckled deep within his chest, "I'm sure. Come, sit down, and let me get you something to eat before I answer your questions." Pete knew how bizarre this all must seem to her.

Meranda let Pete lead her to a couch made of the most beautifully grained wood she had ever laid eyes on, and a wooden coffee table made from a slice of tree the diameter of a tractor tire. It had to be at least one hundred years old or more, according to all the rings it had in the grain.

The couch and chair frames were made out of notched logs, and the suede cushions looked so soft she couldn't wait to sit on them. A large Persian rug covered the cave's floor giving the room an articulate completed look. The room was magnificently decorated, yet had a masculine tone, just like Pete's cabin cruiser, and his office at the Environmental Protection Agency.

"Do you live here?" Meranda finally managed to form a coherent sentence.

"This is one place I live and work." Pete raised an eyebrow. He decided it was best to answer the questions as they came.

"Where are we? When can I go home?" Meranda was unable to resist the warmth of the fire or the smells of the food cooking. Despite her hunger, her stomach tightened and threatened once again to cut off her air, before she collapsed on the couch.

"We are deep within the sea caves along the northern shores of Lake Superior." Pete's eyes lifted up to meet hers as he gently cleaned her bloodied fingers and waited for a reaction, but none came. He grabbed two bowls from a carved out shelf alongside the hearth and began dishing up what looked like stew.

"Where did this food come from and who made it?" Meranda reached for her bowl closing her eyes as she inhaled the mouthwatering aroma.

"There are others; other scientists who live here in the caves year round, and they made the stew." Pete waited to see if that satisfied her curiosity.

"Others…?" Meranda struggled to wrap her mind around the word, *others*.

"Yes, other folks." Pete was starting to feel uncomfortable. "Meranda, I think it would be best if you rested awhile and let your arm relax; you have been through quite a lot."

"But I don't understand, how can…"

"Here drink this it will help with the pain." Pete interrupted.

"What is it?" Meranda sniffed at the glass.

"A very old wine, so smooth you will not even feel it slide down your throat, I promise." Pete was proud of his wine cellar and the wines he had collected over the years from different regions of the world.

As Meranda drank the wine, she eyed Pete suspiciously, and wondered again who Pete Moss really was. She tried to piece together a list of things she knew about him. True to his word, the wine was soft and soothing, as her tongue played with the velvety liquid in her mouth. She soon felt warm and fuzzy.

"I think I need to lie down." Meranda yawned as she got up and started to stumble, Pete flew to her side to catch her. "I want some concrete answers, Mr. Moss! And I want them now. Well, maybe after I rest a bit."

"I know, and I assure you, Miss Michaels, I will answer all the questions I can, just know that you are safe." Pete guided her toward the bed so that she wouldn't cause more damage to herself. The bed was downy soft, and Meranda was so tired it didn't take her long to fall asleep. Pete pulled the fur blanket around her injured shoulder taking care not to bump it.

He stood looking at her running his hands over his stressed face and wondered how he was going to resolve this situation. With everything he had going on right now, he didn't need complications. He went over to the hearth and put another log on the fire to keep the place warm, hoping she would sleep awhile and allow her body to heal.

He sensed his brother was near before receiving a telepathic message, *"Brother, may I have a word with you?"*

"In a moment, Zane." Pete messaged back.

"It's rather urgent brother," Zane insisted, his muscular arms crossed against his dark brown sculpted chest. His chiseled face was surrounded by shoulder length dreadlocks making him look like an African God, but it was his ability to command that made him a valuable member of this family.

"I will meet you in the commons." Pete messaged Zane more firmly. His first concern was Meranda's wellbeing. Pete checked her one last time before he departed knowing he needed to get updates on any new developments that may have surfaced while he was above ground.

3

"Brother, how are you?" Pete inquired.

"I am well. I didn't want to interrupt, but the rift has become very active." Zane was the commander of the patrols that guarded the ten thousand year old Mid-Continental Rift, at the bottom of Lake Superior. "The rift's gap has widened."

"Have any other changes occurred?" Pete knew Lake Superior had a delicate eco-system and that the balance was unique, making it fragile.

"No, sir, there is nothing else to report."

Pete and Zane continued to discuss all that had taken place while he had been away on the mainland. Once Pete felt he had enough information, he knew his father would be waiting to be updated.

"Brother, if I may be so bold as to inquire about the girl? Will she be joining our family?" Zane cast his eyes downward in respect.

"I don't know. Everything happened so fast. All I know is she has been through a traumatic near death experience and I thought it best she rest first." Pete's face deepened with concern.

He felt bad about leaving her when they first had gotten to the caves and she almost died again. He went to check on her once more before heading off to speak with the other team members. She was knocked out cold. Pete notice her soft snores and how they sounded like she was purring. He felt like he was invading her privacy, and left.

The once empty commons began to fill with family members as they gathered to report on each of their stations and welcome him home. After Pete had been briefed he stood to go meet with his father when the room fell quiet and Salmonia appeared. She didn't look happy.

Pete beat her to the punch before she could unleash all the fire he saw in her eyes. "Sal, good you are here. I need a favor of you sister." Salmonia was one of the few females in their family, and was the lead scientist for the invasive species project. She was a huntress with a fiery temper that matched her flaming red hair, making her emerald green eyes look darker.

"Absolutely, long lost brother of mine...." Salmonia replied in a sarcastic sounding voice as she emerged from the pool port. Rainbows of colors reflected off her skin. Pete smiled at his beautiful sister knowing how important she was to him and this mission. He had missed his family and the serene atmosphere of the caves. She must be extremely angry if she was communicating verbally instead of telepathically.

Pete asked Sal to sit with Meranda while he caught up with all the activities and met with his father. "I need you to befriend our guest. Her name is Meranda." Pete's face changed slightly when he said Meranda's name, making Salmonia instantly aware that this girl was special to him.

"I am not a babysitter brother--my plate is full." Salmonia was mainly responsible for the food and supplies, as well as a scientist.

"I know Sal, but this was an unexpected situation, and I need your assistance. Besides, I'm asking you as a favor for which I will grant a favor in return." Pete got his message across without making it a command.

"I will be glad to babysit your pet," Salmonia smiled through her gritted teeth.

"I wouldn't ask if it wasn't important, and I am fully aware of the price I will be paying. Now, on to other business—do you have anything to report?" Pete was eager to move on.

"No, did you get the supplies I needed?" Salmonia asked raising her right eyebrow emphasizing the meaning of her question.

"I did, and Zane has gone to retrieve those very supplies. We were caught in the crossfire of two storms, which is why things haven't gone as planned." Pete decided to leave the explanation at that. Sal quietly departed.

"Pete..." Meranda quietly called out, as she listen to how many times her voice echoed off the cave's walls. All she had to do was say Pete once and it would bounce back five times before it faded. Mentally she was feeling better, but fear and panic were close to the surface.

"Hello..." Meranda's throat tightened and her voice quivered.

Pete popped his head around the corner, "Meranda, you're awake. How do you feel?" He could see she was rested, but confused, and she had every right to be. "How is your pain? Pete felt at a loss as he watched her struggle to stand up.

"I will live. Enough small talk," she answered sharply. "Where am I?" Meranda's temper momentarily took over the fear she had been wallowing in when she first woke.

"You're in the caves along the North Shore, a few miles past Gooseberry Falls. You are familiar with Gooseberry Falls aren't you?" Pete felt satisfied that he successfully answered her question with a fair amount of ease.

Wrong. Meranda's face turned red, "Yes, Pete, I know where Gooseberry Falls is." Her sarcastic tone made it clear that she did not appreciate being pacified.

Pete knew immediately that that was the wrong approach, "Meranda, I'm sorry. I just don't want you to feel alarmed, let me reassure you—you are safe, and I will explain as much as I can."

With her good arm, she had her hand on her hip and her jaw jetted out, "When can I go home? And what is this? Why are there people down here? You said you would answer my questions. I would appreciate some answers now."

With Meranda, it was never a good combination when her fear and anger mixed, she could become quite difficult. She was stubborn and the old saying, *cut off your nose to spite your face*, applied to her. Her stomach tightened and the suffocating feeling began to climb up into her chest, and she swayed slightly.

"Meranda, please sit. I will explain what our operations entail and why we are here…please sit down?"

MLJOSI925NBB

TRY OUR NEW GRILLED CHICKEN

*With Purchase of Small or Larger Fry and Drink

FR

©2016 Quality Is Our Recipe, LLC

BECAUSE IT'S DIFFERENT

Dave's SINGLE™

Pete motioned toward the couch afraid she was going to fall. He started to explain. "I will bring you home as soon as I can arrange it."

The team had been monitoring the lake beneath the surface for past ten years. This environment has been home to all who have been on this project, and living down here in the caves made them a part of the lakes environment.

"Brother, excuse me, but you are needed in the commons, it's urgent." Salmonia's sudden appearance and her intense eye contact with Pete, sent jolts of adrenaline shooting into Meranda's limbs making her jump up from the couch.

Pete introduced Meranda to Salmonia and explained that her mission here was to oversee the invasive species project and study their reproductive cycles.

Meranda responded respectively to a fellow female scientist, however, she did not miss the eye exchange that took place between Salmonia and Pete. "I'm sure Sal would love to tell you more about her projects." Pete tried to quickly take his leave, but as he passed by Salmonia the look in her eye was lethal. Pete stopped in his tracks and gave Sal a look of warning.

"Sure, I would *love* to keep your pe... your *friend* company until your return." Salmonia replied with a smile.

"Excuse me then ladies," Pete quickened his step and took his leave.

"If you are busy, I am fine to wait alone." Meranda was equally capable of giving off an icy persona and she was in no mood for people treating her with kid gloves.

"I apologize, Meranda is it? Tensions are high right now and none of that has anything to do with you." Sal wanted to put her at ease. Meranda had unfortunately been thrown right in the middle of troubled times within the lake.

After talking with Meranda, Sal found herself liking the young woman. She never had any close girlfriends, and admittedly was curious about the girl Pete had brought to the caves.

Meranda was not be able to take her eyes off Sal and how translucent her skin was. Her fine features and flaming curly red hair accented her green and gold flecked eyes, making her positively captivating. Her movements were graceful and flowing. She wore no jewelry, except a necklace that looked Scandinavian by design. "Meranda…"

"I'm sorry. What were you saying?" Meranda was so entranced by Sal that she hadn't heard the last part of the conversation.

"I was just saying that this lake has a bite at times." Salmonia was trying her hardest to be friendly, but she had no prior experience with girlfriends to reference.

Meranda was easy to talk to and so Sal continued to explain what her part in this mission was, and why they lived in the caves. "Basically, it makes more sense to study the lake by being a part of it."

"Where are you from?" Meranda couldn't get over how lacking in color Sal's skin was, as if she had never seen the sun.

Salmonia tried not to think of her home in Trondheim, Norway, because it made her homesick. Her family could easily be traced back to the Viking Era and since no one had ever left Norway, except her, this made her family's tree easy to track. Sal being a specialist in invasive species, had allowed her to travel all over the world, wherever she was needed. "Our team has worked together for the past twenty years and we consider ourselves family. We have devoted our lives to protecting the oceans, and now the largest fresh water lake in the world."

"Oh, that explains why you and Pete look nothing alike." A giggle erupted from Meranda's throat. Anytime she thought of Pete, a reddish hue tinted her face. "That sounds very exciting traveling all over the world."

"It is, but at times I miss being home," Sal lowered her eyes hiding the shift in her mood. Meranda felt the need to change the subject, "So, how will I get back above--um, I mean-on land?

"I think that is a question for Pete, Would you like some tea?" Now it was Sal who wanted to change the subject.

Meranda sat with her hands in her lap, eyes half mast, and nodded yes, "please if it isn't too much trouble." Sal rose in one flowing movement.

When Sal left the room, Meranda dropped the veil that held the pain in her arm at bay, but the sharp pains and throbbing were becoming harder to ignore. She thought about that wine Pete had given her earlier. It not only made her sleepy, but had dulled the pain immensely.

Meranda looked around, still unable to wrap her mind around being in a furnished cave. The whole "in a cave" thing was the mind blowing part, and not being able to gauge what time of day it was felt strange.

Sal had been gone for what seemed a long time. Maybe something had come up? She did say she oversees many operations. Meranda went over to the bed and ran her hand across the soft fur covering. She was sleepy and could use a pillow to rest her shoulder on. Meranda flopped back on the bed and wiggled into the softness, watching the fire from the hearth flicker on the walls.

She had drifted off to sleep, and was woken by some commotion coming from the back of the cave. Her head felt heavy as she pushed herself up wincing from the pain. She slid off the bed and made her way toward the back of the cave.

Her eyes slowly adjusted to the dim light cast from lanterns. She didn't trust her sight so she hugged the wall letting her fingers lead the way while her feet checked for solid ground. The partition ended and she cautiously rounded the corner, and froze. There was Salmonia pulling a man out of the water.

"Meranda can you help me?" Sal's eyes were wild and pleading. She shivered remembering that icy cold water, and rushed to help Sal.

Meranda locked her good arm under the man's arm and found a rock to use for leverage and pushed against it. Sal counted to three and they pulled the man out of the water, almost….

Meranda lost her grip and flew backwards landing hard against the rock wall.

"Meranda! Are you all right?" Sal glanced over her shoulder worried that she had reinjured herself. Sal was struggling to keep the man from slipping back into the water. She knew Pete was going to be furious with her for involving Meranda in the first place and if she reinjured herself, well Sal couldn't think about that at the moment.

"I'm alright; it's hard to keep your balance with one arm." Meranda didn't divulge the fact that she hit her shoulder on a rock and pain was radiating throughout her arm, shoulder, and chest making her suck in her breath and bite her lip to hold back from moaning.

Sal had repositioned herself so that she could grab both of the man's arms and straightening her body, she leaned backwards pulling him completely out of the opening.

Immediately, Sal began pulling small lamprey off him. He was covered with the snake like parasites. He had lost a lot of blood and had a grayish tone to his dark brown skin. She had forgotten about Meranda for the moment in her hast to remove the nasty blood suckers. Her main concern was to stop the bleeding. She needed her salve. Looking up she saw Meranda standing behind her with her mouth open, staring at the man.

"Meranda--are you okay?" Sal asked cautiously.

"H-he has a tail."

"Yes Meranda, he is a merman. He helps protect the lake."

Meranda couldn't take her eyes of this half human/half fish creature. "The folktales are real. There are mermaids"

Sal cracked a smile because that was not the reaction she was expecting from her. She was taken back at the discovery of a merman, but she was not running away screaming. "They are real, and technically, he is a merman."

"Those are lampreys hanging off him," Meranda, in part, asked a question while making a statement. "We studied them in school. We were trying to find ways to rid the lake of them." Sal could see the fascination coming alive in Meranda's eyes.

"Is he going to be okay?"

"I don't know. I need to get some salve, it's in the bathroom on the top shelf," she added. Salmonia knew she had to stop the bleeding if Zane had any chance of surviving.

Assessing whether to ask Meranda to stay with him or not fluttered through her mind. "Meranda, I need to get some salve to stop the bleeding. He won't hurt you; in fact, I doubt he will gain consciousness anytime soon."

Sal started to get up when Meranda offered to go and get the supplies. If memory served her right she knew that the lampreys saliva contained an agent that stopped the process of clotting, rendering its victims to bleed out.

Meranda returned quickly grabbing all the containers in the cabinet, not sure which one Sal needed. Sal smiled and asked for the cobalt jar and began applying it to the bites with one hand and pulling off lamprey with the other. Sal raised her eyebrows at Meranda, when she kneeled down next to Zane, and began pulling off lampreys, so that Sal could apply the salve.

When the bleeding was under control, Salmonia turned to Meranda, "I need to go find Pete. I will send someone to watch over him."

"I can watch him. You said he won't hurt me, right?" Meranda felt the words on her lips but wasn't sure if she had actually voiced them.

"No, Meranda, he won't hurt you. Are you sure you're okay with all this? It's no trouble to send for someone?" Sal knew Pete was really not going to like this, providing he hadn't met the same fate as Zane.

"I doubt he will wake, but if he starts to bleed again, can you apply more salve?"

"Yes, I got this." Meranda took the jar and looked Salmonia solidly in the eyes, showing no fear.

"If he wakes up, try to get him to drink some broth. I will have the kitchen staff bring you some." Salmonia knew time was of the essence for finding Pete. If Zane looked like this, she knew there had to be casualties, and she also knew Pete would have gone looking for survivors.

"Go!" Meranda reassured Salmonia, who looked conflicted.

Salmonia nodded at Meranda and left. She smiled to herself gaining a new respect for Pete's friend.

4

Pete's eyes narrowed and his jaw clenched tight as he looked around the commons. He sensed something was terribly wrong. Guilt nagged at him for spending too much time on land, and neglecting the seriousness of the situation below the surface.

He had repeatedly tried to contact the patrols out in the lake and no communication was returned. He paced back and forth trying to organize his thoughts before deciding to take what troops were available and go to the rift. His commander, Zane, had been patrolling the area heavily since the gap had widened in the earth's crust. The centuries old rift was like an inactive volcano that had suddenly come alive.

Pete suited up and with the few troops that were available, they dove into the lake.

As soon as Pete was in the water Sal sensed his absence and her internal alarms went off making her skin prickle. She knew he had headed to the rift. Salmonia hadn't wanted to leave Zane hanging onto life, but she had to find Pete, it was her job to protect him.

Sal sent Pete a message, *"Where are you?"* She waited momentarily for a response that never came. Her temper flared. He knew better. He should have guards with him at all times when he's out in the lake, and she should be one of them. After all, she was a highly skilled huntress and warrior.

Sal gathered her weapons and tried to get a read on Pete, but her temper interfered with her senses and clouded her ability to communicate telepathically. Zane had been giving Pete updates about the trouble brewing at the rift, therefore, that would be the most logical place to start. With no reinforcements left in the compound, she swiftly departed armed with as many weapons as her body could support.

Just as Sal had predicted, Pete had raced to the rift. After seeing the condition Zane was in, Sal knew the danger they were in. If something was able to do that much damage to Zane, a fierce warrior, the rest of them didn't have much of a chance. She felt like she had been punched in the gut thinking of Pete meeting the same fate.

Salmonia hoped she wasn't too late. The bite marks on Zane's back flashed through her mind, as she tried to imagine what could have left such a large mark. Had something emerged from the rift?

Sal smelled death before she saw it. The absence of life unnerved her long before she saw the scattered remains of the patrol. Salmonia's body shifted to high alert, as she cautiously descended to get a closer look. Terror shivered through her body. The men had the same large bite marks as Zane. Only they were gray, and their skin clung to their bones. They had been completely drained.

Other than Zane, there were no survivors; Sal calmed herself to try to get a read on Pete. She didn't see him amongst the dead, so she felt hopeful that she got there in time.

In all her years, she had never seen anything of this magnitude. Mermen always stayed in pods and were telepathic, cutting the risk of injury or death in battle. She had witnessed fights in the oceans against two thousand pound sea demons, and the casualties were minimal.

"*Take cover!*" Pete blasted through Salmonia's head.

With her senses already on alert she torpedoed toward a crack in the mountainous rocks. Once hidden she instinctively changed her coloring to match her granite gray surroundings. She peered out of her hiding place not daring to move a muscle. The slightest movement in the water could disclose your location. She waited for further word from Pete. He was alive.

A shadow darkened the entrance to her cavernous shelter and Sal held her breath remaining motionless. A snake-like serpent's head appeared in her view and she cowered farther back into the crevice, despite her hunter's instincts to remain still. In her one hundred twenty-five years, she'd encountered dangerous marine life, but she was not prepared for this. Not here.

Sal started to count off in six foot sections; the average length of a merman to determine the size of this thing. However, more disturbing than the serpent, was the size of the lamprey that surrounded the two hundred foot snake. And before she knew it, she had a front seat view to a fight between two giant lampreys.

With their tails entwined, they reared their heads back, to deal a deadly blow to their opponent. They were equally matched in size and length, and it looked more like a dance than a fight.

One lamprey struck low, bouncing off the leathery skin leaving itself vulnerable. The other lamprey opened its mouth and unlocked its jaw exposing its tusk size fangs, and sunk them into the flesh behind the eyes of his opponent draining all the essence of life from its body.

When the engorged victor released his fangs, the dead lamprey's flattened body began its final descent, waving like a ribbon in the wind, and sank. The victor swam out of Salmonia's sight, returning to peer into her hideout with its red bulging eye, letting her know it knew she was there before retreating to the serpent's side.

Everyone remained hidden for what seemed like hours until they were sure the area was secure.

"Sal, join me. They are gone." Pete could sense Sal, but scanned the rocks trying to locate her. With her ability to blend into her surroundings it made it impossible to pinpoint her exact location, and only when Pete swam past the opening she had hid in, did she reveal herself.

"What were those things?" Sal knew they were up against a much bigger problem than she had previously thought. *"Was that a serpent? Did it come through the rift?"*

Pete didn't respond to Sal's questions as he solemnly looked around at the flattened bodies that looked like paper cutouts scattered on the lakes floor. He swallowed the bile that burned his throat as he checked each of his warriors for any signs of life. Their beautiful colored tails waved up and down with the motion of the water as if saying goodbye. Never, in all of Merfolk history had so many men been lost in a single battle. It was a massacre.

"Pete, we have to go, it's not safe here...Pete?" Salmonia asked him several times before putting a hand on his

shoulder. Pete turned around with tormented eyes and nodded in agreement. Neither, Sal nor Pete, wanted to leave the men behind, but they knew they were still in dangerous waters. They headed back in grief stricken disbelief.

Pete spoke first, *"I-I can't believe all the soldiers we lost."* Pete came to a stop in front of Sal and put his hands on her shoulders looking her straight in the eyes, *"Sal, I didn't see Zane's body. I'm so sorry, but I am sure he went down with his men."* He knew Sal and Zane had a special bond. Pete's face turned murderous as he thought of the parasites that took the lives of his comrade and warriors.

"That's because he's alive, at least, he was when I left him back at the compound. He made it back to warn us, but he is barely hanging on to life. I left him in Mer-ran-da's care...." Sal flinched as she tried to suck the words back in, knowing Pete was not going to be okay with her decision.

Pete jerked his head up, *"What do you mean, in Meranda's care?"* Panic gripped Pete chest, *"Start talking, now!"* Sal just stared at Pete. She had never seen him look at her with such anger. *"Whatever your reasons for your lack of judgment there will be consequences. I am, the Son of the Lake, and when I give a command it is to be obeyed."* Pete shot ahead.

Against her better judgment, she caught up with him and fired back, *"She's okay, Pete. She's stronger than you think. She found me pulling Zane's limp body from the pool port and came to help. What choice did I have? Let him die? After she saw his tail she was a bit taken back, but recovered quickly. Then she began helping me pull the lampreys off of Zane and helped stop the bleeding."*

Pete couldn't believe what he was hearing, *"She what?"* Pete was relieved that Zane was alive, but stopped listening to Sal's insane justifications. *"You left her there alone-I ordered you to stay with her and protect her?"* Pete bellowed inside Salmonia's head.

He was losing control from the grief of losing his men coupled with his fear for Meranda. His emotions exploded and he sped ahead to put some distance between him and the huntress before he did something he would regret.

Sal caught up with Pete again, only this time she was determined that he was going to hear her. *"Stop yelling at me Pete...I am responsible for you."* Sal calmed herself and regained control. She knew Pete held himself responsible for the loss of his men, but he had to understand Sal had no choice in leaving Zane with Meranda.

Sal spoke more softly, *"What was I supposed to do? It is my job to be at your side, and that order comes from your Father. I had no choice between securing Zane's safety and yours."* She had taken Meranda at her word when she said she could handle things, and that she would continue to tend to Zane's wounds. She also knew she couldn't let the Son of the Lake face the unknown by himself, especially after seeing the marks on Zane's back.

Sal felt like she was trying to talk sense into a wall, so she gave him some space. However, she stayed close in case another attack occurred before they reached the safety of the caves. She knew she had made the best choice she could, yet it still stabbed at her heart to feel the angry vibrations roll off Pete directed at her.

Pete arrived at the pool port in the common's room stopping just under the surface to scan for Meranda's presence, and came up empty. He immerged from the lake as a merman, and transformed to his human form and quickly got dressed. His only concern at the moment was to get to Meranda.

On the way to her quarters, Pete received an internal summons from his father. He knew he should respond immediately, but he could not ignore the urgency he felt in every fiber of his body as it pulled him towards Meranda.

Since the first day he had met her, he felt the need to protect her. Not because she was weak, but the opposite, because she was so strong. As he walked toward the alcove, his mind searched for an explanation, and there was none.

Pete entered the room clearing his throat so that she knew he was there, but not before he took a minute watching her tend to Zane's wounds and feed him broth. Salmonia was right. "Meranda are you...how are you doing?"

Meranda put her finger to her lips and hushed him, inclining her head in the direction of the hearth. She pulled the furs up over Zane and stood up, adjusting her balance to the contour of the cave's floor. "I'm fine Pete." Meranda's voice was stiff, "Is there anything you would like to tell me Mr. Moss, because I think now would be a good time to have that conversation you've been avoiding."

"How is Zane doing?" Pete wanted to ask Meranda again how *she* was, but didn't dare, seeing the fire that shot from her eyes.

"I think he will recover, but I am no expert on...on mermen, is that what he is-*Pete?*. Is there an in-house doctor that can see to him?" The more Meranda talked the less control she had on her anger that now was bubbling over.

Pete began to open his mouth to explain when he received a stronger signal from his father. "Meranda, please understand when I tell you this, I will disclose everything upon my return, but I have to report to the ...I have some urgent business." Pete hated to leave her just then, but when the Father of the Lake called, he knew anything short of death had best not delay you. He cast his eyes downward before looking into her eyes and seeing the hurt and betrayal. The hurt he alone had caused.

"Just go!" Meranda turned toward the hearth to get some more broth for her patient hiding the tears that threatened to spill down her face. She would not give him the satisfaction of seeing her cry. He didn't trust her with the truth even when she asked about the mission down here, he felt he had to lie to her.

Pete thought about saying something more, but his words seemed to carry no meaning, so he just turned and left. As Pete headed to answer his father's summons, Salmonia entered the room. Pete paused and said nothing, but Salmonia didn't feel the anger she had felt earlier from him, his eyes looked to where Meranda was, *"Will you please stay with her until I get back, sister?"*

"Yes, brother, I will." Sal could see the strain on his face and forgave him. She knew he carried the weight of protecting lake and the pods that lived within it.

"How is the patient doing? Sal asked.

Meranda swiped at a tear, before turning to answer, "I was able to get most of the bleeding to stop, but he still has some break through bleeding. I dribbled broth in his mouth and he is feverish. Don't you have a doctor or caregiver down here?" Meranda was relieved that Sal was back. She trusted Sal; after all, she didn't treat her like she was a fragile little girl who couldn't handle the truth.

"We had a caregiver as you call him. A Shaman, but he's not in the area at this time. Most Merfolk recover on their own." Sal quietly approached Zane. His coloring had returned to its normal deep brown and the skin no longer hung on his beautiful sculpted face. Sal had breathed a sigh of relief before hiding her emotions from Meranda.

"How are you holding up? I know this has to be a lot to take in, especially when you weren't prepared for it. The storm, the caves, and now the discovery of the Merfolk have to be a lot to deal with." Sal laid a hand on Meranda's shoulder showing the appreciation that she felt for this woman who had stepped up.

Meranda gave Sal a small smile then walked over to the couch, giving Sal some privacy with Zane. Sal thought she hid her feelings, but Meranda hadn't missed the obvious connection between them. Sal turned and walked over to Meranda, "I want to thank you for caring for Zane. He is a very important member of this family."

"I was glad to be here to help. Is he going to be okay?" Meranda had decided that whatever feelings she thought she had seen on Sal's face, it would be better, if she kept them to herself.

"His coloring looks good and he is breathing easier. I am confident that our commander will recover." Sal retained her huntress demure. "If you don't mind sitting with him for a bit longer, I have a few things to see to?"

"No--not at all." Meranda smiled.

5

"*When I summons you, I expect a prompt response.*" Pete's father was angry which strengthened his mental energy as it bounced around Pete's head to the point it was painful. "*What has happened son, I sense turmoil and danger?*"

"*Something erupted from the Rift. It killed the entire patrol, except Zane. He had escaped to warn us, but is still fighting for his life.*" Pete's body tensed as the images of the battlefield flashed through his mind. His father was able to see the devastation through his son's eyes.

Upon feeling his son's pain for the loss of his men, he softened his tone. Using his voice Pete's father asked, "*Do you know what came out of the Rift that could take out twenty eight mermen?*" Pete's father was two thousand and thirteen years old; an original guardian from the homelands.

Pete kept his eyes downcast, "*Father, I lack the words for what to call it. A snake or possibly a two hundred foot serpent of sorts--that was as big around as an ore boat.*" Pete looked into his father's eyes searching for an answer. He had only heard stories as a boy of the sea serpents, but he had never actually seen one.

Pete's face had gone slack as his eyes moved back and forth, while the images of the slaughtered men played through his head like a movie. *"That was not the only discovery. There were hundreds of lampreys surrounding it like it was the mother of all lampreys. The lost men had large bite marks on them and were drained of all their blood."* Pete ran his hand through his hair and continued shaking his head in disbelief.

In all the years Pete had served this great lake, he had never seen anything like it. Some of the lampreys were four feet long and as thick as a mer with fangs that resembled small tusks surrounded by circular rows of razor sharp teeth.

Pete was overwhelmed with sorrow and grief, *"I would suggest, son, you call for reinforcements from the old country. There aren't many Nordic Warriors left, but you don't need many, either. They have fought ocean serpents for centuries."* Pete's father also ordered that no one goes out in the lake alone, and only if it is necessary at that.

His father retreated back into his shelter. The natural layers of slated rock created the perfect crevice for his twelve foot, four hundred pound body. In his youth he was half man, half fish, but was regressing back to his ancestral form of an ocean born sturgeon.

Pete turned to leave when his father entered his mind, *"Send a fully armed party out to see to the dead. One more thing son, what of the human girl? Will she be joining our family?"*

"No father, I wish to bring her back to land." Pete knew her return would have to be timely, but with all the danger in the lake; her safety came first. Pete took his time climbing up the winding stairway from his father's quarters. He knew he had to get back to Meranda to offer some sort of explanation.

Pete slumped against the tunnel wall, expelling long sighs. How could he begin to explain any of this to her? Coming up empty, he decided that the truth was the only way to go. She had already discovered their secret.

When he first saw Meranda tending to Zane she looked natural, not freaked out or scared. If he hadn't known different he would have thought she had known of Merfolk all her life, after all, she was a marine biologist. She had to have somewhat of an open mind. It had been his diversion from the truth every time she had asked about the operation that had hurt her. Then he remembered what Sal had said; *"...trust her, she is stronger than you think."*

He rounded the corner running his hand over the smooth contour of the walls. Pete sunk down and sat with his back braced against the cool stones feeling some of the tension leave his body. He watched the light filter down through the cracks and dance around him. It always amazed him how a ray of light could reach down this deep catching the gold and silver flecks in the granite imitating the stars in the skies above.

Pete knew he was stalling, but needed a moment to regroup. He stood up squared his shoulders and walked into the commons. There he found family members in prayer for the lost men, Pete stopped in his tracks, the room echoed with pain.

When they had finished their prayers, they turned their tear stain faces to him and he knew he should say something as Son of the Lake, *"My brothers and sisters, we will destroy these monsters that took our brothers from us. We will avenge them, and send that snake back to the hell it came from. Our warriors will not have died in vain. Until then, we need to stay in groups, and no one will go out into the lake."*

Pete sent an internal message out to the pod, issuing a high alert. No one was to go out into the lake without permission. Pete knew he had to do more, but he was emotionally spent, and had nothing more to say. He stood there absorbing the grief that filled the room and carried that pain close to his heart. The wrenching sobs seem to make the stones weep. He had to bring the fallen home, so that the healing could begin.

The weary lines on Pete's face deepened as he approached what use to be his quarters, and he paused outside the doorway. He could hear Salmonia and Meranda talking softly and hated to interrupt. Lifting his chin and taking a deep breath, he entered the room. The talking stopped "Hello ladies." Pete said with a stiff upper lip.

The women eyed him warily, before Meranda looked away, unable to look him in the eyes. Sal stood up and bid Meranda goodbye, then stopped to check on Zane who was healing at a merman's speed. On her way out, she raised an eyebrow at Pete, *"trust her, brother."*

The air was thick between them. Pete thought he would lead off by asking Meranda about her own welfare, "How is your arm feeling?"

"Stiff and sore--I'll live." Meranda's replied.

"Good, good. You should try to move it throughout the day so it doesn't freeze up." Pete offered his unsolicited advice as he moved closer to the hearth.

"I *have* been moving it, thank you." Meranda turned sitting at the edge of the couch and waited for the explanation to begin.

Nervously, Pete walked over to Zane, who appeared to be sleeping soundly. He noticed that his coloring had returned and he no longer had that death undertone to his face. Meranda decided to give him an update on her patient, "He is doing much better. I have gotten the bleeding to stop, and he has kept down some broth. Sal said, *mermen*, can heal themselves fairly fast. Oh yeah, I have been keeping his *tail* moist too." And there it was the opening sentence.

Pete turned and intensely looked her straight in the eyes, "Meranda, I don't know where to begin...."

Meranda's eyebrows pinched together, "How about start with the merman I have been nursing back from the brinks of death. That would be a good place to begin, Mr. Moss." Meranda placed her hands between her knees to stop them from shaking.

Pete cautiously sat down at the far end of the couch, "Meranda--I, everything has happened so fast." His eyes darted around not wanting to look her in the eyes, and when their eyes finally met, all he could see was hurt. "So, maybe I will just let you ask the questions, and I will do my best to answer them."

Her anger subsided seeing how uncomfortable this confident man had become, "I don't know what to ask, my mind is reeling from all that has happened in the past few days."

"It is a lot to take in, I'm sure." Pete tried to look at it from her perspective.

Without anger fueling her, she felt rather demure and her tone softened, "Okay, apparently mermaids are real. I-I, how--I mean--where do they come from?"

"Well, first of all, mermen not mermaids." Pete only wanted to satisfy the questions at hand; because the less she knew the easier it would be to return her to land.

"Are you a *merman*? Is Sal a *mermaid*?" Meranda looked straight into his very blue eyes as her temper threatened to blow steam out her ears, with his short, condescending answers. She remembered something her father had said to her a long time ago, *Meranda, not all doors are meant to be opened, because they can change you forever,* although, she didn't open this door. It blew open and she happened to be on the other side of it.

"Yes, to both your questions." Pete braced himself.

"Have you always been here--in the lake? How is it that you have legs and walk on land? You're the CEO, of the Environmental Protection Agency." Meranda's mouth slacked open as she visualized him sitting behind his desk at her interview.

"Some can transform, and some cannot. It depends on age and origin." Pete cringed slightly. It seemed every answer he gave opened more doors leading to more questions. "And no, I have not always lived here."

"Origin…so you're not all from here? Are there mermen and mermaids all over the world?" With her palms up, she shrugged her shoulders emphasizing her confusion.

"My pod is originally from Norway. It is written in the legends that we are the original mermen, and that we evolved out of a need to keep the oceans in balance."

"Go on."

"We were summoned to Lake Superior because the eco system was deteriorating. So, to answer your question, we relocated here twenty years ago to maintain the balance of the largest surface fresh water lake in the world," the creases on Pete's face deepened as he rubbed his hand over his face.

Meranda softened, she knew he had been through a devastating ordeal, but she felt betrayed. "I have one more question: When are you taking me home?"

"Meranda, it's complicated. It's not safe out there--

Cutting Pete off she put up her hand, "No, I am done listening to excuses and lies. You will take me home tomorrow! I don't even know if it is day or night." She stood up to leave, but looked around realizing she didn't know where to go. Frustration poured from her.

"Meranda, I give you my word, I will take you back as soon as I can. It was never my intent to put you in this situation. Know--that you are safe amongst us. Please, rest, and give yourself time to heal." Pete hadn't realized he had stood up and was now towering over her.

"Fine, I will have to take *your word* at face value, but I want to leave here as soon as I can." With her fists clenched at her side she turned and walked to the farthest corner of the cave.

"You should rest awhile. You look...." Pete stopped talking when Meranda turned on him slightly hunched like a caged animal ready to fight. "I mean--do you need anything?"

"I can take care of myself." Her shoulder pain was excruciating and she wasn't able to hold back the tears for much longer. "I would like you to leave." Meranda whispered needing some time to sort through things and calm down.

"I understand. There is food and drink, please make yourself at home," he turned and left.

Tears spilled down her face. She wiped the tears away and sniffed. She shook her head as if she had been dreaming, and began taking stock of what was available to her. The cave's wall curved around to the left of the bed, so she began to explore her temporary home.

Meranda let out a small gasp when she pulled back a bear skin curtain exposing a well-stocked wine cellar. Her fingers bounced from one bottle to the next as she looked around the dimly lit room. It had more bottles of wine than she had ever seen. Definitely more bottles than the Aurora liquor store back home. She continued to familiarize herself with her surroundings.

On her way back to the main area, she dipped into the cellar and grabbed a bottle of wine. She knew nothing about vintage or what kind it was, and she didn't care. She was in pain and thirsty. There were glasses made out of beautifully marbled agates tucked in a carved out shelf next to the hearth. She poured herself a glass of wine and sat down. It was so quiet within the rocks. The fire was soothing and the wine dulled her shoulder pain. She curled into the couch and fell asleep.

She woke to delicious smells that made her belly start grumbling. She was wrapped in a blanket that held the warmth of her body in. For a moment, she had forgotten where she was and sat straight up trying to regain her bearings.

"Hey--how are you feeling? I see you found the wine cellar and have a taste for very old wines." Pete was setting the table.

Meranda turned around and looked at him, "How long have I been asleep?"

"I'm not sure. I have only been here for a few minutes. I didn't want to wake you. You needed to rest. Are you hungry?"

"I am, thank you." She didn't want to let go of the blanket so she wrapped it around her and carefully got up.

"I hope you like seafood stew. Please, sit." Pete had come around and pulled out the chair for her, and filled her glass with wine. He then filled the bowls with stew and cut the small loaf of herbed bread.

Meranda felt foggy from the wine she had drank earlier and softened at the tender gestures Pete was doing for her. "I still have questions." She couldn't think of anything at that moment except how hungry she was.

"I'm sure you do." Pete smiled and Meranda felt her anger subside. "I will do my best to satisfy any and all questions your marine biologist's mind can come up with."

She inhaled the aroma's coming from her bowl, and lifted her eyes and for the first time in a while and she smiled softly at Pete. He looked relieved and smiled back. He knew she had been through a lot: nearly drowning, injury, discovering that mermen and mermaids were real.

They ate in silence listening to the fire crackle. Pete filled their glasses with the last of the wine that Meranda had opened. He knew it would help ease her mind and her pain.

She was full, and fuzzy and lightheaded from the wine, "Thank you, the stew was fantastic. Who made it?"

"We have kitchen staff."

"Well, please thank them for me. I still have many questions, but I think they are going to have to wait until tomorrow. I need to lie down." Meranda started to sway when she stood up and Pete was at her side in a flash to steady her.

"Tomorrow is fine. You will feel better after a goodnight's sleep." He guided her by the elbow to the down filled bed that was piled high with soft furry blankets. With her one arm out of commission she clumsily climbed into the bed. He pulled the blankets around her and started to leave.

"Wait! How is Zane?"

"He is making a speedy recovery and has been moved to his quarters. I can't thank you enough for your help, Meranda." Pete's voice was so sincere she knew he meant every heartfelt word.

"Good, I'm glad he is going to recover. Goodnight." Meranda went to sleep immediately upon laying her head on the soft pillow.

The wine helped her pain, but it also made Meranda dream. She was pulling into her driveway back at the farm and as she neared the house she saw the sheriff's car; it was Andy. She could hear Blue, her old lab, barking in the house and lathering himself into a near stroke. Meranda had slowly gotten out of the car and smiled at Andy. He was Mitch's little brother.

It was hard for her to be around Andy at times, he had Mitch's eyes and smile. Eight years had passed since that fatal night, yet she could still feel the last kiss on her lips after Mitch had proposed.

Meranda's smile had begun to fade as she approached Andy; she could now see his tear streaked face. Her heart had recognized something was wrong and she had begun to tremble, "Hey Andy."

He wiped his tears away with the sleeve of his jacket, "Meranda—it's your dad. There was an accident at the mine--your dad," his shoulders began to shake and he looked at the ground shuffling his feet before gathering the courage to look her in the eyes. "Your dad didn't make it. I'm so sorry." Andy broke into a fresh round of tears.

Meranda couldn't understand what he was saying after, "he didn't make it". She could see his lips moving, but it sounded like a foreign language. Her vision was closing in around her and everything had gone blurry. Meranda could no longer feel her legs and grabbed at the air on her way down to the ground.

Andy had caught her before she hit her head and when she came to she was on the porch cradled in Andy's arms. Her vision cleared and she noticed her hands had gone white from the death grip she had on Andy's jacket. She began to sob a sob that sounded like something was dying inside of her.

"Meranda wake up...Meranda. You're okay, you're safe." Meranda woke clutching the pillow she had been sobbing into. It took her a minute to realize she was in the cave and Pete was stroking her hair trying to comfort her.

She quickly wiped the tears away and sucked in a ragged breath, "I'm okay. I'm awake."

"I came to check on you—

"I'm okay, thank you. I was dreaming. Now if you will excuse me, I need to use the bathroom." Meranda turned to shelter her face from Pete.

"Yes, of course. Are you sure you are okay? Do you need some more wine for the pain?" Pete offered.

"No, thank you." Meranda felt she had dreamt enough. After Pete had left, Meranda stumbled to the back of the cave where the bathroom was and slid down the cool smooth wall and cried. She finally was able to stop crying when the pain that gripped her heart loosened its hold.

She stuffed it back into the box she carried her sadness in, and her father's voice entered her head,

"Freckles you'll be okay, embrace the life you were meant to lead." Meranda smiled, her dad had told her those words so many times throughout her life.

Sal knocked softly, "Meranda are you okay?"

"Yes. I'll be right out."

"Pete wanted me to stop by and check if you needed anything."

"I'm fine Sal, and no, I'm going to go back to bed."

"Okay, goodnight Meranda, sleep well."

Meranda made her way back to bed.

She woke feeling rested and more resolved about all she had learned. She stretched her legs and was in the middle of arching her back when she heard someone bustling about. "Hello?" Meranda swung her legs over the edge of the bed trying to see who was there.

"Morn, morn," spoke a girl with a very Scandinavian accent.

"Kan jeg få deg noe?" The girl slowly approached Meranda.

"I'm sorry, I don't understand." Meranda put her hands up to gesture that she didn't understand.

"My name is Meranda," she tapped on her chest like me Jane, you Tarzan.

"Mitt navn er…sorry, my name is Eira."

"It's nice to meet you, Eira." Meranda didn't know what else to say.

"Are you hungry ma'am?" Eira asked.

Meranda shook her head no, "I just need to use the bathroom, thank you."

Eira stood there not knowing if she should help her or not. Meranda steadied herself before looking up at the girl, "You can tell Pete that I'm okay and can take care of myself," she smiled politely and shuffled off to the bathroom. It wasn't long and she heard Pete.

"Good morning. May I come in?" Pete stood at the door waiting for an invite in.

Meranda did a quick check at her appearance and made sure she didn't have any sleep in her eyes, "Good morning, and yes come in."

"I spoke to Eira and I apologize, I assumed you might need some assistance with your arm and all." Pete scrunched his face up knowing he hadn't thought that one through.

"I took the liberty of asking Eira to bring some scones and fruit for breakfast--if you're hungry."

Meranda's stomach let out a loud growl and she grinned sheepishly, "I am very hungry. Thank you."

"Do you want to eat alone or would you care for company? I thought you might want to ask a few more questions and I have some down time this morning." Pete was trying very hard to regain her trust. It was important to him.

"I do have more questions." Meranda smiled at him.

"I thought you might," the right corner of Pete's mouth gave a hint of a smile expressing that he was ready to answer any questions she may have.

Breakfast was served and Meranda ate everything put in front of her. She sat quietly across from Pete trying to organize her thoughts on what she already knew about Merfolk.

Every now and again she would look up at Pete giving him a slight smile. Meranda went over to the couch and wrapped herself in the blanket and faced the fire. She loved the feel of a blanket around her; it made her feel safe. She was ready to hear more, and looked over her shoulder, and invited Pete to join her.

Meranda tried not to notice his long muscular legs and how graceful they carried him across the room or how they bulged tightening the material of his pants when he sat down. He sat quietly watching the firelight play in her hair and waited until she was ready to ask the questions.

"Can all of your kind walk on land" Meranda's brain was struggling that she was even having this conversation.

Pete's head jerked up at her sudden question, he too had gotten lost in his thoughts. "No, my father's generation cannot shift into human form. It was my generation that had evolved to meet the needs of the changing times."

Pete patiently explained how the Merfolk began and that as long as there is a need or danger in our waterways the mer would be called to duty. He peered over at her with an eyebrow cocked to see how she was handling the information.

Meranda thought it made him look irresistibly boyish when he looked at her that way. "How is it that you work at the EPA?

"It seemed the most logical place to have the access needed for our research. I became the CEO because I had transferred from the Norway branch when this locations CEO retired." Pete had never questioned the reasons why he was in his position, just that he had a job to do.

"So, let me get this straight, your generation evolved to land walkers?"

"Not all Merfolk from my generation can transition from land to water or water to land. It is a skill that takes centuries to learn and intense training." Pete straightened which made him look more massive in size than he already appeared.

Once the flood gates of Meranda's mind opened the questions poured out. She wanted to know ages, where they were from. How long they had lived in Lake Superior. Meranda cleared her throat, "How old are you?"

"I am 532 years old. I come from the waters of the North Atlantic, also known as the Norwegian Sea. We have been called to the Great Lakes because of the environmental issues and growing invasive species threats.

We have been monitoring the lake for the past century, but have recently made camp here for the past twenty years to patrol and study the lake and its waterways. We are the guardians of this lake and all others." Pete forgot himself for a moment as he explained about his people with pride.

Meranda put up her hand for him to stop. Looking away she shook her head. Her train of thought was scrambling trying to understand something she had once thought were bedtime stories.

"Meranda ..." Pete was worried that she was not dealing with the information very well.

"Yah, give me a minute. I'm trying to process all of this.., it's kind of mind blowing." Meranda felt exhausted. Between caring for Zane and healing from her own injuries, along with her newly acquired knowledge of Merfolk, she just needed a damn minute.

"Maybe you should rest awhile. You look ….." Pete was careful with his suggestion.

"I have more questions. I am just drawing a blank right now." Meranda decided her mind was full. "Oh yeah here's one…when am I going home." She tried to control her voice but the words shook in her throat.

"That is the one question I can't answer yet. I will get you home, I promise." Pete looked down knowing she had no reason to believe anything he said.

"I need some time alone. Pete." He set the plates on the captain's table that was made from White Pine which reminded her of the White Pine trees that line her driveway back home, and she felt homesick. Pete could see how distressed she was and honored her request and left.

Meranda stayed wrapped in the security of her blanket and laid her head on the back of the couch and fell asleep. She woke to Eira at the hearth stirring the stew and wondered what time it was. It was getting on her nerves that she never could tell if it was day or night.

She waited until Eira left to avoid any uncomfortable communications attempts before she jumped up to use the bathroom. On the way back she grabbed a bottle of wine out of the cellar. Heck it had to be happy hour somewhere.

Meranda poured herself a glass of wine and closed her eyes trying to block this whole nightmare from her mind. She was hoping that when she woke, it all would have been a dream, but it wasn't.

She dished herself up a bowl of stew and sat mindfully at the end of the long table and ate her dinner. She went back to the couch and curled up and watched the fire. She needed to make some sense out of everything that had taken place. Nonetheless, it was nice to have alone time, she wasn't use to people around all the time.

Her eyes searched for something she could entertain herself with when she spotted a small bookshelf. Many of the books were about shipwrecks and navigation, except one, *Serpents of the North Sea*. She settled in and began to read by the dim candle light.

Pete had come to check on her. He stood outside her door not wanting to disturb her if she was resting and heard her turning the pages of a book and smiled. He made a mental note to find reading material for her. He went to look in on his comrade and friend, hoping he was up to talking about what he remembered.

As Pete neared his room, Zane's tormented vibes hit him. *"Brother, were there any survivors?"*

"Don't waste your energy, for I am alone, we may speak freely. I'm sorry, but you were the only survivor, and I am thankful for your life." Pete kneeled down to pour some water into Zane's mouth when Zane propped himself up on his elbows and took the cup from him.

"I see you are recovering?" Relief washed over Pete.

"I am. Your lady friend took good care of me" Zane said with a twinkle in his eye.

"Are you up to telling me what happened out there, and your thoughts on the size of the lamprey—or where the serpent came from?" Pete was hesitant to question Zane so soon, but he had to know what they were up against.

"I have never seen lamprey that big and have only heard of sea serpents in the stories my father used to tell me back in our homeland." Zane just shook his head in disbelief.

"They advanced upon us so fast—and there were so many, the size of their fangs." Zane flashed on the horrific scene as it replayed in his mind. "Normally it would take a hundred small lampreys to drain a merman, if he was rendered unconscious. Instead--all it took was one of those giant lampreys' minutes to drain the life force from a warrior."

Pete felt sickened remembering all the lifeless bodies scattered about. Thank Odin that Zane would not have to revisit that, Pete would make sure he was spared.

"There was no time to save anyone. The serpent was visible one moment and invisible the next, then reappearing encasing around our pod. I saw an opening and shot out toward the rocks knowing there was nothing I could do--I had to try and warn you."

Zane's eyes were cast down in shame. "Just as I rounded the corner I came upon a lone lamprey and before I could find shelter he latched onto my back. He must have thought I was dead and left me. In many ways I wish I had died with my men." Zane broke down and wept.

"Brother it is not your fault. When Salmonia and I went to search for survivors we had to take shelter from the serpent and the overgrown lamprey. You didn't have a chance. And when it is safe we will retrieve the bodies of our fallen soldier. You did the right thing Commander, which is not always the easiest choice." Pete tried to comfort Zane, but knew this would mark his soul forever.

"I for one am thankful you are alive." Pete reached out and squeezed Zane's shoulder. "Now rest. We will need you to lead us in our fight against these giant monsters and send them back into the abyss." Pete sensed Salmonia's presence before she entered the room.

"*Is he awake?*" Sal messaged Pete.

"Yes, and he is getting stronger with every hour. I have some business to attend to could you stay near? I assured Meranda I would watch over her patient while she rested." Pete knew Sal was there to reassure herself that he was alive.

"I will watch over him and will report to Randie as well," Sal blushed at her slip up, showing her emotions for Meranda.

"Randie?" Pete raised his eyebrows at Sal.

"Don't you have urgent business waiting for you, and yes, Meranda, my friend." Salmonia squared her shoulders and stood a little taller as she turned to go sit with Zane.

"Nia…" Zane tried to sit up, but after his manly show of strength with Pete he fell back.

'Please, rest." Sal fought back the tears as she thought of how close she came to losing him. That she never told him how she still felt about him, nor had he voiced how he felt about her, but everyone knew.

Loretta Rose Didrikson

6

Pete still had a lot of explaining to do and bravely set out to make himself available to her. Meranda was pushing to go home which was the one question he couldn't answer. When he got to her door he knocked softly, silently wishing she was sleeping.

"Just the man I wanted to see. Have you figured out when I get to go *home*?" Meranda glared at Pete waiting for her answer.

"It's not that easy Meranda. For one thing your arm has to heal." Pete didn't know how to explain the complexity of her request. He figured that people on land would have considered her missing at sea, making her reappearance suspicious; therefore, a timely explanation of her disappearance was crucial.

"And why is that Pete?"

"Because Meranda, everyone thinks you're at the bottom of the lake." Pete closed his eyes trying to suck back his words.

The harshness of his answer took Meranda's breath away. People thought she was dead…Jena thought she was dead. She didn't have much family left other than her brother and Jena. Her eyes filled up with tears as she tried to muster the courage to ask, "Am I ever going home?"

"Yes, it just might take a bit of careful planning." Pete felt bad that his words came out so harsh and cold. He hated seeing tears spill from her beautiful green eyes. "I'm sorry for everything. I didn't plan on this, the storm, the massacre." Pete's eyebrows were straight with concern.

Meranda sat down on the couch. She was speechless, "Jena thinks I'm dead." The thought made her heart ache. She wondered if they had had a funeral for her. Squeezing her eyes shut she willed the thoughts away, there was nothing she could do about anything right now. "I won't tell anyone about you and your family Pete, I promise."

Pete didn't know how to make her understand that it was her reappearance that was the problem. "I will do my best, Meranda, to get you home as soon as I can. In the meantime, do you need anything?"

"No." Meranda could feel the tears burning her red rimmed eyes.

"I will leave you then." Pete turned stopping for a moment to look back at her. He wanted to comfort her and ease her pain, but what she needed he couldn't give her right now. Meranda sat with her arms around her knees and pulled them close to her chest and stared blankly at the fire as sadness fell from her eyes.

Days grew into weeks and Meranda's arm healed. She kept doing the stretches so her shoulder wouldn't freeze up and she regained a full range of motion. They had retrieved the fallen soldiers and gave them a proper burial.

The recent loss of her dad and the fallen mermen mingled together in her head giving her nightmares. Not knowing if it was day or night messed with her internal clock and she was either sleeping too much or not at all. Meranda paced; her temper laid near the surface and she felt explosive.

Restlessly, Meranda started exploring the caves and tunnels that fed out from them. She got to know the pod members better, and who could transform and who couldn't or refused to try.

They all seemed rather normal and human like, despite the physical differences. She listened to the discussions of how they were going to deal with the threats in the lake. The marine biologist in her started to surface as she thought about the problems the lampreys were causing, in general.

Pete was growing restless and tried to think of ways to cheer Meranda up, "Now that you know our secret-- would like to go do some sightseeing? That is if you are up to it?" Pete's face looked younger, more relaxed, at not having to hide his true identity.

"I would love to!" Meranda felt resolved about her uncertain future and she let Pete off the hook, for the moment. "Do you have diving equipment down here?"

"No, but I do have a wet suit to help protect you from the water temperatures." Pete added quickly.

"That is all good Pete, but how am I going to breathe?" Meranda's expression said the rest.

"Here's the deal, remember when you first came here?" Pete slowly approached the events that lead her here to begin with.

"No, it's all pretty fuzzy."

"Hmmm-okay. The reason I brought you to the caves was because we were too far down to make it back up to the surface. You would have drowned or froze to death. The day I brought you here I had um…."

"Just spit it out Pete, not much can shock me at this point." Meranda crossed her arms and with her chin tucked she raised her eyebrows.

"The mer can produce a membrane from a gland we have, and by placing it over your airways will keep's the water out allowing you to extract oxygen from the water.

Frogs have this same membrane that allows them to breathe under water or on land. It is how amphibians evolved further and further away from the water."

"Yes Pete--I get it, being a marine biologist and all."

"When I knew I couldn't safely get you back to the surface I placed this film over your nose and mouth."

Pete continued explaining how everything went down after *The Freya* had sunk, and that the caverns were closer offering her the best chance at survival. "Like I said, you would not have made it to the surface." Pete stopped explaining because Meranda was staring at him with a blank look on her face. "Meranda are you okay? Say something. Please."

"I-I didn't know how I got here or that I almost drowned." Meranda looked down twisting her hands feeling ashamed, she had been so angry at him. "Thank you. I mean-- thank you for saving my life."

Pete looked surprised. "No, I wasn't telling you any of this except to explain how you can breathe underwater. That you have already done it." Pete didn't feel he deserved a thank you. As far as he was concerned he failed her.

"Actually, I'm sorry your life has been interrupted and it was my fault that you almost drowned in the first place. I should have known the weather was changing. I should have been more careful with your life. I'm the one that is sorry." Pete looked riddled with guilt, after all that Meranda had been through, she was thanking *him*.

Meranda walked over to Pete and looked straight into his crystal clear blue eyes, and rested her hands gently on his, "You saved me and for that I'm thankful. So, please, this is not your fault. I would love to go on a tour." Meranda's soft pleading eyes were almost more than Pete could stand, he wanted to grab her in his arms and kiss away the tears that ran down her cheeks. "Okay…?" she asked.

"Great, it's settled then, we will go on an outing." Pete felt all soft inside.

"I will check with security to make sure it is safe to venture out tomorrow. Now, for more pressing business-- are you hungry? I know I am." Pete was relieved that this discussion was over.

Meranda's stomach answered for her with a loud growl, pressing her hands to her belly she tried to quiet the rumbling noises and giggled.

"I will take that as a yes and get some spirits." Pete headed to his wine cellar to retrieve a bottle of wine from the 1600's.

Meranda and Pete sat down to enjoy a boiled dinner made with rutabagas, carrots, onions, celery and a variety of fish brewed together in a broth. The air between them felt lighter than it had since she arrived. Life actually felt somewhat normal and Meranda babbled on about what her suspicions were with the overgrown lampreys.

"What a wonderful dinner." Meranda yawned.

"The company was enjoyable as well," responded Pete

Meranda felt her face flush, "I think the wine is making me sleepy." Meranda attempted to stifle another yawn.

"If all is okay with security, we will plan to go out tomorrow and tour the area. That is if you are sure you are up to it?" Pete had not inquired about her shoulder in a few days; however, she looked like she was moving it fairly well.

"My arm is a bit stiff, but otherwise it is pain free. A swim would probably do it good. I'm feeling stir-crazy and would love to see life under the surface, escorted by a merman." Meranda had a mischievous gleam in her eyes.

"I will bid you goodnight then." Pete rebounded.

"Goodnight Pete." Meranda said through a yawn.

Meranda couldn't settle down. She was so excited for a tour of her beloved lake. Never in her wildest dreams would she have thought any of this was even possible, and now she was going on an underwater adventure with a pod of mermen.

Eventually, the exhaustion, full stomach, and the wine all came together and she drifted off to sleep.

7

The next morning Sal entered Meranda's cave, "Rise and shine. We have places to go girlfriend."

Meranda came out of the bathroom fully dressed with her hair braided and looked fresh as the mornings catch. "Good morning Sal. How are you this fine day? "

"Well, I see you're anxious to get a start on the day."

"I am. Did Pete get the clearance?" Meranda was trying not to get her hopes up.

"Yes, and I am happy to report we will be leaving within the hour. So, eat some breakfast and report to the commons area. Oh, I almost forgot, here is your wet suit and some grease. Nothing goes on under the suit except the fish grease. You need to apply it from you neck to ankles before you put on the suit. This will provide a layer of fat to help insulate you and aid in getting into the suit." Sal had returned to her matter of fact huntress self.

"Thank you." Meranda took the wet suit from her friend looking at it suspiciously.

"In an hour then," Sal turned to leave and had a lot to do in order to secure a safe outing. Sal was happy for Meranda, it would do her good to get out and exercise both her mind and body.

Sal knew it could mess with your endorphins being in a cave with low light, especially for humans who seem to need more sunlight than the aquatic species.

Meranda headed back to the bathroom to get ready. She held up the wet suit wondering if they gave her the wrong size; it looked child size. Meranda heard the suits had to be snug, but she had personally never worn one.

Once in the bathroom she removed her clothes and began to spread the fish grease on her legs. It didn't smell bad; actually it didn't have any odor at all, which surprised her.

She held the suit up again shaking her head at the size of it and stepped into the right leg first as the tight material encased her ankle. It was way worse than stretching a pair of nylons fresh out of the package to ten times their original size.

Meranda continued to squirm and grunt, tugging and stretching the very small suit over what she thought to be a normal body size. It didn't help that her shoulder was stiff and she didn't have complete use of it yet. She was able to grease all of her but her back.

After contemplating the problem, she pulled the top half of the suit around to her side and smeared extra grease on inside of the suit before pulling it the rest of the way up. Meranda had the suit almost up to her injured shoulder when she was startled by a knock on the door.

"Meranda are you okay in there." Pete asked concerned from all the noises that were coming from behind the door.

"Yes, I'm fine. I'm not sure if Sal gave me the right size," Meranda replied out of breathe.

"Does it feel like it is going to crush you?"

"Yes."

"Then it's the right size. Do you need help?" Pete offered.

"No!" Meranda was horrified that he would even think of such a thing.

"No, I didn't mean me; I would get Sal to help you?" Pete smirked at the thought though.

"I will manage." Meranda snapped.

"Okay, I will see you in the commons then." Pete headed toward the exit still grinning ear to ear.

Meranda continued to force the suit to conform to her body. The suit became her second skin snapping into place and allowing her to finally get it zipped. She stood back to look at her accomplishment and realized that she looked naked except with different colored skin.

Her face turned bright red. Meranda thought about having to go out in front of who knows who…Pete. She grabbed a nearby towel and wrapped it around her feeling very exposed. Then reconsidered thinking about how foolish she would look entering the commons area in a towel, so she discarded the towel, took a deep breath, and headed out in all her glory.

"There she is," Pete jumped up to meet her, his eyes ablaze scanning over her from head to toe. Her face turned beet red exposing her emotions and her body.

Meranda held her head high, "I hope I didn't keep everyone waiting?"

"Not at all, we just finished the preparations." Sal stepped forward to take Meranda by the arm before Pete could get to her. Sal looked over her shoulder at Pete, "*Get your eyes back in your head!*"

"Do you have any questions about how the mask will allow you to breath?" Sal looked her squarely in the eyes wanting her friend to do well.

"No. Nothing I can think of. I'm sure you know what you are doing?" Meranda wasn't sure if that was a question or a plea for reassurance.

"It has been done for centuries Meranda, and I want you to know that I would not put you at risk in any way." Sal's calm take charge manner gave Meranda the confidence she needed.

"Let's do this." Meranda tried to sound carefree as she let out an extra-long breath.

Sal explained the procedure of the placement of the mask, and that it would protect her eyes and allow her to breathe without taking in water. She informed her that it would feel like she couldn't breathe at first, but her lungs would adjust to the condensed levels of oxygen.

Sal tried to put Meranda at ease by telling her, that if at any time she felt she wasn't okay with how she felt, she would bring her back up. That it might take a few attempts before she succeeded, and not to worry if she couldn't do it the first time. "Remember: sometimes you have to crawl before you can walk?" Sal hoped she didn't scare her.

"I'm ready," Meranda smiled weakly.

"I will close at all times, Meranda. Oh one last thing, "you can do this." Sal smiled and let go of her only female friend as she felt her tremble. Meranda's eyes took on a determined look giving a nod that she was ready.

"I am going to put the mask on now...just breath deep and force your lungs to override its distress mode. Ready?" Sal turned away but Meranda saw something ooze out from under a scale by her hip.

Meranda realized that Sal was in mer form. It still caught her by surprise to see half human half fish, but she got over it and was moved by the graceful beauty of Salmonia's true form.

Her tail was wispy at the ends, and each scalloped scale was silver blending into a brilliant aqua color, and outlined in black. The top of her tail rounded her hips before dipping into a v where her white almost translucent skin jetted out into her human form. Her fiery red hair cascaded in waves down her back ending in a sharp point past her waist; she was mesmerizing.

She looked every bit the huntress, with her black leathered vest stretched across her small full breasts. A crested moon made out of bone joined the vest together while leather straps belted around her small waist held her albacore handled daggers. She had matching knives that laid at her sides. Thin leather braids were weaved into straps that disappeared over her shoulders to hold a bouquet of white feathered arrows and an ivory carved bow.

Meranda's mouth slacked slightly open; she couldn't take her eyes off of her friend. Sal noticed Meranda taking it all in, and couldn't help but smile at her in an affectionate way.

When Meranda eyes lifted, she met Sal's eyes and realized she had been staring, so she quickly looked around, her eyes settling on Pete. It was her turn to look him up and down and he was breathtaking.

He too was in mer form. His shoulders were defined balls of muscles tapering into roped upper arms. His bulging forearms twitched back and forth above the hammered metal bands that ended at his wrists.

Her eyes darted across his well-developed chest and continued downward landing on his narrowed waist. He definitely had a swimmers body.

His stomach defined a sculpted eight pack and was lightly covered in soft brown hair descended in downward line giving promise to a—a tail?

Meranda snapped out of the lure of desire she had gotten sucked into, her eyes shooting up to meet his smiling eyes. She narrowed her eyes at him and stomped off toward Salmonia.

Everyone was finishing the preparations for the outing, except her, as she stood there feeling useless. Sal picked up on her friend's uneasiness and quickly assigned her a chore.

Putting some distance between her and Pete was probably a good decision on the huntress' part. Meranda gruffly became mindful of her task of spooling up the rope, but her eyes were drawn back to Pete.

With her head down she peered through her lashes at him to get a look at his tail. Where his human part ended his tail began semitransparent as it rounded on his hips dipping dangerously low in the front before the color turned solid. You could see his hip bones, as if he was wearing a pair of low rider jeans.

His tail was a shimmering bluish gunmetal gray. The outer edge of each scale was outlined in a dark emerald green. His tail fin was not feathery like Sal's, but instead had clean lines that formed twin arrowheads streaked with dark forest green, with blue spikes that were tipped in white. He too was armed to the hilt.

With her curiosity fulfilled, she waited for him to make eye contact. His eyes found her and he broke out in that knee weakening smile of his. His eyes danced with excitement.

Meranda noticed his face had the same look as he did that day on the boat. He had stood on deck with his face was to the wind as if he belonged there, and now she knew he did.

Meranda smiled back in return, "Let's do this."

Pete stepped up and took her hand. "Are you sure you're ready, Meranda?" Pete locked eyes with her searching for any doubts.

"Yes, sir," Meranda's excitement overrode her fear and she realized that she had grown to trust Pete and Sal with her underwater life.

They walked over to the pool port, Pete on her right and Sal on her left. She barely noticed the mask that had conformed to her face and she felt she was ready. "Here we go, just remember to breathe hard and that your lungs are going to do everything to get you to panic." Sal looked straight into her eyes, "You can do this and *you* will be okay."

Meranda held tightly on to Pete's arm and they jumped into the icy cold waters of Lake Superior. At first Meranda found it hard not to hold on to the last breath of air from above. Her eyes revealed her uncertainty as she slowly expelled the air from her lungs.

When the water engulfed her, all the memories of her near drowning came rushing back. She began to struggle as if she had forgotten how breathe. Pete grabbed her by the shoulders knowing she was panicking.

He wrapped his arms around her so she couldn't move and made her look into his eyes. *"Breathe Meranda, breathe hard."* Meranda eyes were wild with fear and Pete was just about to take her back up, when she shook her head no. She sucked in so hard that the cords in her neck became defined. She just kept gasping in and blowing out.

Finally, the pain in her lungs subsided as they slowly filled with oxygen. She vividly recalled Pete telling her to breathe the day she almost died, before waking up in a different world beneath the lake.

Meranda wiggled free from Pete and gave a thumbs up to signal she was okay, and then held up a finger asking for a minute. Pete and Sal exchange looks and breathed a sigh of utter relief. Neither had realized how worried they were about this particular human and the sense of responsibility that had emerged from those feelings. Meranda gave the nod that they could precede.

Zane, Sal and the rest of the patrol headed out ahead of Pete and Meranda. To her surprise it was calm and serene beneath the surface. Soon the patrol was out of sight and Meranda felt like it was just the two of them and she relaxed into Pete.

His voice appeared in her head again, *"I am going to hang onto you from the back so that you can see all the beautiful sights. Just nod or tap me if you understand or want to stop."* Meranda nodded her head that she understood and Pete gently started to move his tail and they were off. *"Are you getting enough air?"* Meranda nodded yes.

Everything looked clear, just softened, in this underwater world. With her hands by her sides, Pete held her waist, and she felt like she was a part of the pod. With her legs together, Meranda began to move her legs up and down in a rhythm that matched Pete's.

She gobbled up the scenery noticing that everything looked like it had a soft mossy carpet over it. The jagged cliffs walls were stacked layers of rock that jetted hundreds of feet above the water's surface.

The water had a slight greenish blue to it, yet she could see fifty feet all around her. When they rounded the corner there was a shipwreck, Meranda tapped Pete pointing down toward the ship. *"Do you want to go take a look?"* Pete infiltrated her thoughts.

Meranda overly answered with a concession of nods, and in the next moment they were descending toward the sunken ship. A school of Coho scattered as they neared the bow.

It looked frozen in time. No rust, but evenly covered with sediment. She peered into the windows trying to record to memory, the last moments of the crew's lives. Plates and cups were scattered and barely visible through years of sitting undisturbed in their final resting place.

She saw a shoe, but no skeletons; actually she saw no evidence of the crew at all. This surprised Meranda, because in all the songs written about Lake Superior and how she doesn't give up her dead, made her wonder where the bones were. Maybe they just wore away until they were gone. She made a mental note to ask Pete.

For now, she had seen enough and motioned that they could move on. His body shifted and angling his tail from a three o'clock position to a six o'clock position, set them on an upward climb.

Meranda felt like she was swimming toward the sun's rays that were streaming through the water from above. She closed her eyes and remembered what the warm sun felt like on her face, not realizing until that moment, that she missed it.

It reminded her of how the rays would filter through a break in the clouds after a rain. Meranda drifted back to a day on the farm, when her father was sitting on the porch smoking his pipe.

Pete entered her head bringing her back to the present *"Are you okay Meranda?"* She nodded yes. It was like he could sense when her moods changed. They had connected the first time they met as if they had previously known each other; maybe she had been a mermaid in another life?

Meranda noticed that the rocks had changed from slated layers to gigantic stones. The protrusion took them farther out into the lake. She noticed the wall had large black cavernous splits in them, and shivered at the thought of what might be lurking within.

Pete shifted their direction staying close to the wall as they headed into the belly of the lake. Meranda hadn't seen any of the pod members since they had first left the pool port, making her feel vulnerable the farther out they went.

She started rehashing the warning Pete had issued earlier about staying in a group, but she felt safe with Pete and dismissed her worries. With nothing to look at but the monstrous wall, Meranda began to wonder how far up the shore they were compared to the highway above.

Meranda thought she could see the end of the wall, but couldn't tell for sure. The water took on a bluish-black empty color that made goosebumps prickle the back of her neck. They rounded the corner and began heading back toward the shoreline.

Meranda felt relieved until she felt Pete's body stiffen. She looked over her shoulder at Pete, and followed the direction he was looking in. Of course, she couldn't see very well in the dim light, but she did see the shimmering black mass quickly descending on them.

The closer the mass came the clearer she saw what they were, giant lamprey, and they were circling them. Their fangs were the size of a bull's horns. The eel like parasites were so close that Meranda could see their beady red eyes and suction cup mouths lined with rows of razor sharp teeth. Pete wrapped his body around Meranda as she sunk further into him trying to feel less exposed.

The lamprey were agitated and their fangs lengthened. The water was still, yet seemed charged with an electrical current. Pete remained still as a rock as one of the lamprey shot behind him leaving him exposed. It took a lot of control for Pete to remain motionless, as he watched the lamprey become energized from their own taunting's.

Meranda didn't know that Pete was in survival mode and that by not moving a muscle was his best defense. He was sending out danger signals hoping the pod had not met the same fate as the others had the day of the massacre. Which would leave Pete and Meranda on their own. Logic took over and Pete realized that someone in the pod would have sent out a warning.

Peering out, Meranda caught a glimpse of silver flashing behind the gang of lamprey. In unison the lamprey turned with their tails toward Pete and Meranda and faced outward. Meranda saw the patrols surrounding the lamprey like the third ring of a target. The circle of lamprey was twice as thick as the outer circle of mer. They were outnumbered.

"Pete-when the fighting begins you search for an opening and find shelter." Sal signaled Pete. A lamprey lunged Sal testing the waters, before retreating back to its original position.

"I will not abandon my family. You are outnumbered and need my help." Pete radiated back to Sal.

"You will endanger us further; do I have to remind you that it is our job to protect you, the Son of the Lake? Get safe-- that is how you can help save us." Sal's coloring was a flaming orange now matching her ignited temper.

Pete stood down knowing Sal was right and would comply with the huntress. He signaled back, *"I will obey and will pray for your victory."*

At that moment, the lampreys shifted position, every other lamprey faced Pete and Meranda, and the other half faced the outer circle of mermen and Sal. The ripple in the water turned turbulent and Meranda could no longer see anything that was happening. She was in a torpedo barreling toward the blackened caves of the huge mountain behind them.

Once stuffed safely inside a cavernous sinus, Meranda strained to see over Pete's shoulder. She couldn't see much, nor could she tell by the tension in Pete's physical demeanor the fate of her friends.

There were flashes of black and silver flickering before their hideout...and then Meranda saw a cloud of red. She closed her eyes praying that it was not the blood of any mer and buried her head into Pete's back.

In the next moment, she felt a shift within Pete as he leaned forward trying to get a better look hopefully not disclosing their location.

The sound of the battle had changed and Meranda could hear the clashing and whooshing of what sounded like metal echoing off the rocks. The water was murky and moving in all directions, making everything clouded.

Pete moved forward to get a better view of the battle when a giant lamprey bared its fangs. He instinctively flew back deeper in the cavern as the tip of a walrus size tusk grazed his arm slicing it open. Luckily the lamprey was too large to fit any further inside their shelter.

A shadow darkened the entrance of the cavern they were stuffed in, and the water turned a blackened red. Screams echoed off the rocks and half a lamprey erratically swam by them.

The water stilled and Pete waited anxiously for Salmonia's signal that the battle was over. Instead, the signal came from Zane, *"Pete the area is secured."* Pete injected into Meranda's head, *"Wait here!"* And before she could respond, he was gone.

8

Pete scanned the grounds in search of a flaming head of hair. It was hard to see through the stirred mixture of silt and blood, mingled with pieces of lamprey suspended in their watery coffins, before descending to the lakes bottom.

Zane rested his hand on Pete's shoulder and felt his muscles contract. *"She is over there brother. We have lost some, but they lost more today."* Zane's solemn words were overshadowed by, a Norse Viking Merman; four times the size of any of Pete's pod members with Sal in his arms.

In a thunderous voice the Viking interjected, *"Your huntress will live."*

Salmonia looked like a rag doll, small and withered in arms bigger in width than her body. Meranda was now next to Pete and reached out to remove the tangled hair from her friends beautiful brave face, when she noticed a crimson cloud around Salmonia's head.

As if the sun was blocked by a solar eclipse, shadows darkened around them. Meranda adhered herself closer to

Pete. Her mouth dropped open, as she stared wide eyed, at five of the largest mermen she could ever imagine, in her brief knowledge of mer.

They had lost a few; however, the outcome would have been negatively different, if it wasn't for the Viking warriors Pete had sent for the day after the massacre. The mildly wounded helped gather the severely wounded and they headed home.

The day had started out as a relaxing tour of the northern shores of Lake Superior, and in a moments time almost turned into another devastating slaughter. Pete knew this had to get resolved soon.

It seemed like forever to get back home, Meranda hadn't realized they had gone so far up the lake. She had been distracted by the beauty of this underwater world, and now she just wanted to make sure Sal was okay.

She also wanted to find out more about those giant mermen and where they came from? Why were they so big? They looked like they popped out of a folklore. All dressed in armor and carrying seven foot long swords sheath at their hips.

The five warriors covered an area that would take fifty normal-sized mermen to fill. Each warrior the size of a killer whale, yet graceful and fast as they sailed through the water surrounding her and Pete.

The pod began their descent to the caves hidden entrance beneath the rocked cliffs, that had become home to Meranda. She hadn't noticed when they began their journey that they had gone through a narrow tunnel before coming out into the lake.

As they neared the wall, Meranda jerked back. She couldn't see an opening. Only a crack in the rock that didn't look big enough to fit through, but each merman disappeared single file. Zane went in with his back first as he pulled Salmonia through the entryway.

Next, it was her and Pete's turn, as he nudged her toward the opening. Meranda kicked her legs and with her arms at her sides followed the mer in front of her. The tunnel widened just past the entryway until it opened into the pool port.

Meranda was surprised when she popped up like a bobber and was lifted out of the water. With the return of her body weight she flopped onto the rocks sprawled out like the days catch.

In moments, Pete appeared alongside of her. "Do you feel okay Meranda?" He reached over and peeled off the film that covered her face. Meranda leaned back and took in a huge breath of air, even though it hurt her lungs to inflate them to their full capacity and nodded yes.

While catching her breath, Meranda turned around catching a glimpse of Pete's well-muscled backside before he finished pulling on his pants. Meranda felt a giggle in her stomach and she quickly turned back around to allow him his privacy.

She would have to ask him how he changes from a tail to legs and back again, apparently it doesn't include clothes. As she sat there in her giggly mindset she was lifted to a standing position by Pete.

"You better get out of your wet suit before it cuts off the circulation...do you need any help?" Pete had that mischievous twinkle in his eye with one brow raised. Meranda turned a deep shade of red as the image of her stolen peek flashed in her mind.

"No! I think I can manage to dress and undress myself...I mean undress and dress myself." Meranda shakily turned and headed to her quarters, well technically Pete's quarters.

"You had better hurry it appears you need some…umm, refreshments." Pete yelled out. Meranda knew exactly what Pete was really thinking, that she needed to get more air to her head. "I need to go see to Salmonia. We will meet for supper, as I am sure you have a question or two." Pete turned leaving Meranda wobbling and squishing toward her room.

Pete ran his hand through his hair realizing what a close call today had been, and that they had almost lost Sal. He cautiously approached her quarters, "Zane, how is she doing?" Pete asked.

"I am doing just fine, thank you." Salmonia tried to sit up but fell back.

"I'm glad you are making a speedy recovery and have regained your faculties. I will leave you in Zane's company, as I must see to our guests from the old country." Pete turned switching to telepathic mode, *"And by the way sister, thank you, for saving mine and Meranda's life."* Pete shook his head and thought that he would never in a thousand years, figure out the female species.

"You are most welcome, brother." Sal softened her tone knowing that it had been hard for Pete to obey her command on the battlefield. He cracked a small smile and gave Zane and Sal some privacy. He wondered if those two would ever find their way back to each other. He knew that it would make their eight year old daughter Roselyn one happy little mermaid.

She was the most enchanting youngster. She looked like Sal, except her skin was a radiant caramel color. She had big brown eyes and chocolate brown ringlets that cascaded around her face. Hues of her mother's coppery red hair shined through, adding to her beauty. She had her mother's keen senses and father's gentle nature; until she felt slighted, then she was all Salmonia.

Pete headed off to report to his father and see to the comforts of the Vikings. They were not as old as his father, but the next generation thereafter. Neither generations could walk on land and they would evolve back to the North Atlantic sturgeon they had evolved from, completing the full circle of a merman's life.

The warriors were 1500 years old, and Pete's was 532 years old, yet the difference and size between them was huge. Pete guessed it was true that the aquatic species would only grow as large as their environment. Lake Superior may be the largest surface fresh water lake in the world, but it was no ocean. Regardless, Pete was thankful that the Nordic Warriors came so quickly to their call to duty.

"Pete, come meet our guest." Pete's father rarely involved himself with Pete's duties, but it was rare that a Norse Warriors traveled this far from home.

"I'm on my way father." Pete telecommunicated back. Pete headed down the caves corridor that led to a larger cavern deep beneath the commons area. This was where Pete's father would remain until he made his final journey home to the rivers in Norway, his birthplace.

The area was spacious enough to accommodate the Vikings. It was partially submerged in the water with natural carved out seats in the rocks, so that the warriors could rest while allowing them to leave their tail in the water. Like most amphibians' they can stay under the water for long periods of time, but have to surface occasionally to replenish their systems with a fresh supply of air.

Pete entered his father's quarters, and immediately felt small next to these giants. *"This is my son, Pelias. Pelias, I would like you to meet Folkor the guardian of the people, Gunnar, the elements of the gunnr war and arr warrior, Hallvardr the rock defender, Logmar the lawman, and lastly Sigurdr - the guardian of victory."*

"Welcome warriors, I am humbled and grateful for your timely arrival. May I offer you food and wine?" Pete felt in awe of these powerful and monolithic warriors.

In booming voices they all returned their greetings. Pete bowed to his father as he excused himself to set forth a feast worthy of these heroes. *"I shall return upon the hour with food and drink."* He bowed to the Norse mermen and took his leave.

Pete started back to the commons, he sighed releasing the anxiety he had felt in anticipation of their arrival. He could hear the deep echoes of their conversation and roaring laughter as they reminisced with his father. He hoped that the warriors were not shedding a bad light on the handling of today's attack.

Normally, it would have been Salmonia's job to accommodate their guests, had she not been injured in the battle.

Upon reentering the commons, Pete shouted orders to the servers, "Eira! Einar! I need one hundred pounds of salmon, many flasks of red wine, and many loaves of bread within the hour for our guests: The twins scrambled in opposite directions to see to the preparations wanting to make Sal proud.

"How would you like the fish prepared sir?" Eira asked.

"Raw please, and the freshest catch we have. Thank you." Pete knew that one hundred pounds was a lot of fish, but wanted his guest to feel the gratitude he felt for saving their lives.

Pete went back to his quarters to see how Meranda was fairing. When he approached the entry to her quarters he heard crying. "Meranda where are you? Are you hurt?" Pete found Meranda by the hearth rubbing her feet.

Meranda tried to wipe away the tears with the back of her hand, "I 'm fine...it's just that my feet are burning-- they must have gotten frostbitten."

"They probably did, and had it not been for the attack I would have never kept you out there that long. The best thing to do is soak them in cool water." Pete lifted Meranda off the floor and set her on the couch. He did not know what it felt like, but knew it had to be painful. "I will be right back with water to soak your feet in." He wrapped her feet in a fur blanket first.

Meranda nodded her head with her arms wrapped around her knees and her head buried between them, she tried to stop crying. It had been quite a day. She could've done without the attack, but the rest of it was like a dream come true.

Pete returned with a large shallow bowl. It was an agate with golden swirls that spiraled down toward the bottom of the bowl. Pete set the bowl on the floor before her and gently took one blue foot at a time and submerged it in the cool water.

Of course, Meranda couldn't feel what temperature the water was until it splashed up on her ankles. The pain subsided as her feet start to turn pink and white except for her toes which still were a blackish blue color.

"Does that feel better? Pete knew the answer by looking at Meranda's face. He added warmer water to the bowl as her feet thawed.

"Better thank you, the pain is lessening." Meranda gave him a small grateful smile.

A cast iron pot hung over the hearth, as steam escaped from the bubbling lid waking Meranda's stomach, which began voicing its complaints loudly. Pete was already on his way over to dish them up a couple of bowls.

Setting them down on the carved coffee table to cool he handed Meranda a warm cup of wine. She wrapped her hands around the cup and soaked up its warmth. Once her feet thawed and she had food in her stomach, she would be heading to bed.

"The food, warm wine, and company earn five stars." Meranda had almost finished her wine and felt its soothing effects and clumsily reached for her bowl. It looked delicious with bite size chunks of Coho and salmon peeking out from a creamy white sauce laden with: small pearl onions, carrots, and garlic. As it hit her stomach she could feel the warm nutritious food spread throughout her body.

Pete was sitting at the other end of the couch watching her nourish herself back to a rosy pink, "Do your feet feel better?"

"They do, and the color is almost back to normal. Thanks again, I have frost bitten my feet before, but never frozen them almost solid." Meranda let Pete remove her feet from the water and he dried them off with a towel. He reached in a drawer producing slippers lined in rabbit fur and slipped them on her feet. They felt like a piece of heaven and she would be sleeping in them. "Thank you! The pain is gone and my stomach is full."

"That is the recipe to a satisfied guest." Pete smiled feeling pleased with himself.

"Feel free to retire, we can talk tomorrow. I have to see to some important matters." Pete gave her a hand up making sure that she could stand on her injured feet. Meranda felt guilty, because she was enjoying being pampered. "I can take it from here Sir, thank you and goodnight."

"Very well, goodnight." Pete let go of her and took his leave as she climbed into bed.

The next thing on Pete's list was to check in on Salmonia, and see how she was fairing before he himself retired. As he neared Sal's cavern, he heard Zane, Sal, and Roselyn's soft chuckles and decided to leave them have their time. He turned to leave when he received a message from Sal, *"Thank you for allowing us this quiet moment as a family. Rosie needs to feel all is safe. I am doing well and will meet with you in the morning. Goodnight, brother."*

Loretta Rose Didrikson

9

Pete sat on the couch in the guest quarters, which had become his room since Meranda arrived. With his head in his hands he tried to sort through the day's events. His hands slipped off his head; he had fallen asleep.

The camp was quiet and all was taken care of for today, so he climbed up into his fur lined bed and allowed his muscles to relax. He hoped tomorrow would shed some light on what they were up against in the lake and how to proceed to correct the imbalance.

Morning came quickly and Pete woke to Zane treading patiently in the pool port, "*It's about time you woke brother,*" Zane's playful voice roused Pete from his unconscious state more quickly than he would have liked. It was impossible not to notice that Zane was in an exceptionally good mood. His commander expression was usually stern and business like.

"Good morning Zane. How is Sal this morning?" Pete sat up running a hand through his bed head hair.

"She is doing well and is seeing to our guest's needs already." Zane didn't sound too happy about that, but he knew there was no talking to that red head.

"Excellent, I will be conversing with my father later this morning and would like you to join me. I am going to suggest a gathering of all the pods to collect information. I would like to hear about their encounters with the giant lampreys and serpent."

Pete felt it would be best to get all pods on both the north and south shores involved covering the mass majority of the lake. The more information they had to arm themselves with, the better their chances of defeating this invasion.

The lines in Pete's face had lessened some, but his dreams had been turbulent. "If you would ready the seagulls and send messages to the Native American, Apostle, and the Devils Island pods, then join me at my father's quarters and we can seek advice from the warriors before deciding our next move."

"Very well, and thank you again for the privacy last night, Roselyn needed to be reassured after having both of us injured recently." Zane started to depart when Pete agreed that things have gotten too close of late, and that they needed to remain in high alert until this matter was resolved. Zane responded with a nod and headed out to ready the birds.

Pete slowly gravitated towards Meranda's quarters when he ran into Sal, "You look lovely this morning Sal, how are you feeling?"

"I'm feeling fine brother." Sal decided to let the "lovely" comment slide. "Meranda is looking for you." Sal had just left her, "I think she is heading to the commons in search of you."

"Thank you, and Sal...I would like to get together with you later this morning to discuss a council meeting." Pete knew there would be no rest around here until they figured out how best to deal with the lakes current situation.

"Very well I will be in my quarters." Sal winced from stabbing pains as she limped to the galley to make sure everything was underway in welcoming their guest; she never said she was one hundred percent.

Pete saw Meranda enter the commons and thought how natural she looked, as if she had always been a part of this mission. Meranda looked up and made eye contact with Pete and broke into a huge smile. "Good morning" she said as her step quickened.

"Good morn to you, how are the feet?" Pete was concerned her frostbitten feet would suffer permanent damage.

"Good--a bit sore, but good. I have something to ask you."

"Shoot." Pete felt he could handle any question she had at this point.

"Do you have any kind of testing facilities down here—a lab of some sort?" Meranda had been giving the lamprey issues some serious thought and had a few theories. "I saved a couple of the lampreys I removed from Zane, and have been observing them. I would like to do some testing on them to see if I can figure out why they are getting so large."

Pete cocked his head and raised an eyebrow at her, "Yes, of course we have a lab, and you are more than welcome to use it. If you could find some answers, it would be most helpful. I just never expected you to …."

"To what Pete, be of some use. Did you think I would be so distraught at the discovery of Merfolk that I would curl up and hide in a corner crying for mommy and daddy?" Meranda immediately felt bad that her sharp tongue had reared its ugly head.

Actually, there were times when she had wanted to cry out for her mommy and daddy. "I'm sorry, I have been feeling extremely restless."

"No apologies necessary, with all that has taken place I hadn't given your usefulness any thought, my apologizes...." "Have you had breakfast yet?" Pete's stomach grumbled.

Meranda eyed him suspiciously; she had discovered Pete's talents at changing the subject. "Yes, I have had my breakfast." She was determined to make the best of her current circumstances and take advantage of this rare opportunity to observe life beneath the water's surface.

Pete didn't say anything at first, so she immediately continued with her request. "As I said, I would like to investigate what's going on with the lamprey--why they have grown to unheard of sizes, and why they are so aggressive. It could shed some light on things."

"I think that would be of great help if you are sure you are up to it?" Pete looked a bit surprised.

"I too would like to know what is causing this unusual growth. Lampreys are normally 8 to 12 inches long and as round as a garden hose. This hybrid version could wipeout the habitat in this lake." The biologist in Meranda was out in full force this morning.

"In addition, the danger it presents to the safety of the guardians and the eco system of this great fresh water lake..." Pete added. "Come, I will show you the lab."

"Great, let me just grab a few things and I'll meet up with you." Meranda was excited to do something useful and had been itching to do tests on the lampreys she had been observing. "Where should I met you?"

"I'll wait for you at the east tunnel south of the pool port." This was an unexpected resource he had not thought of. No one had made use of the lab since Pete had had it updated. He waited by the entrance pacing with thoughts of how helpful this could be. *It must be fated.*

Meranda arrived and Pete led the way. The descent was steep and the wide stairs made Meranda take two steps to get to the next step of layered rock. The walls had thicker concentrations of the sparkled slate and a larger marbling of gold and silver.

She thought of the investigation they had been doing on nickel mining to see if there was enough nickel to harvest. She would have to say, there was, but she would never tell them. It would result in the disruption and destruction of these ancient rocks.

Meranda thought how amazing it was that all precious metals and essential minerals came from the earth, and within these rocks was ash from the "big bang" era of the universe.

Pete's stepped up his pace as they neared the entrance to the lab. He wanted to see her face when she walked through the door. He stopped in front of what looked like a rock wall; a dead end. He push on the wall and the rock door opened. He stepped inside and lights came on and turned motioning for her to come in.

Meranda's mouth dropped and her eyes lit up as she looked around at a high tech lab in-a-cave. Her eyes were drawn to the back wall, "Is that an aquarium across the whole wall?"

"No, actually it is a window to the lake." Pete enjoyed watching her. She was like a young child on Christmas morning.

On the left wall there were all sorts of stainless steel cupboards and an agate counter top with high powered microscopes sitting on them.

Along the back wall, under the lake's window were: computers, data machines, Richter scales, temperature gauges, and some machines she had never seen before. This was one of the only places in the caves where electricity had been piped down from above.

On the right wall, there were glass beakers, test tubes, and all the testing supplies you could think of. And of course, a pool port with a log couches and chairs off in an alcove. There was a hearth, refrigerator, and bunk beds all built into the walls.

"Well--what do you think?" Pete was proud of his underwater lab, and to think, the EPA thought they had a set up to be envied. Pete had always felt bad that they were governed by a budget, but it worked for gathering surface activity and down a hundred feet or so. The rest of the 1200 foot abyss was left to the guardians. "It is yours to use as you see fit Meranda, and if there's anything you need just let me, Sal, or Zane know."

"I-I don't know what to say Pete. It's beautiful! I'm scared to touch anything." Meranda's eyes sparkled as she took it all in.

"I hope you touch something, otherwise the lab will just sit here and we won't unlock the answers we need to best those beasts." Pete looked hopeful, but couldn't help wonder again if all was meant to be as the universe wanted it.

"I will find the answers. I just don't know where to start." Meranda regained her composure and all the knowledge she had learned started to awaken.

"I will let you get accustomed to where everything is and send someone to get some samples for you." Pete thought Meranda belonged amongst all this equipment.

"Not necessary, remember, I already have two lampreys for testing; one regular lamprey and one hybrid.

Fear immediately flooded Pete, "you need to be extremely careful when handling the lampreys Meranda, if one latches on to you it can cause serious bleeding."

"I realize that Pete, and I will be very careful. I have seen what they are capable of doing." Meranda sternly replied. Pete didn't like the thought of her handling those parasites, but knew how helpful the information would be. It could mean the difference between winning the battle or losing.

"I will leave you to explore then, or would you rather come back later?" Pete was not sure if she was ready.

"Absolutely not, I want to get started immediately. I will need the specimens brought down here." There she went again giving orders to the Son of the Lake.

"Specimens…? Oh yes, your pets…" Pete was leery, but knew there was no other way to move forward. Of course, he would have preferred if they were dead specimens. "There are larger storage containers under the counter." Pete's eyebrows were almost joined in one straight line above his eyes he had them pinched together so hard.

"Thank you. I mean it Pete, thank you for the best opportunity of my life, and thank you again for saving my life." Meranda looked like she was about to cry and Pete couldn't handle that.

"You're more than welcome, but I think it is me that is indebted to you, especially your help as a biologist." Pete turned to leave and had to ask one more time. "Are you sure you are up to all this right now?"

"I am more than up to it and ready to be of some assistance around here and earn my keep." Meranda spied some freshly pressed lab coats and slipped one on.

Pete looked over his shoulder before he left watching Meranda busy herself, as she got accustom to where everything was. It didn't take her long to immerse herself in preparation of the task at hand.

Meranda stood in front of the glass wall that allowed her to observe the lake when she heard a noise coming from the pool port. "Hello?" Meranda shook her head and decided that she must be hearing things, until she heard it again.

It was the quietest movement of water. She walked cautiously over to the pool when a head popped up out of the water. Meranda flew backwards distancing herself from …a girl or rather a young mermaid that looked a lot like Salmonia, except darker skinned. "Hello" Meranda relaxed realizing it was a mermaid.

"Hi, my name is Roselyn." Roselyn had been so curious about the human that she had snuck down to the lab without her parents' permission. They were too busy with the visitors and all the adult stuff they were always doing, leaving Roselyn to amuse herself.

"Hello, I don't suppose you are Salmonia's daughter?"

"Salmonia is my mother and Zane is my father." Roselyn announced her parentage with pride. Even though she had to spend a lot of time alone she was extremely proud of both her parents.

"Well it is nice to finally meet you." Meranda smiled trying not to intimidate this young mer-maiden.

"So you are human?" Roselyn was as honest and blunt as most youngsters her age are.

"I am." Meranda let Roselyn set the boundaries of their budding friendship being careful not to scare her off. However, what Meranda did not know was that scaring her would be next to impossible. Since Meranda had arrived Roselyn couldn't think of nothing else, but the human girl. "How old are you?"

"I'm eight, almost nine." Roselyn immerged farther out of the water resting her arms on the pool ports shelf.

"You look like your mother and your father," replied Meranda.

"That's what I've been told." Roselyn seemed distracted as she looked around checking to make sure no one else was there.

"Is it okay for you to be here alone?" Meranda felt that was a fair question.

"Yes, all the ports are safe. Once in a while my mom will let me go hunting with her, but not since the compound was placed on high alert." Roselyn accepted the rules that her parents had put down for her, at least for the most part.

"That must be fun." Meranda wished she could just jump in the water and go instead of always needing help. She felt like she got treated like a child too.

"So can I help you?" Roselyn got right to the point.

"I am not sure how you can help, but I would love the company...that is if it's okay with your mom and dad, and Pete." Meranda hated to state the obvious so quickly, but she didn't want to break any rules or get Salmonia mad at her.

"I will ask them ...later" she left as quietly as she came.

Meranda smiled to herself and began opening drawers and cupboards trying to get acquainted with the lab when a shadow flickered across the wall from the lakes window. Meranda let out a shriek flattening her back against the rocks.

There in the window was the largest sturgeon she had ever seen. It was at least seven feet long with a human like face peering in at her. Meranda's legs turned to rubber, yet she couldn't take her eyes off the human fish when words started entering her head.

"Greetings, Meranda" the fish man spoke.

Meranda nodded like a bobble head until she found her voice, "H-hello."

"I am Pelias' father, my apologies that I have not properly welcomed you sooner. I am very interested to find out what you will discover. I will let you get to your work. I wanted to introduce myself and meet the young human my son talks so fondly of. If there is anything you need--please just ask. Good day Miss Micheals." Pete's father disappeared into the darkness.

Meranda sat down to digest the last few hours, heck the last few minutes, when Sal showed up carrying two closed containers with the lampreys in them. "Here you go. Where do you want them?"

"Over there, and thanks. Sal the strangest creature just stopped by and talked to me." Meranda still had a shocked look on her face.

Salmonia laughed, "Did he look like a fish?"

"Yes--a sturgeon actually, except with a human face." Meranda still was shaken by the strength of his telepathic voice.

"That would be the Father of the Lake." Sal cocked one eyebrow to see if her friend was handling everything okay. "Are you okay?"

"Yeah, I am just in awe of the different ...I don't know... the different creatures I have met. Speaking of which, I met your daughter." Meranda didn't mean to reveal that right away, but at the moment had lost her filter to stop thoughts from spilling from her mouth.

"You did, hmmm--was she bothering you? I was wondering how long it would take her to seek you out. " Salmonia knew her daughter could get pesky at times.

"No--not at all, she is delightful." Meranda sounded a little too excited.

"Delightful-huh," Sal was trying to feel out whether Meranda was just being polite knowing her daughter was full of non-stop questions.

"Yes, in fact, she asked if she could be my assistant..." Meranda paused giving Sal a moment, "...and I told her it would be fine with me, but she would have to have your permission first. So heads up." Meranda appeared excited to have someone to hang out with and mentor.

Sal agreed and thought that would be good for her daughter and her education. She also knew that girls her age talked a lot and asked a lot of questions.

Sal was happy for her daughter, but wanted Meranda to know she had to set boundaries. "How about we give it a try, but I will expect you to be honest with me whether it's working out for you having her down here or not." Salmonia was a straight forward person, a trait that had clearly been passed on to Roselyn.

"I will, but really Sal, the company will be nice and there are a lot of things I could use a hand with. I won't let her do anything dangerous or work with chemicals, just some recording and note taking. She really is enchanting." Meranda was sincere and Sal picked up on that.

Meranda didn't have a lot of experience with kids, but felt if you didn't ask questions you will never know the answers. She worked with the youth groups at the library in Aurora and loved their energy for the most part. She truly would appreciate the company. Meranda found Roselyn refreshing. "When do you want her to report for duty?" Sal was punctual and expected everyone else to be as courteous in return.

"Tomorrow is good, if that works for you. I'll be here at 8 a.m." Meranda didn't know where everyone went during the day, but it was awfully quiet at times considering the number of Merfolk that lived here. Yet another question for Pete or rather Pelias. Meranda couldn't say his proper name without a giggle threatening to erupt.

"8:00 a.m. it is. I have to go and show the old timers a tour and see if they can pick up on any clues or find the mother of these wonderful hybrids." Sal jumped in the pool port "Tomorrow, my friend," in a splash she was gone.

10

Salmonia joined Pete as a united front before meeting with the Father. On the way down the corridor, she stopped a moment, noticing how silky smooth the walls were. Something she rarely took the time to look at, but after a brush with death all things seemed noteworthy.

Being in the Father's presence always made her nervous, but meeting with the Viking Warriors put her over the edge, making her feel more female than huntress.

She was excited to meet the legendary warriors, and that overrode any other emotion she felt. The closer they got, the clearer Sal could hear their deep vibrating voices. When she entered the room, they all stopped talking and bowed to greet her.

"Welcome huntress, we are glad to see you are in good health. We have been informed, that when you are well, you will be giving us a tour of the area. It will be our pleasure to be in the company of such a beautiful guide." Folkor, the guardian of the people, spoke

as his powerful voice resonated in her head making her feel shy.

"The pleasure is mine Folkor, guardian of the people." Pete felt Sal tremble slightly, but she hid it well, *"Shall we go at sunrise, after you have rested from your long journey?"* Sal looked like a smelt compared to these massive Norse Viking Warriors.

"Please, do me the honor and call me, Folkor, as my friends do." Folkor's smile was genuine and spread widely over his face.

"If you feel you are recovered huntress, we would be honored to help hunt as not burden your pod with our large appetites." Logmar eyes were kind putting Salmonia at ease.

Pete and Sal watched as Eira and Einar brought in platters of fish, flasks of wine, and fresh warm bread. Sal was pleased with the bountiful feast that had been set before the warriors. *"We will leave you to your meal."* Sal bowed joining Pete by the pool port.

Sal went directly to speak to the kitchen crew, "Eira and Einar you have done me proud. Thank you." Sal smiled at the twins who beamed with pride that they could be there for their huntress when she needed them.

Sal and Zane joined Pete in his quarters and they discussed the outing, before retiring for the evening. Sal knew the hunt would tax her, but she was looking forward to showing their guests around the lake.

Pete went to the lab; he had a feeling Meranda was still there. "I see you're still hard at it. Have you stopped for supper?" Pete said warily.

"I did, the twins brought me dinner down here. It was so thoughtful. You look as tired as I feel." Meranda laughed feeling the stress in her shoulders, and preformed a few shoulder rolls. "I'm just about to call it a night."

"Shall I wait and walk you to your quarters?" Pete rubbed his large hand through his hair.

"No, that won't be necessary, but thank you. Are the warriors settled in?"

"They are settled and Sal is feeling better, in fact, we are taking them into the lake tomorrow to assess the situation and show them the unique structure of this great lake. We are leaving early, so I probably won't see you until dinner, at which time I will give you a full report." Pete's eyes twinkled knowing Meranda would want to know every detail.

"I will see you for dinner then. Be safe." Meranda's young face was creased with exhaustion and worry. She knew she would be on edge until they returned safely; however, having massive mermen along gave her comfort.

Morning arrived early and the cave filled with a busy hum. Once Pete, Zane, and Sal were suited up they huddled together making sure they all knew the plan. "*Pete I will go first.*" Salmonia never forgetting that her job was to serve and protect the Son of the Lake.

Sal made sure Pete knew to give her the respect she deserved as his protector, especially in front of the Vikings, but knew he was never comfortable with his role as Prince. He stopped and gave Sal the "after you" arm signal.

Salmonia did not hesitate, and led the way. The Viking warriors surrounded Pete and his father offering protection. Once out in the lake, they headed southeast.

The shoreline began to change from layers of slated rock to broken boulders, and eventually becoming a sandy bottom. They saw the old footings that lead to the shipping lanes that ended at the tip of Lake Superior.

"The clarity of the water is remarkable," commented Gunnarr.

"It is pure and refreshing and reminds me of home." added Sigrudr.

Salmonia smiled to herself and felt proud of this great lake they were entrusted to protect. They continued to follow the shoreline south.

The smell of the water changed, sparking a higher level of awareness, as they cautiously continued they saw a fluorescent green fog that hung thick in the water. Sal veered out into the lake where she thought it would be clearer, but the green fog had only thickened.

"What is that foul smell?" Logmar asked.

"It is coming from the barrels that were dumped in the lake fifty some years ago by the U.S. Army Corps of Engineers. They are documented to contain ammunitions scraps and other waste from a Twin Cities Army branch and claim to have zero radiation." Salmonia informed the warriors. *"I have never seen this green mist before."* Salmonia added as she captured some of the mist in a bottle to bring back to Meranda.

When they swam over the barrels, they noticed hundreds of small lampreys engaged in a feeding frenzy. They were scavengers, so it was no surprise.

The group continued toward the southern shores of Wisconsin, and the water became clear again. Sand barges being the more prominent landscape.

The south shores vastly differed from the northern shores, but both had their own unique beauty. The pod spotted schools of Salmon and Coho, at different territorial depths, heightening the hunter in them all.

"Anyone interested in breakfast?" Salmonia's skin started to tingle at the thought of a hunt. It had been a while since she had been able to hunt.

"Folkor and Sigurdr stay with the King and Prince," commanded Gunnarr. *"We will help the huntress gather fish,"* and in a silvery flash they were gone.

The father of the lake hadn't been in open waters for a long time, but seemed to be enjoying the southern shores of Lake Superior. It consisted of more islands and caves and a flat desert like floor. Some places were shallow stretching far out into the lake before it dropped off into the deeper colder waters.

The Apostle and Madeline Islands were very popular tourist attractions from above. Devil's Island; however, with its less accessible shores of jagged rocks were known for their dangerous waters. It also housed the most primitive pod of mermen.

Pete's body stiffened putting both Vikings on alert. There was a fast approaching pod from the south that was heading their way. When the threat was within one hundred feet, the approaching pod sent out a message, *"State your business in our waters."*

"Stand down for the Father of the Lake is present." Pete replied.

"Our apologies, but may we inquire the nature of your business. I am Marius, the leader of the Devil's Island pod."

"We are gathering information on any encounters or attacks with the invasive species." Pete replied stiffly.

"Yes, we have engaged in frequent attacks of late." Marius stood in submission, despite his dislike of the northern pod of Royales.

"There will be a gathering in two days' time at our compound and are requesting representation from each pod to share information on these attacks." Pete looked small and non-threatening compared to his two Viking body guards. Marius and his pod couldn't take their eyes off the massive warriors, they had never seen mermen that large.

"We will inform all southern pods, and help in any way we can. Until then," Marius turned and set out to pass the word about the meeting. It wasn't often the Royales called for a gathering and Marius looked forward to seeing how the other side conducted their compound.

Pete relaxed as the distant grew between his father and Marius' pod. He gave a moment's thought to the Devil's Island pod. They were a younger more primitive group, and not as evolved as other pods that shared this lake. Even their appearance was strikingly different.

They looked more fish than mermen. They had spiny knobs that started at the top of their heads and ran down their backs, ending at their thorny tails. They're faces resembled a sturgeon, with sucker type lips and feeler whiskers jetting out before their gills. Their bulbous eyes were set deep in their small egg shaped heads exaggerating the size of their arms and chests. Their hands were webbed with claws extending from their vaguely recognizable fingers.

The Devils Island pod was seventy eight years old and still possessed strong predator instincts. They were about survival, and if a ship sunk in their waterways the crew was certainly never found. They became the meal.

Whereas, the more evolved pods of the northern shores saved the people they could and returned them safely to land. If that was not possible they were given a second chance at life below the water's surface serving the lake.

Sal sent out a signal that they had been very successful in the hunt and were returning to the caves. *"Is all secure with you and your father?"* She inquired before heading back.

"Yes, we made contact with the Devil's Island pod and will be heading back to the caves as well. Be safe my sister." Pete knew she was in good company.

During their return to the caves, there were no sightings of giant lampreys or the serpent. The father of the lake sought out his quarters immediately to rest from his adventure.

He was becoming weaker and knew it would not be long before he made the final swim to his place of birth in the rivers of Norway, completing his life's cycle.

Upon his return, Pete's first priority was to see Meranda, making sure she was unharmed after working with those blood suckers. Once inside the safety of the caverns, he was able to bid his protectors good bye. Pete used the port to get to the lab being it was the quickest route.

He remained beneath the surface listening before emerging onto the ledge. He could hear Meranda in the front of the lab talking to Roselyn and wondered why Roselyn was down here.

He quietly lifted himself out of the water behind the privacy wall, and transformed to his human state. He grabbed a towel and wrapped it around his narrow waist making a mental note to supply some clothes to this port.

He tightened the towel and walked around the wall into the open.

Suddenly, Roselyn was scrambling toward the door, but it was too late. She was sure Pete had seen her in human form. Meranda was engrossed in dissecting a lamprey and was startled to see Pete standing so close with only a towel on, "G-G-Good gosh, you scared me half to death Pete." She tried not to stare at his well-muscled chest and narrow waist and focused on his intense blue eyes.

"You really get absorbed in your work." Pete's eyes darkened taking pleasure in making her nervous by his closeness.

Meranda felt the heat climb up her face, and she quickly returned to the microscope. "How was your sightseeing adventure?"

Pete backed up letting her off the hook, "Uneventful, which was a blessing with my father exposed--despite his giant body guards, I still felt nervous." Pete looked around for Roselyn knowing she was still in the lab. "Who were you talking to?"

"Roselyn—she's my assistant. I don't know where she got off to." Meranda poked her head up and took a quick survey of the lab.

Roselyn had changed into mermaid form and came back around by Meranda who gazed down at her puzzled to why she had changed, but kept her thoughts to herself. "There you are. Sal and Zane both gave their permission for her to be down here helping me."

"I think that's wonderful." Pete smiled at Roselyn.

Meranda did not want to be rude, but Pete was making Roselyn very uncomfortable. "If there isn't anything else, we have a lot of work to get done before we can call it a day."

"I will leave you ladies to your work then... I'll see you for a late dinner?" Pete looked forward to dinning with her at the end of the day.

"I have to get some samples set up first, but I can join you later." Meranda was in her glory doing what she loved best. It was what she had spent the last six years of her life studying.

Pete nodded to both Meranda and Roselyn and headed for the door. When he left the room, Meranda turned to Roselyn, "What's up with changing into mer form?"

"If I tell you, it has to be a secret that you can't tell anyone." Roselyn looked distraught, and never having a friend before made it hard for her to trust anyone with her secrets.

"Okay, I pinky swear," Meranda offered a slightly curled pinky.

"Pinky swears...I don't get it?" Roselyn just stood there not knowing what Meranda wanted her to do.

Meranda smiled and then explained that when you pinky swear you make a sealed promise that you will do whatever it is you agreed to. Meranda felt like she was eight years old again.

She hadn't pinky swore since her and Jena were in the barn, and Jena told Meranda that she kissed Logan. Meranda felt pangs of homesickness thinking about her friend.

Roselyn reached out and hooked her pinky around Meranda's to seal-the-deal in hopes that Meranda would get happy again. "I pinky swear back."

Meranda gave a sniff and forced a small smile on her face making eye contact with her young friend, "It's a deal."

"Umm...no one knows that I can transform to a land mammal. And I don't want anyone to know, especially my Mom and Dad." Roselyn looked scared that she shared the information with Meranda.

Meranda saw the fear all over her face and quickly reassured her that she pinky swore and was bound to keep her secret. She did inquire on why she didn't want anyone to know that she could transform.

"It's just something that's usually learned over time and I just did it one day on accident. I don't want my mom to get mad at me--I'm waiting until the right time to tell her, that's all." Roselyn seemed upset over what Meranda felt should be a positive thing, but she didn't know the rules. Within every society and culture there are governing rules that everyone abides by or pays the penalty.

"Is that why you ran and hid from Pete?" Meranda tried to understand where Rosie was coming from.

"Yes, if he knew he would so tell my parents."

Meranda tried to reassure Roselyn that she thought Pete would understand, but would leave it to her to tell her parents. Roselyn twisted her hair and looked worried that Pete might of saw her and would be compelled to tell.

"If the hunting party is back, then it won't be long before my mother comes looking for me. I'll see you tomorrow. Remember you promised," Roselyn inched her way back over to the pool port and disappeared without so much as a splash.

Meranda finished putting the samples away to cure for the night. As she turned off the lights she took a moment before heading up the stone stairs to the upper level, "Look at your little girl now mom and dad, who would of thought I would be living a secret life. I love you, goodnight." Meranda made her way back to her quarters without getting lost. She felt the tightness in her muscles start to soften along the way.

When she entered her alcove, instantly the smell of something wonderful hit her senses, replacing the smell of the chemicals from the lab. She saw Pete setting the table and fantasized about him wearing an apron instead of the towel he wore earlier, sending her into an instant blush. "Hello." Meranda gave a soft shout knowing it would echo off the caves walls.

"Hello yourself, did you get things wrapped up in the lab?" Pete was curious about any findings and had to fight the urge to ask Meranda about her findings before she was ready to tell.

"I did, and I won't know anything for a day or two." Meranda answered him with a timeline knowing he was dying to know. "What is that wonderful smell?"

"It's crab in a white wine sauce." Pete announced like he actually made it himself, he walked over and picked out a fine white wine to complement the meal. "You like crab don't you?"

"I do and it smells wonderful. Just give me a minute to wash up and I'll be ready to eat." She quickly splashed water on her face and took her hair out of the bun. Grabbing her tooth brush she gave a quick brush and pinched her cheeks for a little color. Stepping back she caught her reflection and wondered why exactly she was primping before dinner…it was just dinner, with a friend. However, if she was honest with herself she knew her feelings for Pete had bloomed.

She felt she had taken too long in the bathroom, but when she came out, Pete was just plating up the food. He turned around and broke into that dazzling smile that illuminated his face. What is it about him… all he has to do is smile and she gets all warm and fuzzy inside.

"I poured you a glass of wine." The crystal wine glass caught the flickering firelight and exploded sparkling droplets on the wall and ceiling like a disco ball.

"It's beautiful…look Pete." Meranda was looking all around and didn't notice that Pete was watching the fire reflect off her hair. "The colors are magnificent. The smallest light catches the gold, copper, and silver flecks in the walls."

"Beautiful." Pete was watching how the fire brought out the auburn hues in her hair causing its own display. He needed to change the mood before he forgot himself and allowed his feelings to turn into desire. This woman had stirred feelings in him from the moment she walked into his office for her interview.

Meranda turned around proclaiming how a hard day's work always made her extremely hungry.

Pete pulled out the chair for her taking her by surprise. She was blushing again and had nothing to blame it on this time. It had been a long time since anyone had made her feel—well anything, and it caught her off guard.

Mitch was always a gentleman, and would open her door and pull out her chair. He made her feel loved without making her feel too girly. She forgot how nice it felt to look forward to seeing someone at the end of the day, someone to share your day's events with.

After Mitch and her graduated, they were going to go to Isle Royale and rent a cabin for the summer and explore the untouched ecosystem, hoping to find an artifact or a fossil. Isle Royale was truly a last frontier, and many parts of the island, still held secrets from the past.

"Hello…Meranda," Pete had asked Meranda twice now if she wanted some bread.

His voice finally reached her bring her back to the present, "Sorry--I get lost in my thoughts sometimes." After they shared a satisfying meal coupled with conversation and a few glasses of wine, Meranda stifled a yawn.

"I think I better let you retire." Pete gathered the dishes and put them on a tray to be picked up.

"I'm sorry--this day has caught up to me."

"You've been in the lab for at least ten hours. It's understandable that you're tired. Pete chuckled at her. "Sleep well Meranda."

"Thank you--and you too, Pelias." Meranda giggled.

Pete turned around and looked at her knowing there was only one person who called him that, his father. "Aye--you met my father."

"I did."

Loretta Rose Didrikson

11

"Mama…" Roselyn woke up screaming from the reoccurring nightmare that had been nagging at her, but tonight it was vivid. Salmonia went flying out of bed to get to her daughter's side.

"It is alright baby…it was just a dream." Salmonia didn't understand why her daughter had night terrors because she lived a rather sheltered life.

"But mom… it seemed so real. There were serpents and giant eels and they were killing merpeople and humans. They had you and daddy. I couldn't help you--I could only watch."

"It was only a dream. Try to go back to sleep. I know a little trick. If you start dreaming that same dream again change the dream by having some big strong Viking Warrior come to the rescue." Salmonia worried there could be more to these nightmares than she cared to admit to herself right now.

"I'll try mama. Will you stay with me for a while?" Roselyn looked up at Salmonia with those big brown eyes and Sal's motherly instinct to make her baby feel safe melted her heart.

"Of course sweetie, slide over." Merfolks didn't need a mattress bed but rather a down filled waterproof pallet that was always near a pool port. Even still, Roselyn had as girly of a room as a little mermaid could have. She loved agates and had been collecting them for years.

Actually her dad, Zane, started the collection with some very large frosted tear shaped agates he called mermaid tears. Since then she had filled her cavern walls with large and small agates from Lake Superior. The collection was probably worth a fortune in the human world.

It wasn't long before Roselyn fell asleep when Sal heard movement coming from the port. *"She's sleeping Zane."* Salmonia said tenderly.

"I heard her cries." Zane slipped up on the pool ports ledge.

"She had that same nightmare again. I am beginning to wonder...it seems her dreams line up with what has happened or is about to happen." Sal was finding it hard to dismiss the timing and alignment of her daughter's dreams.

"I'm sure it is just her anxieties about us both being injured. Maybe we need to tell her that if anything ever happened, she would be cared for. After all, she is not a baby anymore, she will be nine soon." Zane worried that his and Salmonia's line of work could very well leave Rosie an orphan.

"Yeah, maybe" Salmonia was not convinced that was all that was going on.

"I will leave you. I just needed to make sure she was alright, goodnight Nia." Zane slipped back into the water.

Sal stayed and listened to her daughter's steady breathing and knew she was in a deep sleep and no longer in danger of visiting the dream world. She slid off the pallet and went to her own station. She laid awake thinking of the dreams her daughter has had and the correlation to the recent events, she felt sure there was a pattern.

It was written that some Merfolks had special abilities, of how mermaids could sing alluring tones drawing men to their death. That the men would hear the siren's song and walk or jump into the water and drown, maybe there was some truth to those old stories. Sal made a note to talk to Pete or his father about the legends. After all, legends were built around some root level of truth.

The waters were calm for now, and the morning was off to a peaceful start. The mer community began their daily tasks. Roselyn was up and ready to get to the lab and help her best friend.

"Hi baby, how did you sleep?" Sal decided she would leave it to Rosie whether she wanted to talk about the nightmare or not.

"Good mother and you?" Roselyn didn't seem to remember the dream.

"Good, I slept well. Yesterday's hunt must have tired me out, but the holding tank is full and that is always a good feeling. I feel I should get more though, with the Norse warriors here, they consume a lot of fish. Sal had noticed they fed while they were out exploring the lake as not to burden the pod's food supply.

Still, Salmonia worried about how much food they had stored up with all the threats going on in the lake. She would like to have the two back holding tanks full of fish as well as both front tanks.

"I'm off to the lab." Roselyn could barely eat she was so excited to be Meranda's personal assistant.

"Alright Rosie, mind your manners and try not to disturb Meranda when she is busy." Sal was not sure if her baby heard her because she was gone before Sal could turn around. She liked seeing Roselyn excited about something and felt bad that there were no other mer children to play with. Sometimes, she questioned whether coming to the Great Lakes was the right decision.

She didn't have Roselyn at the time, but she knew she would be coming into season within a few years of her arrival here. The mer reproduction did not happen often and that made Roselyn very special. Salmonia wondered just how special.

"Good morning Pete. How do you fair this morning?" Sal had not sleep well after her daughter had cried out.

"Not well. I laid awake all night thinking about giant lamprey or serpents. I don't want to leave the rift unguarded, but I don't want another massacre of our people either." Pete took a deep breath letting it out slowly.

"I agree. Pete--sometime soon I would like to learn more about the legends of our clan." Salmonia tried to sound casual, so as not to raise suspicion about her daughter.

"Sure, when things calm down we can share stories from our ancestors. I am sure Meranda would love to hear them too." Pete was used to having Meranda as part of their world.

Sal was curious if Pete or Meranda had come to a decision if she was going to join their family. If she was to leave it would definitely impact Roselyn, and if Sal was honest with herself—she too would miss her friend. She also knew Pete had feelings for Meranda, more than he allowed even himself to acknowledge.

Meranda had become endeared to many of the pod members and her knowledge of marine life was valuable. Sal shook off the *"what ifs"* from her thoughts, she would find out when the decision was made.

"I should hunt today. I would like to get all the holding tanks stocked with salmon while under the protection of the warriors. You never know if we will have to hold up in here for a while and with extra mouths to feed.

"I agree, but I want you to take plenty of soldiers and a few of the Vikings along." Pete wasn't comfortable about any of his pod being out in the lake until the dangers were resolved. He did feel better with the Vikings amongst them.

"Not a problem. Shall I go see who wants to go on a hunt?" Sal was getting more comfortable talking with the warriors.

"I can talk to them if you wish; I have a meeting with my father this morning." Pete suggested.

"Very well, I will prepare the nets." Salmonia disappeared in the pool port to start the preparations.

Pete got part way down the tunnel and decided to check with Meranda first and found her room empty. He figured she was in the lab, and hopefully would have some answers today. The council meeting was set for tomorrow and he felt that some scientific information would be most helpful.

Pete was heading toward the lab when he received a summons, *"Son--I need you to sit in on these talks."* Pete quickly turned about and headed toward his father's quarters to see what was so urgent.

"Pelias, the warriors and I were discussing our situation and we have decided that no one goes out into the lake unless necessary, and then only accompanied by a warrior. Has Meranda been able to shed some light on anything yet?" Pete's father was on top of everything and Pete admired his ability to lead. He hoped to be as great a leader as his father has been.

"I only know that she is in the lab this morning, and I have yet to check with her. I will give a report as soon as she knows anything." Pete reported.

"Good, any light that can be shed on the lamprey's unusual growth would be helpful." Pete was relieved that his father had not pressured him about Meranda's future.

"Sirs, Salmonia would like to hunt today and will not be satisfied until she has filled the back two holding tanks." Pete did not have to say any more as all five of the warriors' heads perked up.

"I would be honored to accompany the huntress today," volunteered Logmar.

"Excellent. She is preparing the nets now, so I will inform her that you will meet her in an hours' time outside the entrance." Pete turned to his father, *"If there's nothing more...I will go check if Meranda has discovered anything that could enlighten our situation."* Pete nodded and gave a slight respectful bow.

Pete was relieved that Sal would be hunting with a warrior. The size of one warrior was equaled to ten or so regular mermen. On his way to the lab Pete ran into Sal and informed her that Logmar would be accompanying her on the hunt and would be ready within the hour.

"Wonderful. I will be ready as well. Are you going to the lab?" Sal looked worried.

"Yes, I need to see if Meranda has anything to report. Why?" Pete seldom saw Sal worried.

Sal asked Pete, for Roselyn sake, if he could work into the conversation that everyone is being as careful as they could. Pete's eyebrows shot up, and tilting his head at Salmonia waiting for an explanation.

Sal seeing the concern on Pete's face tried to lessen his worries by offering some sort of explanation, "With the recent threats along with Zane and mine's recent encounters, I think Roselyn's fears of losing one or both of us, and have her feeling insecure." Pete had the feeling that there was more, but didn't push her.

"I will do my best to reassure our littlest mermaid, and Sal, be safe out there and come back as quickly as you can," he added.

Pete made his way to the lab giving some thought to Sal's concerns about Roselyn and concluded that her fears were warranted. "Hello...Meranda?"

"In here Pete. Roselyn can you get me five more test tubes. Thanks sweetie." Meranda quickly had become very comfortable in the lab.

"Hey ladies...how are things going?" Pete sloughed off his concerns and turned on a playful persona.

"Good, but--so far the tests are inconclusive. Look at these samples under the microscope."

"I won't know what I am looking at." Pete confessed.

"The microscope on the left is a normal cellular structure and the one on the right clearly has changes going on." Meranda gave him a quick reference.

Pete looked at one sample and then the other. The normal one was void of any chartreuse green coloring. "The right one is the same color that is coming from the leaky barrels. Is that why the lampreys are growing so large?"

"I'm not sure. I have to do more testing to confirm if there is a connection." Meranda didn't want to speculate, but was fairly certain that the barrels were at the heart of the matter.

"Very well, do you think you will know anything by the council meeting tomorrow?" Pete's face matched his pleas.

"Hopefully--I can come to some conclusions by then." Meranda had a hunch, but needed scientific facts to back them up. Pete poked his head in the back of the lab to give Roselyn a reassuring smile and inquire how she was fairing today before leaving. The opportunity hadn't come up to tell her that all was going to be fine. She was not a girl who could easily be fooled by falsehoods, so he didn't try.

Sal was ready with her nets and a hunting party; however, she was more heavily armed than usual, double checking that her dagger that was tucked into her vest. She then signaled for the hunting party to assemble. Salmonia saw a shadow darken the entrance and her heart skipped a beat, and then saw Logmar's smiling face appear in the entrance.

"Good morn, the rest of the hunting party will be here momentarily." Sal still felt shy around the massive warriors, but she also felt safe.

Logmar nodded and remained alert, too big to enter from this entrance. The rest of the hunting party joined them and they headed out. The pod followed the northern shoreline that headed toward Split Rock, where the last attack had taken place. Unfortunately, it was where fishing was the best as well.

Salmonia's stomach knotted as the horrific scene of the massacre flashed across her internal eye. That deadly day will remain with her forever. Never had they lost so many soldiers in a single fight.

It was a beautiful day to hunt, the clear water allowed for the right amount of the sun's rays to filter through, highlighting the beauty beneath the water's surface. As they neared Split Rock, Sal spotted a variety of fish hiding in the sunken ship, called the Madeira.

The three-massed schooner sunk after being stranded in one of the worst storms recorded; November 28, 1905, and only the first mate was thought to have died. The other ten crewmen made it safely to shore with stories of mermaids helping them. The Madeira's first mate, John, couldn't make it to the surface alive, and joined the mer family. He was given a second chance at life protecting the very lake he loved.

Fifty feet below the surface the Madeira rested in three pieces, she tilted upwards and hung off the cliff still suspended. She had been picked apart by divers, so all that remained was the ships skeleton. Which made a perfect shelter for fish; therefore, making it a great place to hunt. Spotting the fish was easy, rounding them up not so easy. A fish's survival depended solely on their alertness and what direction they scattered in.

Logmar messaged, "I will go deep and flush the fish your way."

Some of the hunting party positioned themselves in a large depression in the mountainous rock wall behind them. Sal and the rest of the crew manned the nets around the cove out of sight.

In this position, the scattered fish should swim directly into the nets making it an easy sweep. Everyone was in place and the focused was on the timing of the flusher, Logmar.

Just as Sal had thought, the fish scattered in the pattern they had predicted. However, she noticed that Logmar had not surfaced behind the fish and large bubbles were coming up from where he had gone down. She wondered if he got hung up on something.

She swam over to the bow of the boat where Logmar had descended only to see him going deeper and deeper-- tail first. He waved her off, *"Huntress find shelter."*

Turning around she used all the strength in her tail to ascend quickly. Only to find the hunting party surrounded by lampreys of all sizes. They had separated Salmonia from the rest of her pod.

Logmar continued to be pulled downward by a thick black rope like tail; the serpent. He descended farther and farther into the blacken depths of the lake, where even light could not reach. Logmar knew that if he did not free himself soon he would drown.

The giant warrior stopped fighting long enough to draw his Damascus steel saber lifting the heavy metal blade against the tons of water above him. His powerful arms shook against the weight and with the last of his strength he brought down his sword striking the serpent. The sword cut into the serpent's tail forcing it to uncoil, freeing Logmar from deaths grips.

The Viking immediately shot upwards to insure the safety of the hunting party. When he reached the sunken ship he franticly looked around for the pod. With both swords in hand he started attacking the giant lamprey that were draining the life from the last of the mermen.

Logmar sliced a lamprey in half, and it screamed releasing its fangs from its victim, but it was too late for the fallen soldier. He franticly looked around and saw the whole hunting party had been slaughtered.

He searched amongst the remains of the flattened bodies for the huntress. There were no signs of her or her body. The lingering lampreys detached their fangs and retreated as the shadow of the warrior blackened over them.

He covered the area over and over signaling for Salmonia. With a heavy heart he headed back to the compound to deliver the news of his failure to protect the pod, and their beloved huntress.

The patrols greeted Logmar outside of the cavern's entrance to help the hunting party with the days catch. Logmar felt so ashamed that he hadn't signaled ahead. One look at the warrior and they knew they had run into trouble. Shocked replaced their smiles. The other warriors had sensed Logmar's emotions before Zane and Pete did, and came immediately to his side.

Logmar's head hung in disgrace as he told of the horrific event, *"We were attacked. All of the hunting party is gone. I was pulled down by the serpent while the lamprey's attacked the rest of the pod."*

Zane pushed his way through, his heart felt like it was being crushed, *"Where is Salmonia?"*

"I do not know--she was not amongst the dead." Logmar looked Zane in the eyes and shook his head in disbelieve.

"We have to go search for her." Zane was blinded by fear.

"I put out a signal that all was clear, I searched for her and nothing." Pete held Zane back as he tried to push past him to go look for his Nia.

"Brother Zane, stand down." Pete commanded.

"No! I have to find her. She could be hurt. She needs me." Zane would not believe she was gone not until he saw it for himself.

"We will regroup and search for her. You need to go to your daughter and be with her." When Zane did not move Pete added, *"That was an order."*

Above all, Zane knew he could not disobey the Son of the Lake. He hung his head to hide his eyes that blazed with fury as he stood down and left to find Roselyn. A conversation he was not sure he could even have with their daughter.

How could Pete order him to stay behind? He just kept rationalizing over and over that Salmonia was a survivor; she was after all the huntress. Her instinct and skills as a fighter made her one of the best. She had to be holed up in a cave, and then the realization hit him, she was not invincible.

Zane could hear the commotion of the merman posse that was forming to search for his beloved; the mother of his child.

12

Zane had no idea how to tell Roselyn that her mother was missing. He couldn't wrap his own head around the reality that Salmonia might be gone. He stood at the labs door watching his beautiful, smiling daughter, so happy and for the moment, still innocent. She loved helping Meranda in the lab and that she had a friend closer to her age.

Zane was not good at hiding his feelings and Rosie would know the minute he entered the lab that something was terribly wrong. He decided he needed a minute to think about what he was going to say. Zane knew he was about to break her heart and then had to try to comfort her, a tall order for a father. Sal was good at parenting, he was not. Sal would've known exactly what to do or say, but she wasn't here.

On his way to the pool port he ran into Eira who had tears running down her face and she informed him they went to look for Sal: the soldiers, the Vikings, and Pete. Zane nodded and headed back into the water, he was ordered to stay behind, but that didn't mean he couldn't sift through the facts.

After some time, he surfaced in the lab, and delivered the bad news. He figured he better tell her before she heard it from someone else. It was the singular most difficult thing he had ever had to do. Roselyn sensed her father was near and transformed back into her mer-maiden form and message him, *"Father what brings you to the lab at this time of day?"*

Zane broke the surface of the pool port and slipped up on the ledge. Roselyn immediately moved backwards and started shaking her head no. She didn't know what he was going to say, all she knew was that it was bad. Bad like her dream.

"Rosie, there's was an attack on the hunting party. O-only the Viking warrior returned. We don't know where your mother is, but she was not among the casualties. Pete and all the warriors have gone to find her." Zane looked at Meranda who was stood frozen by the counter.

"No daddy! She's not dead! I would know…. You have to find her--she might be hurt. Please daddy--you have to find her …" at this point Roselyn slid down to the floor and cried a heart breaking cry that echoed off the labs walls. Her cries stabbed through Zane's heart and he went to her.

Roselyn pushed him away, "Daddy you have to go find her and you are not going to find her here."

Meranda stepped up and laid a hand on Zane's shoulder, her voice barely a whisper, "I will stay with her."

Zane knew his presence was only making Roselyn more upset and decided not to tell her that he had been ordered to stay behind. He and Nia had never talked about what to do if something like this happened. Zane felt helpless and sank back down into the icy cold waters of Lake Superior praying they would find her alive, if not for him, then for their daughter.

It didn't make sense to him, if all the other members of the hunting party were accounted for, where was she? Reasoning began clearing the numbness from his brain. He realized at that moment why Pete did not want him to come. He couldn't risk Roselyn losing both her parents. Zane had to sit and wait, which was not his strong suit, but for Rosie he would endure.

The minutes seemed like hours and the hours seemed like days, but eventually Pete and the warriors returned-- empty handed. Meranda brought Roselyn to sit by the caves entrance, only because Roselyn wouldn't take no for an answer.

When the search party returned the look on Roselyn's face was enough to make the grown mermen want to cry. She didn't shed a tear she tilted her chin up and looked them in the eye, "She's not dead."

Meranda thought of how much Roselyn reminded her of Salmonia at that moment. Roselyn dropped her shoulders back and her chin out and slipped into the port. Zane was right behind her; he needed to keep his little girl close.

When he got to her room he treaded beneath the water for a moment to gather his own raw emotions before emerging to offer comfort to his brave young mermaid. Roselyn all but jumped into her dad's arms and cried like Zane had never heard her cry before.

"Don't give up sweetheart. Your mom is a survivor. There are two ways to look at not finding her; it means there is still a strong chance she is alive. Hey, hey look at me." Zane seldom spoke out loud but he didn't have the mental energy to do otherwise. He wiped her big mermaid tears away that streamed down her face. "Did you hear me baby? Not finding her could be a good thing. We have to stay strong for your mom until she comes back to us."

"I know daddy, mama would want me to be strong, but I can't help it. If I don't let the pain out--it feels like it is going to explode within me. I know mom is alive I can feel her." Roselyn truly believed what she said. "You have to find her."

"I will Rosie, I promise." Zane had no choice but to make the promise to look for her mother and he would, with or without Pete's permission. This wasn't just anybody they were talking about; this was Roselyn's mother, his Nia. "Do you want me to get Meranda to sit with you?"

"Yes, I don't want to be alone," at least Rosie was clear on what she needed.

"Alright baby, I will go get Meranda. I love you." Zane slipped back in the water to find Meranda. He didn't have to go far Meranda was already on her way to check on Roselyn. "Meranda--Roselyn was wondering if you could stay with her."

"Of course Zane, it's the least I can do. I need to feel useful right now or I may lose it and Rosie doesn't need that." Meranda knew what the loss of a parent felt like, and hoped she could be of some comfort. Meranda's eyes welled up with tears reliving the loss of her own mother as she often did when she was faced with loss, anyone's loss.

When Meranda entered Sal and Roselyn's quarters, Roselyn ran into her arms. Meranda remembered how her own mother would comfort her and run her hand gently from her forehead to the crown of her head. It would always quiet Meranda, so she tried it with Rosie and it worked. She started to relax and Roselyn laid her head on Meranda's lap. It wasn't long before Meranda could hear Rosie's breathing deepen, as she escaped her reality.

Meranda tenderly watched Rosie sleep for what seems like hours. She noticed how much she looked like her mother, except in her coloring. Meranda started to look around the cave and then toward the ceiling and asked her mother to look after Sal, wherever she was. Meranda herself had fallen asleep, and when she woke up, she and Roselyn were cuddled up like a bear and her cub.

Roselyn's eyes popped open and Meranda could see that for just a moment she had forgotten that her mother was missing, and then watched as it all came flooding back to her. She sat abruptly up, "I am going to see what they are doing about finding my mother."

"I will meet you in the commons." Meranda had to take the long way.

By the time Meranda reached the commons room, it was empty except for Eira, "Where is everyone?" Meranda had a demanding tone to her voice.

"They are all out looking for the huntress. I am to continue with the preparations for the council meeting," you could tell Eira had been crying.

"Have you see Roselyn?" Meranda inquired.

"I did, and she said for me to stop crying, that her mother was alive. That I should busy myself with the preparations, because if her mother was here, that is what she would expect from me. Then she left for the lab." Eira knew that Roselyn was upset, but she still did not like being disrespected.

Meranda softened her tone and reassured Eira that they will find Sal and headed off to the lab. When she got there, Roselyn was in her human form. "I don't care who sees me in human form. I dare anyone to say anything. I want to continue working on the lampreys." Roselyn's voice dropped to a more respectful tone, "Please."

"I think that's a great idea. Let's get to work." Meranda slipped into her lab coat and they began to pull the samples from the incubator and started to compare them.

The search and rescue party headed back with no evidence of Sal. Where could she be? This was not the M.O. of the previous attacks. She can't live underwater forever. Merfolks needed to come up for air.

Pete too had a feeling she was not dead and something didn't feel right. If she was holed up somewhere injured, someone would've sent word. The pods were beginning to arrive for the gathering and hopefully he'd discover some information that was helpful.

Pete knew he must start greeting guests and hoped Meranda had found some concrete results he could bring to the meeting.

Eira and Einar were doing their best at welcoming the pods, but the pods expected to be received by the Prince. When Pete showed up relief washed over Eira and she was excused. With Salmonia gone, the responsibilities of the kitchen fell on her and if all the pods showed up, there would be around two hundred guests.

Einar was busy directing the guests to the great hall, the large cave's natural design allowed room for many Merfolk. The walls were spiraling layers of slate that formed a circle that started larger at the lower levels and narrowing as it neared the top like the inside of a beehive.

There was an excitement in the air as the pods gathered. So far, there were no arguments and everyone seemed focused on the issues at hand, the lampreys' and the serpent. Few had actually seen the serpent and some didn't known of its existence, but all agreed that something was wrong with the size of the hybrid lampreys.

The hall echoed with voices in various languages. Pods along the northern shores from Canada to the eastern shores of Michigan and the southern shores of Wisconsin were all present.

The Apostle Island pod settled in next to the Whitefish Point pod, and above them were the guardians of the Sault St-Marie locks, the largest pod on the Great Lakes. They guarded the entrance into Lake Superior, nothing entered without their knowledge, except the serpent. However, the serpent didn't come into the lake, it emerged from within the lake.

Representation from almost all pods were present and talking amongst themselves. The room hushed when the Devil's Island pod arrived. Being the youngest and least evolved amongst all the pods of Lake Superior invoked stares and whispers. Marius, their leader, led his pod to an isolated area in the hall. He held his head high and made eye contact with no one.

Zane took over the greetings while Pete slipped off to ready himself for the meeting. He quickly stopped by the lab "Meranda the pods have gathered--do you have anything to report?" Pete was pacing and couldn't stand still; this was his first consul meeting as Son of the Lake.

"I don't have all the data, but what I do have is proof that green toxins are in the cellular structure of the larger lamprey, and it appears to make the cell division more aggressive in nature. Aggressive being that the engorged cells multiply at an alarming rate making them larger in size than normal lamprey."

Meranda notice the look on Pete's faced, and had doubts if he had heard a word she had said. He was trying to follow her, but seemed unable to focused and wasn't retaining the information. "The bottom line is that the samples retrieved from the dump site were the same chemical that showed up in the hybrid's cells." That was a fact Meranda could prove.

"Thank you, Meranda. At least I can present that information and assure them that we're on top of the situation. I know I don't have a right to ask a favor of you, but ...could you relay this to the consul as you just told me? I think that it would send the pods a solid message that we are working to get to the bottom of this, especially having a human biologist amongst us." Pete's eyes pleaded for her help and support.

"I-I have never given a report in front of so many people...I mean Merfolks," but after looking at how stressed Pete was, how could she refuse. "Sure, I will present this to the council."

"Thank you so much. I had better get ready before they get too restless. I will meet you at your quarters and escort Roselyn to the hall." Pete turned to Roselyn, "You are welcome to sit in your mothers place at my side. And by the way...I see you can transform, but we will all be in mer form. Many of the pods cannot transform and that may make them nervous." Meranda and Roselyn jaws both dropped open as he turned and left.

Then at the same time both girls busted out in a round of giggles. "I will be the only two-legged being there" Meranda voiced the obvious and they both begin to laugh again.

Roselyn slipped back into her mer-form and went to get ready. She was so excited. She had never seen any other pods before. She doubted any of them brought their kids, but it would still be exciting. She will make her mother proud. She had to get ready and meet Meranda at her quarters.

Meranda grabbed the notes that she had scribbled haphazardly, and hope to use them as a guide for her speech. She rushed back to her room to get ready.

Luckily, the shirt and pants she had worn on the day of the interview were clean, although, it would be better if she wore a lab coat to make more of an impression. She put her hair in a bun to add to her professional persona.

When Roselyn showed up she looked stunning. She was wearing her mother's emerald necklace that glimmered against her black halter top. Her youth size bow was slung on her back with a case full of white feather tipped arrows, making it look like a bouquet of flowers.

Roselyn felt the need to look like a huntress if she was going to represent her mother. Meranda just gave her a kiss on the forehead and a quick hug. "You look every bit the huntress. Your mother would be so proud, Rosie." Meranda beamed with pride for her friend.

Pete returned shortly to escort Roselyn down to the gathering. Meranda peeked over at him and he took her breath away, and he looked like a prince. The sapphire jeweled vest brought out the colors in his tail and the decorative metal bands that encased his forearms were engraved with a Scandinavian scroll that looked ancient.

"Alright ladies, are you ready? Meranda—I'm sorry to leave you to your own means of travel, but we have to stay in mer form. Zane will be waiting at the entrance to escort you to your seat." Pete hated to leave Meranda knowing she had to be nervous about being the only human in front of two hundred pod members, but he had no choice.

"I'm okay Pete. I will see you there." Her smile was shaky, but brave. She gathered her notes and headed to the great hall. The speech played out in her mind and sounded strong, hopefully her voice would follow suit.

Meranda rounded the corner and froze in the entrance of the hall. She couldn't believe all the mer. There were tails everywhere. Her knees locked and her legs began to shake as her eyes darted around the ginormous room, before her eyes settled on Zane. He stood by the entrance waiting for her with his arms clasped behind his back.

He looked like a Greek god with his thick braids gathered at the nap of his neck before the mass settled between his shoulder blades. She could see the fine boned angles of his African decent giving him a dangerous look. When their eyes met, she drew comfort from the warmth and reassurance that radiated from them, and calmed down.

Upon seeing Meranda, Zane made his way over to her with graceful movements of muscles rippling throughout his tail. Despite the fact that the lower section of his tail remained behind him, he still towered over her shadowing her completely. He offered her his arm and Meranda latched on for the support she wasn't sure her legs would provide.

Zane could feel her tremble and gave her one of the few smiles she had ever seen on his face. Meranda's eyes met his and he nodded, she smiled back letting him know she was ready and he escorted her to her seat. He then took his place behind Pete's pedestal, all the while scanning for any indication of danger.

Meranda looked over her shoulder and stole a glance at how regal Zane looked in his boiled leather vest laced together with what appeared to be shark's teeth. His metal wrist guards were engraved with a lion, and housed his throwing stars. Lions were also engraved on the handles of his daggers that were tucked into his waistband matching the swords that hung at his sides. Being the commander, he was always armed, but tonight he was armed to the hilt.

Meranda's breath caught in her throat when she saw Pete and Roselyn. Where she was seated she could see them through a gap in the privacy wall. Roselyn looked scared until Pete bent and said something to her that changed her look to a beaming ray of confidence.

Pete took Roselyn's hand and they stepped out from behind the wall giving everyone a moment to acknowledge their Prince. Two hundred tails started slapping against the rocks in response to Pete's presence. It was musical.

Pete held Roselyn's hand and when he raised his arms in a welcoming gesture Roselyn's arm rose too. Zane came over to escort his daughter to her seat on Pete's immediate right, where her mother would have sat and then resumed his position directly behind the Prince.

Roselyn beamed up at her dad who glanced down at her with tears sparkling in his eyes. Roselyn momentarily felt shy, until she thought of her mother and sat up with the best posture ever. Zane wished Sal could see her daughter, their daughter.

"*Welcome. Welcome my friends.*" Pete looked like a king with his arms lifted to the guests. On his left arm he wore an armband in the colors of the Norwegian flag, and on the right an armband of yellow that signified he was waiting for the return of a family member. Meranda knew that was for Salmonia.

"*I am thankful you all made it here safely. I will get right to the heart of the matter. I am seeking any information on the invasive species, mainly the lamprey. What encounters, if any, you have endured.*" Pete's voice resonated throughout the hall.

"In our first attack we lost 28 mermen. We requested help from our homeland, and five Viking warriors came to our aid. I would like to take a moment to recognize our guests." Pete motioned in the direction of the five Norse Vikings who stood at attention and did not even flinch as the pods slapped their tails against the rocks clapping.

"It saddens me to say that as of three days ago we came under attack again and we lost three more members of our family and our huntress has gone missing. If any mer has any information that can lead to the return of Salmonia, please see Zane, our commander in chief.

In the meantime, we are investigating these giant lamprey. They are aggressive and can drain a merman in less than five minutes. In addition, a serpent has made its way into our waters. Any information we can gather will help us to rid the lake of these intruders."

Meranda's felt like she was in a silent movie except Pete made sure to include her in the telepathic speech. Pete then turned to Meranda and winked. *"I would like to introduce Meranda Michaels, Marine Biologist."* Pete offered a hand to Meranda to stand and give her report. She was glad for his assistance. She had never imagined that so many Merfolks existed, and some of them looked scary.

Meranda tested her voice trying out the acoustics in the hall with a meek "Hello." She paused to listen for the loudness of her voice. "I haven't much to report, except that the tests I have done on the cellular structure of a normal lamprey compared to the enlarged lamprey show remarkable differences. In the normal lamprey the cells are sluggish and murky in color, whereas, the infected lamprey cells are aggressive and abnormal in color.

The florescent green color found in the "hybrid" lamprey match the substance collected from the barrels on the lakes floor. It is causing the lampreys cells to divide at an abnormal rate, increasing the speed and size in which the lamprey are growing.

In conclusion, it would be safe to say that the toxins leaking from the barrels are genetically altering the lamprey. Thank you." Meranda tried to sit down immediately, but questions were being shouted at her in various languages and echoing off the walls. Meranda tried to address the ones she could understand, but it was hard to know who was asking what.

"I am sorry I didn't quite catch that question?" Meranda's eyes search the crowd lifting her eyes upward, left, and right spiraling up to what would be considered a back row, it made her dizzy.

Zane must have sent out a call to order, because the hall became eerily quiet at once, and hands began to shoot up.

"Greetings, I am from the Native pod of Isle Royale, and I would like to know what is being done about the barrels?" A very regal looking Native American Chieftain stood waiting for an answer. "We have been concerned about the risks and pollution to the lake from these barrels for many years. We have been told they were harmless."

"It's early in my studies and therefore I cannot suggest a solution yet to the effect on the marine life, but only offer an awareness that the problem exists." Meranda felt she had handled that appropriately and after a few more questions, she looked helplessly at Pete. She didn't have the answers.

Pete stood up and thanked Meranda for her report, and then he addressed the floor, "*I would like to open the floor for discussion or if someone needs to consult in private I will also grant that at this time. We need to figure out how to resolve this threat to our people and this great lake. There will be food and wine served shortly, and if any pod needs overnight accommodations, please seek out Einar."*

Pete turned and asked Meranda if she would take Roselyn back to her quarters. With all the strangers in the compound, he'd feel better if she and Roselyn were safe deep within the belly of the caves.

"Sure, but Pete--I think I should come back and hear what is being discussed. You might not think it's important, but I might hear something useful." Meranda made a strong argument.

Pete gave it some thought and then turned to Roselyn, "Very well you may stay, but Roselyn I would like you to return to your quarters or offer to be of some help in the kitchen."

Roselyn screwed up her face, but knew better than to show any disrespect. So, she headed to the pool port and slipped into the water. Zane waited a few moments and then followed after his daughter. He was uneasy with all the strangers present, and he too preferred his daughter not to be in attendance.

Meranda informed Pete that she would return shortly, that she should go check on Roselyn. With her mom still missing she felt the need to keep a close eye on her emotional state if anything. Pete nodded in acknowledgment before turning back to the line of mer requesting a word with him.

13

With Roselyn safely escorted to her living quarters, Meranda stopped by her own room to freshen up and catch her breath before checking on Rosie. When she entered Roselyn's room, she found a very upset young lady. Roselyn felt that if she was old enough to attend an important meeting, she was old enough for all of it.

Meranda explained that they were just being cautious and that if anything happened to her, that when her mom returned, everyone would have to answer to her. Roselyn smiled at the vision of her mother in all her raging glory.

"Okay, but can't I go to the lab instead of helping Eira in the kitchen?" Roselyn tried to persuade Meranda with those big brown eyes tucking her chin for an added effect.

"I'm sorry Rosie, Pete gave you specific instructions. Part of being older is to listen and respect your elders, even if it seems unfair; sorry kiddo." Meranda kissed her head and gave her a wink.

"I need to get back to the gathering and listen to some of the conversations; maybe it will be useful." Meranda reassured Roselyn that they would resume their investigation tomorrow.

"Okay, bye." Roselyn headed toward the kitchen to see what she could help with knowing that it would make her mother happy.

Meranda made her way back to the hall and wished, at times like these, she too had a tail; using the pool ports would be so much faster. When she got there Pete motioned for her to sit with him. She was introduced to the different pod members.

Meranda was fascinated in that some pods were as evolved as Pete's pod and some had two rows of spiny knobs starting from their heads to the tips of their tails like a sturgeon. It appeared that the Devils Island pod were the least evolved and the definitely the scariest. They radiated evil. Meranda couldn't put her finger on it, but they even smelled fishy.

The food was served on platters heaped with raw or smoked salmon, Coho, and whitefish garnished with crawfish. There were ample amounts of bread and flasks of wine available to the guests. When the dinner bell rang many rushed to get their fill as the elders stayed back more interested in solutions than hospitalities.

Meranda turned to Pete when they had a moment alone, "Why are there different levels of evolution among the pods?"

"Age mostly, but like all communities you also have all walks of life. Why do you ask—did you pick up on something?" Pete's chest puffed out slightly as he asked.

"No, nothing like that Pete, it is just that there are dramatic differences." Meranda tried to hide her real concern.

"Hmm, are you referring to the Devil's Island pod by chance?" Pete was getting good at reading her.

"Well I did notice them to be more...shall we say primitive." Meranda felt she said that with political correctness.

Pete couldn't help but chuckle at her. It was the first smile she had seen on his handsome face in a long time. It was true enough that the Devil's Island pod wasn't as evolved as many of the other clans, but it was more than that, they acted like predators. They were whispering and pointing amongst themselves, snickering behind their webbed hands. The leader slapped one of his pod members alongside the head and the mer immediately put some distance between himself and his leader.

Meranda also noticed that they didn't socialize with the other pods reinforcing that her instincts about this pod were on cue. All the other pods were very sociable.

Meranda kept an ear open as each of the leaders came to tell Pete of their encounters with the lampreys or the serpent. Not many had seen the serpent and Meranda thought that was strange considering they have had three devastating encounters with it; one leading to the disappearance of Salmonia.

As the gathering continued, Meranda wasn't really hearing anything useful, so she found Pete, "Hey, how is it going?"

"Fairly well, it should be breaking up soon. I think the biggest concern I have heard is what the progress was on the removal of the barrels. So far, no one has given me any clues or has any knowledge of the disappearance of

Sal." Pete looked tired and the loss of his sister-friend-huntress was taking its toll.

"If you don't need me anymore I would like to go down to the lab and work on a few things, and check in on Rosie again." Meranda felt that as interesting as it was to see the different pods she was tired of answering the same questions about the removal of the barrels. To her knowledge it has been an ongoing battle, but she recently heard that the Native American bands and the environmentalist had won their battle for the partial removal of the barrels. That was all she knew to date.

"Go ahead; I see no reason for you to stick around. Thank you for all your hard work in the lab. I will be by to say goodnight when things have died down." Pete smiled wearily.

Meranda quietly headed off to check on Rosie before heading to the lab. If Rosie wasn't sleeping she could join her in the lab, and hopefully putting her in a better mood than she was when she had seen her earlier.

The commons were empty and the quietness was making the hair on the back of Meranda's neck stand on end. It felt like in the movies where the person goes down the basement to investigate a noise and you are yelling at the television, *don't go down there.*

She continued toward the tunnel that lead to Sal and Roselyn's quarters when something slimy and cold grabbed her ankle. Meranda's feet came out from under her. She was being pulled across the caves floor toward the pool port.

Looking down at her ankle she saw a webbed hand that had claws and she started to scream. She grabbed onto a pillar trying to stop her descent into the pool when the spiny webbed hand shot up and covered her mouth. His fish breath was hot in her ear. "You're a girl," he said and then laughed like a hyena. Meranda looked into his red beady eyes and started kicking and twisting trying to get free.

"I like girls," he repeated. Her hands slipped from the pillar and he immediately pulled her closer to the opening. She dragged her fingers like a rake across the rough floor making her finger tips bleed. She heard the water part as he partially entered the water and she knew she was next.

When her foot found a rock she locked up her knee bringing her to a stop. For a moment his claws slipped off her mouth cutting into her skin as he tried to regain his position. She scrambled back up the slope screaming using every fiber in her body.

He propel himself out of the pool and landed on top of her. Grabbing both her wrists and painfully pinching them together with one hand while clasping her mouth shut with the other, he inched them closer to the pool. Meranda spread her hands apart and grabbed onto a rock hoping it would hold, despite his downward tugging.

He was partially immerged in the pool again only this time Meranda lower limbs were submerged too. She could feel the strength of his tail in the water as he tugged harder. Her bloodied hands slipped away from her lifeline and she was pulled deeper into the water.

She knew if he got her completely submerged she would not survive this attack.

For a split second his hand loosened around her mouth and she bit into his grotesque hand. He pulled his hand away letting out a growl and she let out a blood curdling scream that echoed ten times over in all directions.

The attacker let go of her and departed quickly knowing someone would have heard that deafening scream and they did. Zane was there instantly, he had just come from Roselyn's room. "Meranda, what is it?

Meranda was clinging to the pool ports ledge sobbing, "One of those horrid Devil's Island mermen grabbed me." Zane lifted her out of the water and Meranda clung to Zane as she trembled unable to stop crying.

"He was in here?" Zane looked puzzled.

"Yes and he kept saying how he liked girls." Meranda's skin crawled as she explained what had happened.

"He might have been looking for Roselyn," the horror hit Zane at the same moment it hit Meranda that he was probably after Rosie and that Meranda just happened by.

"Are you sure he was from the Devil's Island pod?" Zane knew this would start some serious issues between the pods.

"I am sure Zane; I looked right into his bulging red eyes. Zane, there's something else…I think I saw Salmonia's dagger on him. I'm not completely sure, everything happened so fast." Meranda tried hard to remember the colors on the dagger. He had taken it out to cut her so that she would let go of the rock.

"Are you sure Meranda?" Zane searched her eyes for any signs of doubts as fury boiled in his blood as he envisioned Sal at the hands of that pod.

"I'm pretty sure. Yes, I'm sure it was Sal's." Meranda's eyes moved back and forth as she searched her memory. "I haven't seen that many daggers in my life and it looked familiar." Meranda wished she could be one hundred percent sure, but under the circumstances, she couldn't be completely sure.

"Are you hurt?" Zane saw blood but nothing life threatening.

"I will be fine." Meranda was starting to get a hold of herself.

"Will you stay with Roselyn? I need to secure the ports." It had never crossed Zane's mind that it could be one of the other pods.

"Sure, but I would like to get to the lab. Can Roselyn come with me?" Meranda had a theory.

"Yes, I will escort her there and to be on the safe side stay away from any pool ports." Zane handed Meranda a dagger of her own. "Keep this on you."

Meranda took the dagger and put it in her lab coat. When she looked up--Zane was already gone. Meranda's legs felt wobbly as she made her way to the lab. When she got there she slid down the wall just inside the door.

Roselyn popped up through the port which sent adrenalin shooting through Meranda and realized it was her friend and quickly tried to pull herself together.

Roselyn transformed and dressed on the run. Meranda was trying to wipe the tears away, but blood smeared on her face. "Ready to get to work?"

Roselyn stopped in her tracks and stared at Meranda. "You have blood on your face and your fingers are bleeding." Roselyn looked so horrified that Meranda had to briefly explain what had happened and warned her to exercise extreme caution. She was shocked that an outsider could invade their private space. "My father will get them and make them pay."

Then this lovely young mermaid ripped off some of her white cotton shirt and wrapped Meranda's worse hand up in it. "Let's get you cleaned up." Meranda's eyes spilled over with tears and she was so glad it was her that was attacked instead of Rosie. Roselyn helped Meranda up and got her to a stool where she could get her wounds cleaned and bandaged.

Pete appeared moments later his eyes wild with fear. Seeing Meranda's bloodied face turned all that fear into rage. "Are you alright?"

"Yes Pete, I'm okay. A bit shook up, but unharmed. When I screamed he let go and left. I bit him. A little self-defense my father taught me." Meranda smiled as her heart warmed with thoughts of her dad.

"Who let go of you?" Pete's face had darkened.

"It was someone from the Devil's Island pod," replied Meranda.

Pete gently took Meranda's hands turning them over for inspection. Roselyn looked straight into Pete eyes, "I got this," she look so much like Sal at that moment that he surrendered.

"Okay. Are you sure you're not badly injured anywhere Meranda." She shook her head yes, unable to speak without the tears spilling out. Pete went to the pool port and pulled an iron gate over the opening so that nothing could get in.

"I'll be fine. Rosie's here to help me. You need to go find Zane." She looked at him and her eyes expressed the urgency that he seeks out Zane. She didn't want to say anything to get Roselyn's hopes up or worry her any more than she already was.

"The patrols will be searching all the pool ports and passages, and will continue to patrol them." Pete nodded at Roselyn and went to leave.

Meranda grabbed his arm to stop him, "Could I speak to you outside for a moment."

Meranda followed Pete outside the lab, "Pete you need to talk to Zane he has some information." Her eyes flashed at Rosie. She didn't mean to be secretive, but she didn't want to upset her, nor let her out of her sight. Roselyn was busy getting bandages and had her back to Meranda.

"I'll go talk to Zane, but can you clue me in about what?"

"We might have a lead on Sal." Meranda whispered.

Zane had been franticly searching for Pete to devise a search and rescue plan. They almost plowed into each other in the watery passage. Zane relayed what Meranda had told him about seeing Sal's dagger.

Pete knew the trouble it would cause if they were wrong, but he trusted Meranda's judgment and it was a lead that made sense. He instructed Zane to gather the warriors, and he would talk to his father.

Roselyn had Meranda bandaged and cleaned up when Pete tapped on the door and motioned for her to step out of the lab. "Zane said you might have seen Salmonia's dagger on your attacker?" Pete had all the information, but wanted a reason to check on Meranda.

"I can't be completely sure, but I did recognize the dagger, and like I told Zane, it's not like I have seen many in my life." Meranda reasoned.

"Well it's enough of a lead for me, and if you are wrong I will deal with the fall out later." Pete felt justified in organizing a posse to search for Sal; any lead was one he had to follow. He couldn't lose his sister. "Please, until we can investigate this lead don't say anything to anyone." Pete and Meranda went back inside. Roselyn was busy labeling test tubes.

"Roselyn, if you need to use the pool ports tonight I want you to call for security, they will take you wherever you want to go. Or use your legs." Pete winked at her.

Both the girls exchanged a horrified look, "Pete please, she hasn't told her parents that she can transform. So I am asking you to leave that to her." Meranda pleaded Roselyn's case for her.

"I know nothing." Pete smiled at how Meranda was looking out for Roselyn. "Thanks, and we will be extremely careful, promise." Meranda wanted to put his mind at ease. He had enough to worry about with Sal.

With Meranda and Roselyn secured in the guarded lab, they all could concentrate on the information Meranda had given him. When Zane reached the great hall Pete was already prepping the Vikings. *"Brother Zane, we have been waiting for you.*

"I am ready, more than ready." Zane knew there was nothing going to stop him from coming with. Pete knew it too--he wasted no time in organizing a search team.

"Let's go." Pete gave the signal leaving Logmar to protect the entrance.

"*Do you have a plan brother?*" Zane was used to leading, but even he knew he was too emotionally involved to execute a logical plan.

"*I do. I am going to first try to respectfully talk to their leader and...*" Pete did not get to finish before Zane exploded.

"*Talk? What will you expect them to say...oh sorry we kidnapped your huntress and...*" Zane was clearly on the verge of uncontrollable anger.

"*That is enough Zane and if you cannot pull yourself together I will order you to return to the compound...as I was saying, while I am talking to their leader the rest of the search party will do just that, search.*" Pete looked angry. Not at Zane in particular, but at the fact that Salmonia may be in the hands of those primates.

"*I'm sorry, my Prince; I will control myself.*" Zane immediately looked down in shame for even doubting Pete's ability to lead; after all, he loved Salmonia as much as anyone.

The posse took the shortest way to Devil's Island which went over the barrels. As they passed over they could see a flurry of small lamprey feeding on the toxic waste like it was candy. Pete would have like to have taken the time to kill them off before they grew and became more of a threat later, but he did not want to waste a single minute if it meant finding Sal.

Everyone was twitchy in anticipation of another attack from the serpent and the flunkies that swam around it. They approached the outer island and split up.

Zane led one of the patrols with Gunnar and Folkor, and Pete went with Sigurdr and Hallvardr as they descended on the caves. They were armed with swords, harpoons, daggers, and four very big Norse Viking warriors. Just the sight of one of the Vikings was enough to discourage most threats.

Cautiously they approached the only entryway into the sea caves; these caves could not be reached by land, except when the big lake completely froze over or by kayak during the summer months.

The jagged rocks on the northeastern side of the island acted like spears guarding the entrance. Not a problem for an angry posse of mermen.

The islands southern side made a perfect lair for the primitive pod, but also made it easier for Pete and his troops to trap them in their caves. Zane with his group of warriors entered into the Mawikwe Sea Cave's entrance, Pete and his warriors went into the hidden entrance that led to the main cavern. With the Vikings towering behind Pete, he asked to see their commander.

These primates had a crested backbone making it easy for Meranda to identify them. As they sat waiting for their commander, the rest of the flunkies moved around in a hyena like fashion pacing back and forth.

"Prince what brings you to our humble abode?" Marius inquired.

"We have reason to believe that you know of the whereabouts of our huntress, Salmonia." Pete waited for a reaction.

"We know nothing of your huntress," the commander flinched slightly when he answered.

"Then you won't mind if we take a look around." Pete came back at him.

"On the contrary, I will find it offensive that you do not take me at my word," returned the commander.

"*My apologies... I mean no disrespect, but we believe she is being held against her will.*" Pete fired back making his accusation unmistakable.

As quickly as the accusation was made things turned violent. Some of the accused pod appeared from behind some rocks armed with harpoons and the tips dripping red with poison. They aimed for the Prince, who was already surrounded by the warriors using their bodies as shields.

The warriors pushed forward, and the pod let loose a few spears that barely pricked the powerful Viking's before bouncing off their muscle bound arms.

The warriors quickly had the primates up against the caves walls and held them there. The weasels were so scared for their own safety, they started to talk. "*The huntress is in the storage cave,*" spilled the one that acted like the leader of the pack.

Sigurdr stayed and held the condemned mermen at bay, that is, if you could even call the cowards mermen. He would have loved nothing more than to squash these low lives like a bug, for taking the huntress in the first place.

Zane and his soldiers were storming through every cavern and crevasse when they came upon Pete, "*They said she was in the storage cave.*" Pete was unsure of where the storage cave was, so Zane went one way and Pete went the other, both sending out signals to Sal.

Sal was barely consciences, but she heard Zane's voice and sent out a faint message. Every muscle in Zane's body froze, until he heard her again. The signal was weak and garbled. "*In here, I'm in the barrel.*" Sal used all her mental energy she had left, in hopes they would hear her.

Zane's head whipped around and he focused on the boulder on his left. He tried to move the huge rock blocking the entrance to the alcove.

Pete's party joined Zane and Hallvardr, the rock defender, who with little effort moved the rock. To their surprised there were about twenty barrels stored in there.

Pete could only speculate what they were doing with these toxic barrels.

"Nia--can you hear me, help me find you." Zane was franticly trying the tops of the barrels to see if any were loose or open.

"In here," Sal banged her head back and forth to make some noise. She herself did not know where she was; only that she was dying.

Pete and Zane reached the barrel at the same time and began prying the lid off. Tears sprang to their eyes from relief and horror. There looking up at them was their green eyed huntress. She was submerged in green slime, but she was alive.

Zane partially lifted her out of the barrel and gently ripped the tape off her mouth before pulling her from the 55 gal drum. Pete was right there to grab the lower part of her body so she didn't injure herself any more than she apparently was. He looked down at her tail; it had been clipped.

Her skin was the color of the slime she had been submerged in, but nothing mattered, they had their huntress back. Her wrist were bound behind her back then anchored to her tail. She bit her lip from the pain as they unfolded her.

"Get me to the water; please." Salmonia wanted to wash the slime off her as quickly as possible. She had been marinating in it since her capture. Both Pete and Zane grabbed her under the arms and hit the clear fresh waters of Lake Superior.

When the soldiers gathered outside of the caves, the Vikings wore a smug look. No one asked them what had taken place, but they all had the feeling that evil pod would no longer be a threat to anyone.

Loretta Rose Didrikson

14

Salmonia reveled in the fresh water, as it cleansed the green slime off her face and body. The pod took the long way back to the compound purposely avoiding the barrels. Her skin still had a green tint to it, but her hair flowed free and vibrant red. She nuzzled closer to Zane, needing to feel safe. The warriors were aware of anything that twitched or rippled in the lake.

All Sal wanted at that moment, was to throw her arms around her little girl and stretch her body out in the familiarity of their quarters. She had been so cramped in that barrel, and forced to breathe in toxic slime, making her feel nauseatingly sick.

She had knew they would come for her after piecing things together. What she didn't know was without Meranda's keen eye during her own attack, it might have been too late.

As they approached the entryway to the compound Roselyn came shooting out the entrance like the birth of a seahorse, and latched on to her mother holding nothing back. Pete let go of Sal, and Zane repositioned himself behind her keeping her in an upright position. Something she could no longer do herself with half a tail. She embraced her daughter who was now crying uncontrollably.

The warriors stood with their backs to the inside circle while Sal, Roselyn, and Zane rejoiced. Zane was nervous about being outside the cave and as soon as he could guide them into the safety the sooner he could relax. The warriors were then able to retreat to their quarters. It had been a taxing, but joyous day.

Once inside, Sal was able to calm Rosie down; she looked up and saw Meranda standing there with tear filled eyes. Meranda couldn't put her feelings into words, but was thankful Sal was alive. Blinking her eyes to clear her vision she noticed the green glow to Sal's skin.

She knew immediately it was the toxicants. What did they do to her…force feed her slime? Meranda's stomach contracted, and she knew she needed to get to the lab first thing in the morning, to check the samples. All Meranda knew at the moment was that Sal was alive; they would get through the rest.

Meranda knew she would have to run some tests on her and try to flush the toxins out of her system. From observing the infected lampreys she doubted that things were going to be that simple.

Meranda wasn't concerned that contact with Sal was dangerous, but felt an urgency to see what was going on internally. Meranda glanced at Pete who was watching her reaction and he knew she was already on it.

Zane decided the party was over and that Salmonia needed to rest. Whisking her up in his powerful arms, he bid everyone goodnight and took his family to their quarters. He wasn't sure if Salmonia's tail would rejuvenate or not, but it paled in the fact that she was home. Meranda on the other hand, was wondering how if it affected her human form.

Once everyone left, Pete sought out Meranda, "A penny for your thoughts while I walk you to your quarters."

"Do you have time for a glass of wine? After a day like today I know I could use one." Meranda eyed him respectfully. After seeing him at the council meeting made her realize, that he was not Pete her boss, CEO of the Environmental Protection Agency, but a Prince, protector of seas.

"What would be your pleasure, white, red, bubbly, or dry?" The lines in Pete's face soften.

"I think a fruity red would be nice." Meranda took this opportunity to show Pete she had become worldlier than the girl who had first come here, at least in knowing her wines.

"I have a sweet red wine from California that I think you'll like." Pete was good at matching his wines with the occasions.

Meranda smiled as she walked over to the cubby and grabbed two long stemmed crystal wine glasses. She loved the reflection the glasses threw off from the fire, and how the lights danced on the walls.

The smile on her face was one of relief that everyone had come back safely. She exhaled an extra-long breath and felt the tension leave her muscles and with a little help from the wine, she should sleep well.

She and Pete sat quietly staring into the embers; he loved how the fire picked up red hues in her hair. His heart gave a squeeze at the thought of letting her go back to the life she was meant to live. Meranda looked up at Pete and smiled.

"I suppose a conversation about what was going through that pretty head of yours back in the commons room can wait until tomorrow." Pete smiled sheepishly.

"It could... but I'm not sure I will be able to sleep with all the possibilities running through my head." Meranda knew herself too well and if her body would allow it she would be in the lab right now.

"Do you care to share your thoughts then, because I'm very anxious as well?" Pete choked back his own fears for everyone's sake, but it was obvious Sal did not come out of this totally unscathed.

"I'm only in the first stages of trying to figure out what the toxins are doing to the lamprey. All I know so far, is that it is doing something to their cells. I can't even begin to think about what it could be doing to Sal." Meranda's eyebrows showed her concern as the arch's straightened out making her look like she was about to cry.

"We can't change what has happened, so hopefully we can find a solution. What do you need from me?" Pete felt helpless, but Meranda appreciated his ability to bring reason into their current situation.

"I don't know Pete. I suppose it would help if I had some healthy mer cells to compare to Sal's if they are infected." Meranda felt that was a good first step. It would be extremely helpful if she knew what type of toxins she was dealing with, and if they were radioactive. A to-do-list was forming in her head.

"I will give you some of my blood and I can try to find out more about the barrels." They're supposed to contain ammunition, grenades, and parts from mines; however, no one seems to be sure of what is actually in them. The push for the recovery of those barrels has been going on for many years, and yet no one seems to have any answers.

"Well regardless of what they say above, we are down here and know they're seeping into the lake." Meranda felt angry with the government for their irresponsible tactics.

"True enough. I will report to the lab in the morning. For now, I must bid you goodnight. I need to see my father and update him. Is there anything you need right now?" Pete was always so considerate.

"Nope--the wine has done its job and relaxed me and I should be able to sleep. Pete, I think it's best if we keep quiet about the testing, so that Roselyn nor Sal worry needlessly. They have been through so much." Meranda didn't like secrets, but until she knew something noteworthy, she would rather keep her thoughts to herself.

"Absolutely, I know Roselyn appears older, but in reality she is only eight." Pete started to head to the door.

"She's almost nine, and at that age, a half of year makes a big difference." Meranda chuckled and reiterated Roselyn's response to her age. Meranda hung her head shacking it back and forth giggling, before she waved goodnight to Pete, and headed off for a much needed night's sleep. She doubted if anyone has slept soundly since Salmonia went missing.

That night Meranda dreamt she was back on the farm, waking up to the birds singing and the sun shining through the cloudy window in her loft. She could smell the coffee that her dad had put on, as it floated up, teasing her nose.

She loved waking up to mornings like that. She could hear Blue's long nails clicking on the wooden floors below, as he searched for breakfast. She could see her Dad in the kitchen making a Sunday breakfast of eggs, bacon, and potatoes. She could taste it.

In that moment everything seemed normal and made her feel happy; but things weren't ever going to be normal--because her dad was gone.

Meranda woke and her head felt fuzzy. There was no sun shining through the windows, because there were no windows. She shook off the fog as the weight of the day settled in. She needed answers yesterday to help her friend who had become her family.

As Meranda's senses woke up, she realized she did smell coffee brewing. Hanging her head over the side of the bed, she could see a blue metal coffee pot hanging over the fire just-a-perking away.

Meranda smiled and felt more at home than she had since her arrival...coffee yum. Pete must be behind this, he is the only one who knows how much she loves coffee. He could be full of surprises at times.

Meranda flung the covers off and shuffled over to pour herself a cup of the delicious liquid. Her was hair ratted from a restless night's sleep. Grabbing her steaming cup of Joe, she made her way over to the couch tucking her feet under a pillow. She smiled and though of how amazing Pete was, and something stirred inside her.

"Good morn. May I join you?" Pete popped his head in.

"Absolutely, did you put the coffee on?

"I put it on the fire, but it was Eira who found it and made it for you." Pete was always straight forward and honest, she liked that about him.

"Would you care for a cup?" Meranda offered.

"No--never touch the stuff." Pete sat across from Meranda and thought she was beautiful, even with her hair all messy.

"I got hooked on coffee when I was ten. Dad would let me have some with him in the mornings, but it had more milk and sugar in it than coffee." Meranda tossed her head back at the thought and laughed.

Pete loved her laugh. "So what time would you like me to report to the lab?" He had at least ten other things he needed to do, but this took priority.

"Give me forty-five minutes and I will meet you down there." Meranda was pretty much a brush your teeth and hair, and you're ready to go kind of gal.

"Excellent, then I will leave you to your coffee."

Meranda enjoyed the moment for a minute longer, until the coffee kicked in and so did her brain. The list started to form on what she needed to do.

She hoped Roselyn didn't show up right away so that she could draw Pete's blood without anyone being the wiser. It would be interesting in itself to see the cellular structure of a merman despite the urgent need to help Sal.

Mental note to self, she must go see Sal after she meets Pete in the lab and gets too engrossed in her work. Meranda had a feeling that it was going to be a long day.

Exactly forty-five minutes later Pete came to the lab and sat down on the stool. Meranda smiled at him as she finished getting her test tubes in order. She decided to assign numbers to each vile giving some organization to her secrecy.

"Ready? Please roll up your sleeves." Meranda was all business like. Pete on the other hand was taking that particular moment to breathe in the smell of her freshly washed hair, "There will be a little pinch." It had been awhile since she had taken blood, but slid the needle in like she had been doing it every day for years.

She drew ten tubes of blood. That way she would have plenty to run a gamut of tests without having to bother him for a re-draw. Meranda put a cotton ball and tape over the puncture even though it didn't bleed.

Pete decided to tease her, "Yes, our blood is red like yours."

Meranda got all flustered, "I-I wasn't, I didn't think anything different. And even if it wasn't--."

Pete just laughed shaking his head as he left to go about his business, "Don't forget to eat."

"Yes, your highness!" Meranda felt a bit foolish he caught her off guard about the blood, because she was wondering. She put a small amount of blood between two glass slides and examined it under the high powered microscope.

She was a little surprised, the cells looked the same as humans, except their polygonal shapes and bulging nuclei were slightly different. If there were no differences, it would indicate that we all descended from sturgeons.

Meanwhile, Sal was getting tired of being fussed over and confined to her quarters. It was getting on her nerves. She loved her family, but decided she needed to talk to Meranda, alone.

Pete stopped by to see how she was doing. He had kept his distance giving their family some time to themselves, but couldn't wait any longer to reassure himself, that she was okay.

"Hello, brother." Sal sounded awfully glad to receive company.

"How are you feeling?" Pete's face wore the same expression as Zane's, and everyone else that was treating her with kid gloves.

"Fine. I need to have a private word with Pete." Sal was trying to be kind to Zane and Rosie, because she knew they had been through hell the past few days. Zane went over and guided Roselyn toward the pool port and took his daughter to find some lunch.

"What's going on?" Pete kneeled down by her bed.

"I need to talk to Meranda alone--and I need you to take me there." After all she had been through, she was angry, and didn't want to take it out on her family.

"No problem I can do that. When would you like to go?" Pete decided it was best to let Sal communicate her needs.

"Is Meranda in the lab now?" asked Sal.

"Yep." replied Pete .

"Then I would like to go *now*." Salmonia whipped her clipped tail off the bed and reached for Pete. As he carried her, Salmonia laid her head on his shoulder and he felt the tears silently drop.

He didn't know what to do but hold her a little tighter. As he neared the lab he could see Meranda bent over looking into the microscope, the same position he had left her in.

Sal reached out and tapped lightly on the door, but it still startled Meranda. The minute she seen it was Sal, her eyes welled up with tears and she rushed over to let them in. Meranda knew what post-traumatic stress syndrome felt like, so she held back from asking her any questions. She just pushed a chair over for Pete to set her in.

"Thank you Pete, now if you wouldn't mind, I need to talk to Meranda, *alone*." Sal was very clear about the alone part.

"I will check back in an hour to see if you want to go back to your quarters." Pete turned and left his two favorite women to talk secretly, he hoped that Sal would find some comfort by opening up to Meranda.

Meranda waited for Sal to talk first, "Hey girlfriend." Salmonia tried to lighten the mood.

"Hey, it's good to see you up and about already." Meranda played nice back waiting for Sal to decide the direction of their conversation.

"Thank you for taking Roselyn under your wing. It was a relief to know she had someone to lean on and wasn't alone. I mean--she had her father, but I'm sure Zane was more focused on finding me."

"She was so brave Sal; she really reminded me of you." Meranda smiled endearingly.

Sal changed the conversation quickly, "They were trying to pickle me in that slime. I believe they were using me as an experiment to see if the same changes and behaviors that the lamprey displayed would occur in a mermaid. I think their plan was to breed with me when I came into season if it worked. To create some type of hybrid mermaid and I am not sure they were far off in their thinking."

Sal confessed to Meranda that she felt sick--toxic. "I don't know what to do. I was hoping you would have some ideas on how to detoxify me somehow…" Sal just stopped talking because she knew if she continued she would lose her composure. That was all she had at that moment holding her together.

"Well I did take samples of Pete's blood to study, but since you are here and are willing, it would be good for me to have some of your blood too. That way I could monitor any changes if they occur. Are you up to that?" Meranda wanted to hug her friend and let her cry it out, but she knew that wasn't Sal's style.

"That's what I am here for...and Rand, could we keep this between us? Not even Pete?" Salmonia was unsure of her future and worried what affect this would have on her family.

. "Whatever you need Sal, I am here for you." Meranda could not hold back any longer and bent down to give her friend a hug. When Meranda went to pull away, Sal tightened her hold for just a moment longer.

Loretta Rose Didrikson

15

Pete returned within the hour to see if Sal wanted to go back, and she was ready. She was exhausted. He picked her up and headed toward the door. Sal shook her head, "Can we take the pool port? I feel the need to be in the cleansing water."

"As you wish huntress," was all Pete said. Pete set Sal down by the port and went behind the wall taking his time to fold his clothes and pull his own emotions together before transforming. They bid Meranda good day and Pete and Sal slipped into the water. Sal held onto his tail to help her balance. She closed her eyes and focused on how the water softly caressing her skin and smiled; she was home.

Meranda compared the tubes of blood from both mers side by side, and you could see with the naked eye that Sal's had a green tint. Meranda shielded the samples from Pete when he had come in to retrieve Sal. She had nonchalantly walked over and put them in the refrigerator to respect Sal's wishes, which was not an easy thing to pull off with Pete's all-knowing eyes. It was part of his survival skills to be aware of his surroundings at all times and reading people was his hobby.

Meranda got right to work examining Sal's blood to see if she saw any contamination in her cellular structure. At first glance she saw the greenish hue, but more disturbing was the cells, they were extremely active.

Hopefully, in time, the toxins would work its way out of her system. Meranda knew that would be the easiest solution, but was doubtful it would go that easy.

She had already been experimenting with the sea lampreys infected blood to see if the cells could be altered or cleansed. Meranda never thought in a million years she would be here doing experiments on infected marine life in a cave beneath the water's surface. Reality check, a marine biologist's dream come true, but one she could never tell anyone about.

Pete escorted Sal back to her quarters where Zane and Roselyn were waiting for her. They had lunch cooking and the table set. Sal felt less stressed having talked over her concerns with Meranda, making her feel more appreciative of the care her family was trying to give her.

However, Sal couldn't shake the aggravated feelings growing in every fiber of her body. Not at anyone in particular, just agitated, especially with what that disgusting pod had put her through.

Pete said his goodbye's and headed back to the lab. He shot out of the pool port startling Meranda who flew instinctively toward the door, which was the farthest point from the port. When she saw it was Pete all that fear turned to anger, "What's the matter with you?" Meranda's eyebrows were so close they could have been joined.

"What do you mean 'what's the matter with me'?" Pete didn't realize that when Meranda was working on something she closed out all other distraction around her and with her own recent attack still fresh in her mind by a prehistoric monster, left her nerves jumpy.

"I wasn't expecting anyone to come back here, or pop out of a hole like a piece of bread from a toaster." Meranda's facial muscles were slowly relaxing and she headed back over to her work station.

"I was wondering what was up with Sal?" Pete was worried about what she might have gone through in captivity.

"I can't betray her confidence, but I can tell you she is traumatized. Who wouldn't be after being kidnapped and put into a toxic barrel? She is just going to need some time." Meranda didn't lie well as her eyes darted down toward the floor.

"Did they hurt her?" Pete was worried.

"Well they clipped her tail so that she couldn't swim away. I doubt that felt very good." Meranda was trying not to let anything slip out, but she was not good at keeping secrets either. For Sal she would do as she was asked. "Is her tail going to grow back?"

"I didn't mean that, I meant 'did they hurt her'?" Pete couldn't choke out the 'r' word. "And yes, her tail could grow back, but it would take a long time." Pete knew that would be one of the hardest things Sal would struggle with, and not being able to hunt.

"I don't think they got around to raping her, she didn't say anything." Meranda knew she had to end this conversation before she spilled everything she knew. "I was wondering, when she's in human form—her feet?" Meranda squeezed her eyes shut trying to rid the picture of Sal being crippled from her mind.

"I'm not sure. I don't think it will make a difference because they clipped the end of her tail off which affects her balance in the water. When she transforms, her feet would be where the cartilage part of her tail is and not the fin part." Pete had never really given much thought about it until now.

"We'll tackle one day at a time." Meranda prayed Sal wouldn't be crippled in either form; and if she couldn't swim, she'd be able to walk.

"Obviously, Sal has sworn you to secrecy, and I will respect that. However, if there is something going on that involves the security of this pod, Meranda, I need to know. Do you understand what I am saying?" Pete looked very serious.

"I do…I mean I understand the priorities. And I would tell you if something came up." Meranda felt in the middle between the two people she cared about most, but she would tell Pete if she felt someone including Sal, were in danger.

"I will leave you to your work. Will I be seeing you for dinner?" Pete had a much softer look on his face.

"A late dinner, I need to run some more tests and then I have to give them time to cure." Meranda was anxious to get back to work.

"Excellent, I will see you later then." Pete went behind the screen before he slipped back into the water.

Meranda stopped for a moment and wondered when it was that she became so comfortable with seeing him as a merman, for that matter, any of them? She shook her head and realized she was like her dad that way, taking things for what they were.

Meanwhile, back at Salmonia's quarters things were not going so good. Salmonia was sick. Her stomach cramped up after she tried to eat, and then she started throwing up. Zane carried her over to her bed and kept a cool cloth on her feverish head. Roselyn just stood back horrified that she would lose her mother again.

Roselyn looked pale "Daddy should I go get Meranda...," but before Zane could answer, Salmonia snapped that she would be fine and needed to rest without all the fussing that was being done over her.

"Roselyn why don't we leave mommy alone for a while and you could come hang out with me at my place." Zane wasn't sure what to do, but grant Salmonia what she was asking for, time and space.

With tears in her eyes Roselyn kneeled down by Sal, "Mama, do you want to be alone?"

"Yes honey, I just need to rest and catch up on sleep, so why don't you go with your dad for a while." Salmonia tried to talk kind to her daughter despite the feelings of rage building inside of her.

"Okay mama, but if you need me just send me a message and I will come right away," Roselyn leaned over and kissed her mother's clammy forehead as she bravely held back her tears. With her head held down she left with her father.

Salmonia laid there feeling half crazed and angry. After all, she was home with her family and safe. She was glad that Zane took Rosie out of there, because the last thing she wanted to do was loose her temper on her eight year old daughter.

Sal tried to calm herself and thought how grateful she was that Meranda had been there to watch over Roselyn. She knew there were many in their family that would've cared for her, but Meranda was closest in age despite the eighteen year difference.

Sal had become close to Meranda since she arrived into their secret world under the water. Sal drifted off to sleep with tender thoughts of her daughter and her friend.

Meanwhile, in the lab, Meranda did not like the results she was seeing under the glass. The infected cells of the lamprey were dividing faster and becoming larger. She started to fear that the same would happen with Sal's blood, but had no clue to the why's or how to stop it. She tried different compounds and hormones to counter act the infestation, but so far saw no results.

Maybe the tests just needed more time to cure. She decided to put some of the samples under a heat lamp and some in the cooler to see if temperature made a difference. She mixed some of the lamprey's infected blood with Pete's blood to see if that would lessen or dilute the cells. Meranda was unsure of what to do so she just kept trying anything.

After she had mixed everything she could think of she put her head in her hands and broke down and cried. Her heart was breaking for her friend. What those monsters had planned for Sal was unthinkable, using her as a living incubator. To be defiled and enslaved as a concubine; to mother a new breed of mer.

"Meranda…are you still in here? Its pitch black--how can you see anything?" Pete was looking for a lamp to light.

"I'm back here Pete." Meranda didn't realize she had been so deep in thought that the lab scones had gone out and she had been sitting in the dark.

When the lights were back on, Pete could see the tear stains on her face, "Hey there, come on it is time for a break. Let's get some food in you. Sometimes when you give a problem some time you can see it with fresh eyes."

"Yeah, I guess. I could use a break. I just feel so helpless. We never studied anything like this is class." Meranda felt so inexperienced.

Pete's chest rumbled, "I don't suppose you did."

Meranda looked up and smiled at the thought of her sitting in a classroom studying the anatomy of Merfolks. Pete had his hand out to help her up and lead her away from the stressfulness of unlocking the mysteries of the barrels, and the effects they are having on the marine life. It was a tall order.

When they got back to her quarters, Pete had had the table set and a bottle of dry red wine opened and breathing. Meranda smiled at the thoughtfulness and care that went into every detail. When she didn't come up at the dinner hour Pete got nervous. He knew nothing could get past the security he had in place, but he still rushed down to make sure she was safe.

"What smells so good?" Meranda didn't realize how hungry she was.

"It is apricot glazed salmon steamed in a parchment pouch ...and wild rice." Pete sounded like he had pulled out his bag of tricks to distract her from her worries.

"Wow... this is quite a spread." Meranda was excited that it wasn't seafood stew.

"I thought you might like a change of pace. I mean it's not a hamburger, but something a little different." Pete himself couldn't stand beef. "Would you care for a glass of wine?"

"I would please." Meranda began pushing the day's worries to the back of her mind.

"Sit." Pete motioned toward the couch then proceeded to pour her a glass of wine. As he walked around the couch he placed his hands gently on her shoulders and started to rub the knots out of her shoulders and neck. It was all she could do not to moan. His fingers were strong and warm.

After a few minutes she put her hand on his and signaled for him to stop. Not only was she hungry, she was starting to feel warm and tingly in places she shouldn't.

"I'm starved, how about you?" Knowing Pete would have waited for her before he himself ate.

"I am. Your seat awaits you Miss." Pete went over and pulled out her chair. Meranda could feel the heat climbing up her neck bursting onto her face. All she could muster was a very shy thank you.

They barely finished dinner when Roselyn popped up in the pool port. "Pete! Meranda! Come quickly--its mother...she's flipping out."

Pete shifted to mer form before Meranda had reached the door, when she looked back all she could see was the last of his tail disappearing in the water. Meranda ran to the lab and grabbed a hypo with a sedative in it and her bag of supplies.

She cautiously approached Sal's quarters. It looked like a tornado or tsunami had hit. Everything was tipped upside down and on the floor broken or smashed. Pete and Zane were holding Salmonia down so she wouldn't hurt herself or anyone else for that matter.

Meranda kneeled down a safe distance from Sal who looked up at Meranda snarling. Meranda let out a gasp,

Sal's eyes were red. She looked like a rabid wild animal and didn't seem to know who anyone was.

Meranda shrunk back for a minute before she found her courage and remembered that somewhere in there was her friend. She opened her bag to get the sedative ready when Sal leaped forward taking a swipe at Meranda.

Every nerve and muscle in Meranda's body filled with adrenalin throwing her back against the wall. Straining to keep hold of her, Zane and Pete got her back under control. The growls and sounds coming from her were like nothing Meranda had ever heard. "Hold her still if you can and I will give her a strong sedative."

Both of the mermen swung her face down as Pete pressed his elbow in the middle of her back for extra measures. Meranda slowly went over to her and jabbed a large syringe into her backside and backed away quickly.

Roselyn started to cry," You're hurting her, stop it! Daddy, please you're hurting her."

Meranda went over to Roselyn and hugged her tightly, "Honey they are not hurting her, they are keeping her from hurting herself or others."

Roselyn hugged Meranda tight and cried a waterfall of mermaid tears.

The sedative seemed to work as Sal's tension filled body slumped and became motionless. Pete and Zane lifted her onto her bed turning to Meranda asking her if she had anything they could use as restraints. Meranda did have some rubber tubing and handed it to them. She was speechless as they tied Salmonia to her bed.

Zane stood up and turned away so that their daughter would not see the tears in his eyes. Pete was still nervous about whether the restraints were enough to ensure everyone's safety.

Salmonia stirred, looking over at Meranda and Roselyn, "Baby, stay away from mommy right now until Randie can figure out what's wrong with me." Salmonia's eyes were green again and it was all Meranda could do to not run over to console her friend.

Sal looked at Pete, "Brother, I want you to lock me up in the quarantine area. I would never forgive myself if I hurt anyone."

Pete did not even flinch knowing that he had already made that decision, "Zane do you want to help me take her there or should I call for someone else?"

"No one will see her like this. I will take her." Zane had his softer side stuffed deep inside where he carried all his emotions. He went over and picked his Nia up to bring her to be locked up in a holding cell.

Meranda asked Zane if Rosie could come and stay with her, and he responded with a nod of his head grateful for her suggestion. Pete followed Zane in case Salmonia started to turn into the red eyed demon again.

Meranda put her arm around Rosie and walked her over to the pool port, but before letting her go she hugged her and looked straight into her big brown eyes, "I will find a way to help her. I love her too Rosie. I promise. I will find a way. Do you need to grab anything before coming to stay with me?"

"I want to grab a few things...my diary and something that smells like my mom. That probably sounds silly." Rosie was trying not to cry again. "Would you mind taking it back with you?"

"Sure honey, I can do that for you." Meranda stepped aside so that Rosie could get her things together. "I'll see you back at my place." Meranda knew all too well that it didn't help to be too coddling.

Roselyn disappeared in the pool port as Meranda looked around fighting back her own tears. She made a promise to herself that she will find a way to help Salmonia, she had to.

When Zane got to the cell he stopped and looked into Sal's eyes, "I'm so sorry, Nia."

Pete silently opened the bars and looked at the floor as Zane brought the mother of his child into the cell and set her down on the steel bed that was attached to the rocked wall.

Salmonia put her hand on Zane's arm, "This is for the best. Remember I asked to be brought here. I want to be here until we can figure this out. It is not your doing."

Zane just shook his head again as if speaking would open the dam that was holding back the storm of emotions he was feeling. Fear for Sal, and anger toward the scum that hurt her. Nonetheless, it didn't help that he had to lock her up. He turned and left not looking back; not now.

Pete shut the door and checked to make sure it was locked, "Do you need anything sister?" Pete had to put safety over all else, even though his heart was breaking. "Are you hungry? Do you want me to stay with you?"

"No, brother, I want you to go and make sure Zane and Rosie are going to be okay. And I want you to help Meranda find a way...to fix this." Sal turned her head so that Pete wouldn't see the tears that were streaming down her face.

"I will, we will. I hope you can get some sleep, and if you need anything or want someone to talk to…" Pete tried to look like he wasn't worried and Sal let him think he succeeded.

He caught up with Zane down the tunnel putting an understanding arm on his shoulder. "I will be staying right here, Rosie is with Meranda." Zane sat down. He wasn't going to leave her down here alone, like an animal.

When Pete got back to Meranda's room, he knocked quietly on the door. Meranda came to open it and put a finger to her lips signaling for him to be quiet as she stepped outside the room to talk to him. "Rosie cried herself to sleep, but at least she is sleeping. I am going to go to bed myself so that I can get an early start in the lab. I'm sure that Roselyn will be right by my side, so don't worry about her."

Pete reassured Meranda that Roselyn was stronger than anyone realized. Meranda put her hand on Pete's arm and smiled at him for his observations on the youngest member of their pod before bidding him goodnight.

16

Meranda said a prayer and promised to work non-stop until she found a way to help her friend before she could fall asleep.

The next day, just as Meranda predicted, Roselyn was glued to her side. They walk down to the lab in silence; both were lost in their own thoughts. When they got in the lab, Roselyn went to the couch and curled up. She was traumatized by her mother's violent actions the night before. Meranda didn't blame her, it was a horrifying thing to witness.

Meranda felt the weight and urgency to find a way to reverse the toxic changes that were polluting her friend's cells. She didn't know for sure if that's what was happening, but she had a good idea that the changes began at a cellular level.

Meranda had skipped breakfast in her haste to get started researching anything and everything. She was curious to see if any of the test slides she had set up the night before showed any results. She wasn't sure what she was looking for or if exposing the slides to different temperatures and compounds made a difference, but it was a place to start.

She checked the slides that were refrigerated and nothing looked different. She then checked the slides in the incubator and again nothing.

In her head she went over her old lectures from her biology and chemistry classes, including an essay she had done on blood and temperatures during the onset of hypothermia. She had only had researched key points for the paper on the biological changes that occurred; she was a biologist not a doctor.

When she looked up, Roselyn was watching her with a worried look on her face, "Rosie honey, don't worry. I always go round and round, up and down, frontward and backwards. It is how I process things. Would you rather go back to the room?"

"No, actually I was wondering what you think of all of this…of us?" Roselyn's sat with her arms around her knees and was looking at Meranda, her large brown eyes taking up most of her face above her knees.

"It was a little hard at first to wrap my mind around it all, but it would be naïve of me to think that humans were the only species in the universe." Meranda smiled reassuringly at her.

"Do you miss it? I mean--miss your pod and land?" Rosie shifted to a laying position with her hands under her chin.

"I haven't had too much time to think about it. I guess I do and I don't. My mother passed when I was seven and my brother ran away with the circus. I lost my father recently in an accident at the mines--so there's just my best friend Jena. I don't have anyone else." Meranda never thought of her life summed up in a few sentences.

"The circus...what's a circus?" Roselyn perked up.

"It's a show that has animals that do tricks, and people that dangle from ropes high off the ground. They have games and lots of food on a stick, and they travel from town to town and people pay money to see the show." Meranda couldn't think of any nice way to explain it; she personally hated the circus and the treatment of those wild animals.

"Your brother ran away with them? What is money?" Roselyn thought that was a strange thing to say about her brother.

"I don't really know if he really ran away with them, I just say that because it is easier than saying what really happened." Meranda didn't want to get in to it, but had a feeling Roselyn was not going to let it go. "And money is what people work for so they can—um, pay for things."

"What really happened?" Rosie sat up; she was ready for the real scoop.

"Well, when my brother was a teenager, he and my dad got into a fight over my brother not going to school and getting into trouble...anyways they got into this fight and my brother left. I haven't seen or heard from him in many years." Meranda instantly noticed a change in Roselyn. She wasn't sure if it was a good shift or a bad shift. Either way it got her up off the couch, as she pulled a stool next to where Meranda was working. She could almost hear the wheels turning in her head.

Roselyn then gave Meranda a hug, "We can be your family." Roselyn closed her eyes as she held on to Meranda and tears rolled down both their faces.

Meranda hugged her tightly back, "You are my family, and we are going to find a way to help your mom sweetie."

Meranda went back to trying different things and Roselyn took notes, and together they worked side by side to save Salmonia.

Pete stopped by asking how the tests were going and asked Meranda to step outside, "I think Sal is getting sicker and more agitated--like last night, just before her eyes turned red."

"I don't have anything yet Pete, I'm sorry." Meranda said in a heartfelt frustrated way silently wishing she was more experienced. "I guess you should have hired someone with more experience." She was sort of joking.

"I don't think anybody but you could've handled the reality that we exist. I think you are the right person for the job, and if there is a cure you will find it, out of sheer determination if anything." Pete knew in his heart she was the right one.

"We will see. Could you have someone bring some food to the lab? We are going to stay at this until we drop." Meranda felt a bit strange about asking Pete to do something for her. After all, he was the Son of the Lake; a prince.

"Not a problem. I will send Eira with some refreshments. Zane hasn't left Salmonia's side. I think I will go sit with Zane for a while if you need anything else." Pete look older carrying the weight of the problems, and with his shoulders slumped he started to leave.

"Keep me posted, and if she gets worse…I can give her another sedative. I would like to know if it comes and goes on its own. Like a fit of some sort." Meranda tried to smile reassuringly and turned to continued her work.

It wasn't long before the food and drinks arrived. Roselyn was so hungry and when she reached across to grab a sandwich she knocked over a tube of blood.

Instantly pulled back she started to cry hysterically, "I'm sorry Meranda; I have ruined your tests."

Meranda went over to Roselyn and took her face between her hands, "It is okay Rosie, and you didn't ruin anything. We're just trying different things to see if something works. Now calm down and eat your sandwich." Meranda wiped her tears away.

Roselyn sat back on the couch and nibbled at her sandwich trying to stop the sobs that made it hard for her to take in a breath, and Meranda went back to the bench to clean up the mess. She noticed that the spilled tube was one of Pete's blood samples and it had seeped into the slide with Sal's blood on it.

Meranda shrugged and placed the slide under the microscope. At the edge of the glass where Pete and Sal's blood had mingled she saw a change. The green hue under that side of the slide had lessened. Pete's blood changed Sal's toxic blood.

She immediately took out a fresh slide and put a drop of Pete's blood and a drop of Salmonia's blood on it and clamped it tight. She knew it would take time to cure, but couldn't wait and only gave it a few minutes to interact while she finished her lunch. When she looked at it under the microscope she could see the healthy red cells over taking the infected green cells. Meranda froze.

Roselyn had been calling Meranda's name asking her if she was alright, and when Meranda finally snapped back, Roselyn was shaking her and pleading with her to answer.

"I'm okay honey. I didn't mean to scare you. I told you I get lost in my thoughts sometimes when I'm working on a problem." Meranda didn't want to jump ahead of herself, but told Roselyn what she saw. "Rosie when you spilled that tube of blood, it made the green blood less green." That was the simplest terms she could come up with at the moment.

"It made the bad lamprey's blood better?" Roselyn was confused.

"No…I mean yes, it made the bad lamprey's blood better…less green. Your mishap might have helped with the solution." Meranda didn't want her to know that it was her mother's green blood she had been testing.

"You scared me. I thought something bad had happened to you too." Roselyn was still unsure of what was going on, but decided to sit back down and finish her lunch.

"We might be on to something kiddo." Meranda's eyes danced with excitement. "I need to go talk to Pete for a minute. Will you be okay here by yourself?

"Yes." Roselyn gave her that I'm not a baby look.

"Okay, don't touch anything. Pinky swears?" Meranda knew she could trust her, but wanted to make sure she knew the importance of her promise.

"Pinky swears! I was just going to write my mom a note so my dad could bring it to her." Roselyn rolled her eyes at Meranda.

"That's a lovely thing to do, and I'm sure it will make your mother feel better. I will tell Pete you want to give your mother a note. Sit tight." Meranda rushed out of the lab wishing she could use the pool port once again; a much faster way to travel down here.

"Pete! Pete! Where are you? I need to talk to you…?" Meranda didn't really know how to seek him out, he usually would just appear, and he didn't fail her now.

"What's wrong Meranda?" Pete's face was frantic with worry.

"Pete, Roselyn knocked over a tube of your blood and it mixed in with Salmonia's blood causing the green in her blood to lessen." Meranda was trying to give hope without giving false hope.

"What are you saying?" Pete looked confused.

"I don't know exactly. I need to do more testing, but it's something to go on. I just wanted to update you, and take a minute to get a grip on my nerves." Meranda wanted to get back and retest with purpose to see if the same results came about. "Hopefully, I will know more this afternoon. I'm going to run some other tests too."

"This is great news." Pete was trying not to get too excited, but it was too late he was already sporting a huge smile, a mixture of pride for Meranda and relief that a cure might be on the horizon. "I knew you would figure it out."

"Well, it was actually Roselyn who stumbled across the mishap." Meranda was giving credit to the one it belonged to.

"Maybe so, but you know what to look for." Pete eyes portrayed how much he appreciated everything she was doing.

Meranda quickly headed back to the lab not wanting to leave Roselyn by herself too long. When she returned Roselyn was sitting there writing her mother a letter with tears running down her face.

Meranda wanted to comfort her, but felt she deserved some crying time. She remembered how much she cried about her mom, except Salmonia was not dead, at least not yet. Meranda sorted through the information she had and set out to test different components that may improve the results.

She mixed different solutions with different ratios of Sal's and Pete's blood. When she reached a half and half mixture, she saw the best results. There still was a few cells that had a green hue, but the ratio was 4:1, four being Pete's healthy blood cells.

By the time evening came, Roselyn, had fallen to sleep giving Meranda the quiet time she needed to concentrate on her theories. Pete knocked softly on the lab door waiting for the signal to come in.

"Hi, how is it going?" Pete lowered his voice to a whisper when he saw Roselyn was curled up.

"I think it is worth a try Pete. Meranda looked into his worried eyes.

"You think what's worth a try?" Pete was confused by Meranda's half sentences.

"I think that if I removed Salmonia's blood to make room for your blood at a 50/50 mixture, her own cells would start to produce normal cells. I would like to wait until tomorrow to see if the test results are the same before I offer it up as a solution."

Meranda was worried that many things could go wrong. She had no idea if there would be side effects or rejection of the foreign blood. Maybe she should start out with a small transfusion ratio first.

Meranda's head felt like it was buzzing, all her muscles hurt. She was tired, hungry, and thirsty. Pete, of course, sensed that she needed some down time.

"I'm going to get Zane and have him spend the night with Roselyn. He can take her to visit her mother. I think that would be good for all of them and you are going to relax over a very good vintage bottle of wine, and a warm dinner." Pete did not give the impression this was up for discussion and Meranda was fine with all of it. She was both physically and mentally exhausted.

"That would be nice." Meranda coyly smiled up at him as her heart tightened and thoughts of melting into the safety of his strength engulfed her.

It wasn't long before Zane showed up in the pool port and was at Roselyn's side waking up his little girl. "Hey baby, do you want to visit your mom?" Roselyn's eye's popped open immediately when she heard, "mom" she quickly looked down and was thankful she had fell asleep in her mermaid form.

"Yes, daddy!" Suddenly Rosie looked like the little mermaid she was.

"For a short visit, I think it would do both of my girls good to see each other." Zane spoke softly with such tenderness in his eyes, and in a flash they were gone.

Meranda cleaned up the lab and shut down the lanterns. She felt every minute of the day in her shoulders; in fact, all her muscles were rock hard with tension. By the time she had reached her quarters Pete was already there with two glasses of a very smooth red wine.

The Dutch oven that hung over the fire was omitting it's usual mouthwatering smells. She didn't care if it was stew again. It was warm and nourishing; she always heard fish was considered "brain food."

"So do you think a transfusion will work?" Pete didn't want to bring it up, but he was so worried about Sal that he couldn't refrain.

"I'll know tomorrow if it is worth a try or not, unfortunately, the test of time will be the answer in the end. If the ratio stays the same for at least twenty four hours, and every hour that passes thereafter, increases the odds of it being the solution." Meranda barely got that out before stifling a yawn. Pete walked behind her to rub her shoulders, and flinched feeling how knotted they were. Meranda was grateful, because she had a banger headache.

The wine and food hit her all at once and she dozed off right there on the couch. Pete came around and picked her up and carried her to bed. She barely woke other than the smile that spread across her face. He pulled the covers over her and couldn't resist placing a kiss on her forehead. He stood there a moment and looked at her beautiful face and noticed how young she looked, his heart gave a squeeze and he left her to some much needed rest.

Meranda slept like a rock and when she woke, just for a moment she didn't remember where she was, but it wasn't long before she heard a splash at her pool port.

In a cheery refreshed child's voice, "Meranda are you up? I told mom we might have a cure. We have to hurry Meranda, my mom looks really sick."

Swinging her legs off the bed, Meranda sat there for a minute letting the blood catch up to her head, waiting for the dizziness to fade. She was foggy and her muscles hurt, "I'm up Rosie, but I am going to need a few minutes to wake up and have some coffee… that was coffee she smelled perking." Meranda slid out of bed and sat at the table where Roselyn joined her in her human form.

"Can I have some coffee too, please?" Roselyn was so happy and excited at the thought that they might have a cure for her mother.

"No honey, I'm not sure your parents would approve of you drinking coffee. I take it that your visit with your mother was good?" Meranda peered over her cup at her young friend.

"Well the visit was good, and mommy was trying to act like she was okay...but I could see how sick she was. That's when I told her that you might have a cure. I know we don't know yet, but she needed to hear something good. She said that just seeing her baby made her better." Roselyn was very intuitive for her age and Meranda forgot how old she really was at times. I guess when you are around adults all the time you think more like an adult than a child.

"You're right Rosie, I don't want to give false hope, but sometimes hope is all we have. Let's go see if the tests show any signs of a possible solution." Meranda went to get cleaned up as Rosie waited patiently for her on the couch.

Meranda approached the lab door and stood there for a moment taking in a deep cleansing breath and said a little prayer asking her mom and dad for any help they could give.

As soon as she opened the door she looked into the faces of her cheerleading team. Roselyn and Zane sat on the edge of the pool port with their tails in the water, and Pete was on the couch rubbing his hands together. "Good morning," all three chimed together.

"And a good morning to you three as well," Meranda grumbled back. Her stomach was so tight she could barely breathe.

Pete joined her at the counter, "Meranda, relax...what will be will be, and anything is better than nothing." Pete could be so sweet sometimes; she truly could see why he was the Prince.

She peeked around Pete to see father and daughter looking anxiously in her direction. They immediately looked down as if they had been instructed not to add to her stress. Meranda looked at Pete, "Let's do this. Let's see if we've found a cure."

Meranda went over to the incubator and pulled the clamped slides out. Then she went to the refrigerator and pulled out more samples with gloved hands. Placing a glass slide under each of the microscopes she took a deep breath before gathering the courage to peer into the scope.

First she looked at the slide from the incubator and the green cells had taken over the healthy cells. Looking up at Pete she shook her head no. Slowly she walked over to the room temperature sample and looked into the high powered microscope…it had stayed the same with little or no change.

Lastly, she walked over to the last sample that had been in the cooler which was set at 40 degrees, approximately the same temperature as the lake. She looked into the microscope and looked again. When she looked up at Pete she had tears in her eyes, and she shook her head, yes.

There were only a couple of faded green cells left between the blood smeared glass. There sat their solution. Pete not really knowing what he was looking at had to look for himself, followed by Zane and Roselyn who had pushed their way to the counter to take a look.

Roselyn ran up to Meranda and hugged her so tight Meranda stumbled backwards, luckily Pete was behind her to steady her. Meranda's knees felt weak and the tears of relief streamed down her face. Roselyn brought her little hands up gently cupping Meranda's face and wiped away the falling tears.

Loretta Rose Didrikson

17

Meranda took a moment to regain her composure, and look again at the sample that gave promise. She couldn't get the smile off her face. She knew she needed to run the tests a few more times making sure the results were continually the same, but she knew time was running out. She had to try something, even if it was wrong, because her friend was growing weak.

Apparently, the differences between a mer being infected and a parasite being infected was the parasite flourish. Salmonia's symptoms were equivalent to stage three out of four on the disease scale. They had to try the blood transfusion and soon. Pete's blood seemed to hold the key to restoring her cells to a healthy state.

Meranda told Roselyn she needed to talk to her mother alone. The young mermaid protested somewhat, but her father put his arm around her and shook his head no. He did whisper in her ear that she could go and start getting their quarters cleaned up. So that when her mother came home, everything would be tidy. Roselyn's face lit up, and she disappeared through the pool port. Pete and Zane followed and Meranda headed off to talk with Sal.

Meranda approached Salmonia's cell slowly in case she was sleeping. She knew Sal would need all her strength to fight the toxic levels in her body. When she approached the cell, Sal was laying there motionless with her eyes closed. For a moment, Meranda thought she was too late, "Hey girlfriend," croaked Sal.

"Hey, how are you doing?" Meranda instantly thought what a stupid question that was. She knew exactly how she was doing…she was dying.

"Oh--I've been better." Sal struggled to sit up; her once silvery translucent skin glowed green.

"We think we have a solution. It's not for sure, but we did see positive results in the lab." Meranda was up beat.

"Great when do we start?" Salmonia said with all the optimism she could muster.

"We can start immediately; I just have to decide the best way to proceed. We will do a 50/50 blood transfusion first and see how that goes." Meranda was more or less talking herself into deciding which way to go.

"Sounds good, you know where to find me." Sal closed her eyes.

Meranda ran through the tunnels to get to the lab to gather supplies. Calling for Pete who heard her summons and shot up through the pool port arriving minutes before her and he hurriedly threw on some sweatpants.

"Ready?" Seeing Pete come out from behind the privacy wall as Meranda busted through the labs door.

"Whatever you need me to do." Pete was glad he could help.

"I'm just going to get some things together for the transfusion and I will see you back at Sal's. Pete she doesn't look good. This has to work." Meranda didn't even look at Pete as she gathered equipment from the list in her head.

"Don't go in there until someone is there with you." Pete was very serious in his command.

"I wouldn't dream of it, besides you will probably beat me there." Meranda shouted back over her shoulder.

Pete called for Zane to be there in case they needed help. Just as she thought, by the time Meranda got there with her bag of supplies, they were all waiting for her.

"Great we are all here." Zane had move Sal's bed over to the bars so it would be easier for Meranda to access her. Meranda kneeled down and began getting everything laid out. "Pete I want you to get comfortable, because this will be slow going. Here's what's going to happen." Meranda explained that she was first going to remove Sal's blood to make room for Pete's.

"Sal you are probably going to feel weak or pass out, and I expect that. Pete, I will get you started with an IV drip and slowly collect your blood. Then I will infuse Sal with Pete's healthy blood. Does anyone have any questions?" Meranda looked each of them in the eyes to see if there were any doubts. Everyone was on board and ready to try anything.

Zane barely whispered if he could be in the cell with Sal. His eyes pleaded with Pete. Pete looked at Meranda for any objections before nodding yes.

"Good, let's get started." Meranda's hands were surprisingly steady when she placed the IV in Sal's arm. She then ran the tubing through the bars and hooked it to an empty blood bag and the siphoning began.

Meranda then turned to Pete and started his IV so that it would begin to fill his bag with the healthy blood. When Pete's bag was full, she shut off his valve and placed the sac in icy water to stay cool. The mer body temperature was close to that of the lakes, but she had gotten her best results at lower temperatures.

Zane looked miserable, but wrapped his muscular arms around Salmonia whispering reassuring words into her delicate green tinted ear.

"Here Pete drink some juice and then some water so that you will replenish what you have lost, because I need more." Meranda put a hand on his shoulder as he tried to get up. She just shook her head and handed him the fluids.

She took one full bag out of Sal and started to draw a second bag, then a third, and as she thought, Salmonia passed out. She was weak to begin with, and losing blood didn't help.

Unfortunately, Meranda needed to get four bags from Sal to make room for Pete's blood setting the stage for Sal's body to regenerate. Letting Sal's body think it was dying would increase the chance that her body would greedily absorb Pete's blood.

Sal began to convulse and shake violently. Zane's eyes shot to Meranda filled with alarmed as he instinctively tightened his hold, "Why is she shaking?"

"She will be okay Zane. We are bringing her to the point of going in to shock, so that when I give her the transfusion her body will do everything it can to make new and healthy cells." Meranda knew this was hard to watch, especially for Zane.

"Your body heat will help comfort her. She'll be okay Zane, I promise." Meranda looked directly into Zane's golden eyes and watched them turn from fearful to determine.

"As soon as I withdraw this last bag from Sal I am going to start infusing her with Pete's blood." Meranda removed Sal's toxic bag and replaced the tubing. Using the new IV site that Meranda had the sense to put in place before they had started this process. She didn't think she would be able to get another IV in her nearly collapsed circulatory system.

The exchange began. She set it on a slow drip and sometime during the second bag of healthy blood; Sal stopped shaking and started resting quietly.

"Do you feel okay Pete?" Meranda knew she needed to get filling another bag from him.

"Absolutely Doc," his eyes were all sparkly and he flashed Meranda that million dollar smile making her cheeks turn pink.

"Here we go then." Meranda started on the third bag and hopefully that would be enough to jump start Sal's body. After that she didn't dare take anymore of Pete's blood, at least not right now.

The introduction of Pete's blood into Sal went on for hours. Pete disregarded Meranda's orders about not getting up and came and sat by her. He removed her hands which were holding her head up and leaned her against his body as she nestled in the crook of his neck.

Once the bags were empty, all they could do was wait to see if Salmonia responded. Zane left for a minute to give Roselyn an update and check on her, other than that he never left Salmonia's side.

In the caves it was hard to tell what time of day or night it was. Regardless, Meranda knew they all had been there over twelve hours. She eventually fell asleep on Pete shoulder; and he too fell asleep, weakened by the loss of blood, his head resting on Meranda's.

Meranda woke to the low hum of Salmonia and Zane's voices. He was helping her sit up and drink some fish broth. Meranda woke first and Pete woke when Meranda tried moving his heavy arm off her shoulder. Pete was confused for a minute, but his coloring was better and the dark circles under his eyes had lightened.

Taking one look at Sal, even in the lanterns dim light, Meranda could see that Sal's coloring was better, and her eyes showed no signs of red. Meranda kept her worries to herself, in that; just because she looked better didn't mean she was. The blood tests would tell the true story.

"Hey Doc..." Salmonia's mood was light.

"I'm no doctor Sal," Meranda could feel the heat crawling up her face.

"Maybe not, but I feel great." Salmonia did look like her old self again.

"Well, we will have to monitor you and do labs frequently until we are sure that it worked." Meranda wanted everyone to know that she was still unsure of the solution they all desperately wanted.

"Anything is an improvement from the awful color combination you were sporting the last few days. I thought it was Christmas with all the red and green that was going on." Pete meant to be funny; instead he took one look at Sal and knew it was too soon for any kind of joking.

Zane had both his arms wrapped around Sal and was whispering in her ear and Sal nodded. Zane untwined his body from hers and headed to the pool port. Meranda figured he was off to tell Roselyn that it was over for now and her mother was doing well.

"I hate to do this to you so soon Sal, but I need to draw a little blood to see what's going on." Meranda had to poke her again not wanting to use the IV port; she wanted it straight from a vein. "I also think it is best if you stay put until we are sure." Meranda was being very cautions.

"I agree Randi, we have to be sure. I want to thank you for looking out for Roselyn while I was sick and for all you've done." Salmonia voice quivered from emotion not only from the trauma her body had gone through, but overwhelmed by the love.

"Hey that is what family does for each other. I want you to rest and keep drinking fluids, you're still a quart low." Meranda wanted to get to the lab and see how things looked internally.

"Brother may I have a word with you before you leave." Salmonia said quietly.

Meranda headed down the tunnel and sat on the stairs to give Sal and Pete a minute leaning against the smooth cool walls, exhaling and letting go of the stress. Looking up she silently thanked her parents.

"I-I don't know how to thank you for what you have done." With tears in her eyes she looked at Pete stammering for words that couldn't even begin to express her gratitude.

"Like Meranda said, that's what family does, sister. Now let's concentrate on getting you back to one hundred percent." Pete tried to lighten the mood.

"I don't think that is going to happen anytime soon with my tail clipped." Sal looked down at her stump of a tail.

"It will grow back Sal, you just have to be patient." Pete wasn't entirely sure about that but he felt that discussion could be had at a later date.

Zane was back in a flash with Roselyn. To be safe he kept Rosie on the outside of the cell, she had to see for herself that her mother was better. After a short visit Zane stated the obvious and announced that Salmonia needed to rest. Roselyn squeezed her mother's hand and told her that she loved her and bid her goodnight.

Pete opted for the pool port feeling the need to feel the cold water that would embrace him and cleared his mind before joining Meranda for dinner.

Sal could sense Meranda was near and called out to her. Meranda left her doctor's bag at the foot of the stairs and came to sit beside Sal remaining safely outside the cell, "I just wanted to ask you that if the news is bad--please don't tell anyone before talking to me. I know I shouldn't ask any more of you--as you have already done so much. I will never be able to thank you enough, but I don't want my family to go through anything more unless they absolutely have to," Sal pleaded.

"No worries, besides it's your information to do what you want with, unless it endangers the pod. I'll stop back to check on you, and please try to rest, that is the best thing you can do for yourself." Meranda was worried even though Sal's coloring was better, she still looked extremely sunken in.

"I will Meranda-and again, thanks." Sal could barely keep her eyes open.

"Hey, this is going to work, and you are going to be okay," Meranda gave the same pep talk to Sal that she had gotten, the day she to learn how to breathe under water. "I will come and see how you are doing before I go to bed... rest!"

Sal slid down under the blankets and closed her eyes.

Pete was feeling better, but not totally back to normal. He too could use some rest and a hot meal. Meranda figured she would insist on both and had set her mind to winning if he thought to argue about it.

Like always, when she got back to her quarters she was hit with delicious smells of dinner. She guided Pete to the couch and served him for once picking out a bottle of red wine. She needed to relax and it wouldn't hurt Pete to have one glass of wine either.

After dinner they sat on the couch and Pete fell asleep. Instead of waking him, Meranda covered him up with a blanket, knowing his body had gone through the gamut too. Meranda was feeling antsy and decided to go to the lab.

Anxiously, she got out the samples she had taken from Sal, and set up the slides to take a look. She knew it was too early to make a call on whether the transfusion worked, but she wanted to take a look anyways.

In addition, she wanted to make some notes on the process, in case she needed to change anything, or if this happened to other mers.

Pete's blood had succeeded in diluting Sal's, and there was just a hint of green that remained. Only the test of time would tell if the results would hold up, and if Sal's body would make their own healthy cells thereafter.

Meranda shut down the lab and went to check on her friend, before calling it a night. When she got down to the cell it appeared empty.

Instantly, she thought that Sal had gotten out and the thought terrified her. Sal sat quietly in human form in the darkest corner of her cell.

"Hello." She said softly.

"Hey—you're awake and in human form." Meranda replied.

"I am." Sal was not only looking better, but seemed to be feeling better within hours after the transfusion. "I had to see if I still had feet."

"I see." Meranda was relieved that having her tail clipped only affected her mermaid form and that she was not disabled in human form. She wasn't sure Sal would have come back from being completely crippled.

"How long will I have to be locked up?" Sal wanted to get out of that cell and back in her own quarters she shared with her daughter.

"I'm not sure. It depends on what the blood work shows tomorrow and the next day. Even if there is some toxins left in your cells and they stay diluted, I think it will be fine for you to be released." This was all uncharted territory for Meranda.

"I agree, and I don't feel aggressive anymore, which will hopefully continue. It gives me insight on what drove the infected lampreys to act so violently. They need to get those barrels out of the lake." Sal no longer had any doubts that the barrels were contributing to the imbalance and growth of the lamprey.

"My thoughts exactly, I do know that there was a group that had been pushing for the removal of the barrels over the last decade. The talks kept being put on hold until recently." Meranda was searching her memory on every article she had read about this subject.

Sadly enough, she now realized that the government had covered up the results and told the public the barrels were harmless. Meranda now knew different, but at the moment there was nothing she could do about it.

"Earth to Meranda..." Sal had been talking to Meranda who was deep in her own thoughts and didn't hear a thing Sal had said.

Meranda laughed, "Sorry, what were you saying?"

"I was just saying that it has been a long day for you, and that you should get some rest." Sal must be feeling better because she was back to running the show and that brought a smile to Meranda's face.

"I will. I wanted to check on you first, and you seem better than I had hoped for this early on. So, if you don't need anything...I will do just that--and go to bed." Meranda's muscles ached so down deep from the intense day that even rubbing them wouldn't help.

Meranda bid Sal goodnight and slowly walked back to her room. Meranda for the first time, felt the need to go back on land and prove to the officials that the barrels were affecting: the lake and the fish. She didn't even want to think what it was doing to the water supply. She thought it would be a good idea if they set up testing sites in the lake to see how far the infestation was reaching.

For now, she just needed to sleep, and when Pete felt better she would have to pick his brain about when she would be going back home. She wondered if everyone really thought she was dead? How long had she been here?

It was time for her and Pete to have that discussion. Just thinking about it made her sad. It wouldn't be so bad if this was her life, in a way, serving the lake was her life's goal anyhow.

18

When Meranda returned to her quarters, she didn't have the heart to wake Pete, instead she covered him up with a blanket and put another log on the fire. She stood over him looking at how peacefully he was sleeping. All the worry lines of the past few weeks had relaxed making him appear years younger.

Meranda smiled down at him and felt a warmth course through her body. She wanted to trace her fingers over his sensuous lips, and reached out for him, then stopped. Her cheeks blazed with color even though no one else was there to witness her actions, as she pulled her arms to her chest, she turned and dragged her exhausted body to bed.

Morning came too quick, but it was made better by the wonderful smell of coffee. She thought for a moment she was home in Palo, Minnesota. Only when she opened her eyes, it wasn't her father sitting there, it was Pete. She had the urge to start crying as her heart remembered her life on land, a life without her father.

"Good morning Doc." Pete smiled looking refreshed.

Meranda's heartbeat quickened and she wondered if she would ever get use to that smile of his. She wasn't even standing and she felt weak behind the knees, "Good morning. Did you sleep well?"

"I did and I feel great. Now get your butt out of bed and come have coffee. I don't see what you see in the stuff, but here you go." Pete crinkled his nose.

"Thank you. I can't believe it...do you have an endless supply down here? Forget it, I don't care, I just want some." Meranda inhaled deeply filling her nose with the wonderful aroma.

"You should try a cup you might like it." Meranda said playfully.

"No thank you, it smells...well, I'll leave it at no thanks." Just then Pete received a summons from his father.

"My father just called for a meeting. I suppose he wants an update. I better not keep him waiting." Pete got up pausing in the entry way, "Thanks again for everything you've done. I'm sure Salmonia will make a full recovery." Pete disappeared out of the alcove to go meet with his father.

Meranda wished she could be as sure as Pete regarding Sal. Today's testing would be a good indicator if the transfusion was going to work or if the infected cells would have taken control over Pete's cells; actually they were now Salmonia's cells. Meranda shook her head; this was way too much to think about before her second cup of coffee.

When Pete arrived at his father's, he was in merman form. The warriors seemed uncomfortable whenever he was in his human form. *"Good morning father, gentlemen."*

Pete could not help his lighthearted mood. The Vikings nodded, *"Good morning Pelias, how is the huntress?"*

"She looks good for the moment, but we will know more as time passes." Pete took his place by his father facing the circle of warriors.

"We are deciding on how we should eliminate the giant lamprey and serpent." Pete's father laid out the details of the plan. *"Is there any added information that would shed light on the problem?"*

"What we have learned is that there are biological changes from the chemicals seeping out of the barrels. Meranda has studied the changes in the infected lamprey, and clearly the results point to the toxins. Not only are the cells enlarged and multiplying at a faster rate. The toxins also makes them far more aggressive." Pete had a flash of Salmonia's red eyes and vicious outburst.

"It's the serpent we are most worried about. The warriors have taken on larger serpents in the ocean; however, serpents are cunning at blending into their environment making it much harder to locate them. We will have to lure it out of hiding in order to kill it. The overgrown lampreys are not a threat to our great warriors." Pete's father had seen many battles take place in his youth within the oceans.

"When you say lure, you know what it will respond to?" Pete had a uneasy feeling.

"The serpent, more than likely, came through the widened gap in the rift, which is where the first attack occurred. It is our belief that is where it retreats for shelter other than coming out to feed. Unless, we get lucky, the only way to lure it out--is with a merman's blood." Pete's father paused letting his son absorb what he was saying.

"Merman's blood...? Pete wondered how they came to that conclusion. *"Why would you conclude that?"*

The Viking Folkor spoke up, *"We have dealt with serpents in the past off the shores of Norway. Centuries ago serpents were more common and caused many shipwrecks. To restore order we had to slay many a serpent. The legends speak of a time when serpents ruled the oceans, of which is not completely true. We ruled the oceans and kept the balance."*

Gunnarr added, *"Of course, there were more Vikings back when serpents were more of a threat. The legends tell of mermen being used as bait, in which no serpent could resist. When a serpent surfaces to feed, that is when they are most vulnerable, and that is when we attack. The sharks would come and do cleanup."*

"So you are saying that we have to use our pod members for bait?" Pete did not like where this plan was going, but if it lured the creature out of hiding, they'd do whatever needed to be done.

Pete's father spoke up, *"Fortunately, we have captured a few of the Devil's Island pod. They are in custody and were the ones responsible for kidnapping Salmonia, so they will be used as bait. Ordinarily, I would not ask neighboring pods to make such a sacrifice, but that issue has been resolved with the actions of the guilty."*

Breaking into an evil smile Pete thought the punishment was justified, *"When do we put this plan in motion?"*

"It will be a full moon the day after tomorrow which is when the serpent will be most active and wanting to feed," added Sigurdr the guardian of victory. *"Knowing the feeding habits of your enemy is crucial to defeating them. We will need an army from your pod to assist with the lamprey, and we will see to the serpent."*

"I am sure my men will be honored to help." Pete knew Zane for one would be at the forefront of that crusade.

"Excellent," was all the Father of the Lake had to add.

"We will meet outside of the main entrance when the full moon rises in two days." Logmar, the lawman concluded. Pete could hardly wait to fill Zane and Sal in on the plans. He would also have to let Meranda know so she could be ready for any casualties.

The talks continued until Pete was fully informed on everyone's part. The father excused himself and retreated deeper in the rock to rest. Pete respectfully bid the warriors good day and disappeared into the pool port. He sought out Meranda and found her in the lab; he popped up immediately announcing himself. "How do things look?"

Meranda still was startled and almost knocked over the test tubes she was working on. She looked over at Pete ready to yell at him until she saw his happy face, "I don't know if I will ever get use to mer-people emerging in and out of a swimming pool." She smiled as the panic left her.

"We have great news. I just met with my father and the warriors. They have a plan to rid the lake of the serpent and its overgrown flunkies. Can you meet me at Sal's home away from home, then I can enlighten everyone at the same time?" Pete had already sent a message to Zane to meet him at the cell. "By the way, how did things look for Sal this morning?"

"I just ran another set of labs and everything looks good. Your cells remained in tacked and infused with Sal's. I couldn't be happier with the results." Meranda hadn't told Sal the good news yet, but Pete and Meranda felt it would be safe for her to go home.

Once they were all gathered at the cell, Pete relayed the plan that would restore balance to the lake. When he finished briefing them, he noticed how quiet Sal had become. Pete figured she would work out what was bothering her as she always did.

Meranda also noticed the change in Sal's mood, and decided that the moment was right to enlighten her on her progress, "Hey girlfriend, you are free to blow this pop stand. Your cells are rejuvenating toward a healthier ratio."

Looking up at Meranda, she just smiled, "That's great" and turned to gather her things. Pete, Meranda, and Zane exchanged confused looks at the huntress' reaction. It didn't take Meranda long to zoom in on what her friend might be feeling. She hung back after the men had departed.

Meranda wasn't as patience, "What's going on Sal?"

"Not much. I'll be happy to get out of this joint. It's just I won't be a part of this mission nor will I be able to hunt." Sal looked down somewhat ashamed of how she was feeling. The truth of it was she didn't know what her future role was supposed to be without a tail, she provided food for the pod and was Pete's protector.

"Let's take today for what it is and today we made progress." Meranda tried focus on the bright side.

Salmonia smiled back at her friend. She caught herself instinctively heading to the pool port before she realized that she couldn't swim. Meranda quickly turned around with her back to Sal.

Meranda could feel the heavy heart of her friend, "I haven't told Roselyn that you were given a clean bill of health, she'll be surprised when you walk in the door."

Sal smiled.

Upon entering the commons room it was obvious that family members were leery of Salmonia. Then she heard a squeal. "Mother you're free," Roselyn all but flew across the room into her arms. "How do you feel? Are you better? I love you mama!"

There is no greater joy than the love of a child. Looking around, Sal noticed that everyone started to relax and go about their chores, "I feel good sweetheart and I'm better thanks to the Doc here. I love you too Rosie." Sal's mood had lightened the minute she saw her daughter's luminous face.

It was going to take time for Sal to adjust, but with Roselyn needing her mother to be okay, hopefully that would help Sal move forward. "Come mama, I have a surprise for you. You can rest, and I will take care of you." Roselyn was probably the only one who was happy that Salmonia was grounded.

Leading the way Roselyn all but dragged her mother off so she could take care of her. She also wanted her mom to see how nice she had made things look at home, after all, she was almost a girl grown.

Meranda stopped by the lab to make sure things were shut down before heading to her own quarters for some well-deserved down time. Pete knocked lightly on the alcove's door not wanting to disturb her if she was resting when he heard her say, "The door's open."

Meranda sat on the couch close to the crackling fire staring into it. Pete admired how the reflection of the fire made her skin glow. He walked over to the hearth and grabbed a wine glass before noticing Meranda already had one out for him. She was waiting for him to show up and say goodnight. It had become their ritual. She looked up at him and smiled.

He returned the goblet to the shelf and turned with a sly look on his face. Meranda's head tilted as she peered through her thick lashes and poured him a glass of wine. She had picked out a very smooth one hundred year old bottle. Pete put his finger on the rim of the bottle tilting it slightly to get a better look at her choice.

Looking up from his hooded eyes, a smile spread across his chiseled face. She had developed quite a palate for aged wines. He sat down closer to her than he normally would allow himself, and to his surprise she leaned back into him. Each taking a deep relaxing breath knowing they had done all they could for that day.

Pete set his glass down and gently rubbed the tight muscles in her neck and shoulders, knowing where she carried her stress, "You were great today," he leaned forward and kissed the back of her head.

Meranda just made a purring sound agreeing that she too felt pleased with herself, "We all did great today."

Pete wrapped his arms around her resting his chin on the top of her head and looked at the ceiling—wondering if he could let this woman go—he loved her.

In his 532 years he had many opportunities to marry, but no one stirred him to the core as she did. Pete finished his glass of wine and bid her goodnight as any respectable merman would do before things progressed. He knew she deserved a chance at the life she was meant to live. Getting her back above, was another day's problem.

Morning had arrived and everyone was bustling around preparing for what was being called, "The Day of the Serpent" or "The Day the Serpent Died"; this was the stuff legends were made of. At the rising of the full moon tonight the plan would proceed in ridding the lake of its unwanted guests.

Pete's jaw was clenched as he saw to the preparations. Between the loss of his men and the hurting of Sal, the anger bubbled beneath his skin. He couldn't wait to send the evil snake to its death and justice to be served to the ones responsible for hurting his sister.

Pete searched out Zane, his comrade, making sure all the troops were clear on their part in the battle. Now was the opportune time to show his father he was ready to step up. It would be more than Pete could bare if his father didn't feel confident to return to his birthplace to complete his life's journey, because of him.

Lastly, Pete went to talk to Meranda to see if she was ready for any casualties. He should have known she would already be prepared. She had cots set up in the lab and plenty of salve along with a backup of blood if needed.

Salmonia had asked if she could assist her, needing to be useful. Of course, her assistant, Roselyn would also be by her side. "We're ready." Meranda set Pete's mind at ease when he popped up in the pool port.

"Excellent, I don't anticipate trouble, but there is always that possibility in war." Pete turn to leave, but he stopped turning to Sal, "You will be with us in spirit, huntress."

Sal gave him a sad but loving smile, "Sikker min bror."

Meranda, Sal, and Roselyn walked down to see the soldiers off to battle. They could feel the electricity in the air.

Meranda's breath caught in her chest when she saw Pete in his boiled leather vest and armed with all his jeweled weapons. Their eyes found each other, filled with unspoken words. His hair fell forward as he shot a sideways glance at her and flashed her that smile, before disappearing into the pool port.

Zane, who was equally impressive, had whispered into Salmonia's ear, and grabbed his dagger cutting off a piece of her fiery red hair to carry into battle. He attached it like a war feather to one of his dreads, then disappeared into Lake Superior.

The commons became eerily quiet and the three women headed back to the lab to nervously wait for the safe return of the men in their family. Meranda had the jitters and busied herself in the lab going over everything that might be needed. Sal and Roselyn stopped by their quarters to light a candle saying a prayer for the safe return of their pod, before joining Meranda in the make shift medical station.

The three women checked and rechecked making sure that everything was in place. All there was left to do was, wait.

It was of comfort, having the Norse Vikings warriors amongst the troops, making everyone feel more favorable about the outcome of this battle. The reality of war was that many things could go wrong and causalities were to be expected.

"By the way, what did you say to Pete back in the commons?" Meranda asked Sal.

"Be safe my brother."

19

The troops assembled outside the caves. The Vikings stood at attention. Their majestic frames shadowed the area as they lined up shoulder to shoulder, creating a massive shield of Norwegian warriors.

Each were eight feet tall. The span between one shoulder and the other was four feet of roped muscle. Their tail fins were five feet wide and fanned gracefully giving the warriors their sylphlike balance. They crossed their hands behind their backs at a soldier's attention, waiting for the command to move out, which made their arms bulge out from their shoulders looking like boulders beneath their skin. Pete and his men looked like small fry next to these ocean born mermen.

Each Viking wore a leather sash wrapped around his scalloped waist with swords that hung snuggly at their sides. The swords alone were nearly the height of a regular merman.

The handles of their weapons were engraved and unique to their personal family's crest. Thick leather straps pressed taunt against their solid expanding chests, before crossing in the middle of their shoulders that housed a dagger. The knife was placed strategically so that one could reach over his shoulder in close proximity and access the blade, allowing them to easily rip the entrails out of their opponent, and gut them like a deer.

The red armbands they wore, emphasized the monolithic volume of their strength, and represented the blood spilled from fallen soldiers. Their beards and mustaches were braided in various designs and embellished with charms, proudly worn by a seasoned Norse Warrior.

At the beginning of the line stood Sigurdr, the guardian of victory, his blonde hair was shaved on each side of his head leaving only the top of his head thickly braided. The braid fell free as it continued past his dense neck, and laid between his shoulder blades. His reddish blonde mustache was weaved into his beard, before splitting into two braids and decorated with charms, and rested on his chest. He had icy light Norwegian blue eyes that were shaped like half-moons.

His family's symbol was the colors of the Norwegian flag as the backdrop to an ivory carved fist holding a lightning bolt. Sigurdr seemed just a little bigger than the rest of the warriors, if that were even possible.

Next in line was Logmar, the lawman. He looked most like the pictures drawn of Triton. His wavy red hair flowed around his neck caressing his shoulders. His light blue eyes twinkled with mischief and good humor. He didn't sport a beard, but had many charms woven into his mustache that hung far beyond his cleft chin.

On the handles of his swords, were the scales of justice, engraved in silver and set against black onyx. His full mouth was clenched tight in anticipation of the battle as his roped muscles contracted beneath his freckled skin, that defined a frame built to fight.

Hallvardr, the rock defender, could easily blend into his surroundings with his gray slate colored hair and beard. His hair was fastened back with many leather ties cascading down his back before blending into the colors of his tail. He looked like a stone statue, except for his black gleaming eyes. His forked beard was knotted at the end to secure the sapphires and rubies that were generously woven throughout his mustache. His olive colored skin stretched tightly across his massive chest. He appeared muscle bound, yet moved gracefully through the water. His swords and weaponry were carved with mountains jetting out of the ocean and set against a sky of turquoise blue.

Fourth was Gunnar, the element of gunnr war and arr warrior. His long silky brown hair danced in the water. His dark skin and almond shaped brown eyes drew you to in. He bore no facial hair giving his high cheekbones and brilliant smile center stage. His swimmers build was slender. His long smooth muscles tapered seductively to down to a semi-transparent tail that showed the swells of his well-defined buttocks. When his tail became solid, it was smooth and without scales fanning into a variegated vibrant blue fin.

Cobalt handled swords hung at his sides, matching the cobalt throwing stars slipped into the slots of his vest. His family crest was a dolphin riding an ocean wave.

Finally, at the end of the long span of Vikings was Folkor, the guardian of the people. His jade color eyes radiated from his face surrounded by white blonde hair that sat in ringlets on his shoulders. His beard was cut close to his face emphasizing his arrow straight nose. He wore his mustache just long enough to fasten a charm at each end. He was the most social, and when he smiled, it seemed to take up half his face, making the creases around his eyes smile too. His symbol was of a man and a woman who held a child to her breast.

Once everyone had assembled outside the cave's entrance, the warriors presented the three Devil's Island mermen, bundled together with their arms tied behind their backs. Their tails had been clipped in the same fashion they had clipped Salmonia's.

Individually, without the support of a Viking they would have sunk to the bottom of the lake. It would take the effort of all three convicts to remain upright in the water as they dangled from a rope. Pete gave the nod, and they headed toward Split Rock, where most of the attacks had occurred.

The protectors of the lake leisurely swam to their destination, as they waited for the sun to set and the full moon to rise. The sky treated them to different hues of pink as the last rays of sun disappeared behind the horizon.

The stars began to appear cluster by cluster, Venus being one of the brightest. The constellation of Orion also appeared, as if to bear witness to the righting of those who had been wronged.

The Vikings and mermen turned warriors, hid amongst the rocks and remained motionless. Patiently waiting for the moment, when the serpent would be lured from the abyss for his evening meal.

The moon now high in the night sky, threw off beams of light that showcased the baited sacrifice. A luminous view allowed all to see the fear on the condemned evil faces. Zane's eyes burrowed into the demented freaks that kidnapped his Nia, and he waited for justice to be served. He could smell their fear, but felt they were getting off easy with death.

The stillness in the water felt eerie, except for the erratic movements of the prisoners that dangling above the darkest depths. The anticipation felt unbearable until the calm water started to ripple. Large air bubbles escaped rushing to the surface before dissipating.

Electricity echoed through the water making the wait painful with the forbearance knowing that the fight would begin soon enough. The beast, was awake and hungry.

The serpent's senses picked up on the jerking movements above, signaling every nerve in its body that something was injured. The ripples increased, before turning turbulent.

Every muscle in each Viking was filled with adrenalin and they were ready to strike.

The serpent shot straight up from the split in the earth's crust, and all that could be seen was a gigantic mouth. With its jaws unlocked, it seemed large enough to swallow a ship. Its fangs were extended and ready to pierce the prey; ending its life. The circular rows of pointed shark like teeth lined its jaws and were clearly made for shredding.

The sea monster was a master of disguise. The body appeared invisible except for its large scaled head and a mouth full of teeth. When the jaws closed around all three mermen in one engulfing motion, they were gone, but it signaled the beginning of the battle.

The sound of metal clashing on metal, like a butcher sharpening his knife, rang throughout the water. The camouflaged serpent appeared, then disappeared. With its tail in its mouth it had circled the Vikings rounding them up like cattle, before closing in to squeeze the life out of them.

The Vikings formed their own circle with their backs facing inward covering all angles. With the inner side of the serpent's body camouflaged, Gunnarr squinted his eyes searching for the slightest ripple. He caught a slight glimmer and his body shot forward swords extended. In a swinging motion he brought down his steel blades cutting through the water. The ripple was gone.

They remained still like statues searching for any movement. Folkor left the circle and shot downward hoping to get on the other side of the snake, the side that was visible. He remained suspended outside the protection of his brothers looking for any visible signs of the beast.

The serpent turned his invisible side outward, breaking the circle, as it propelled at Folkor with its mouth wide open.

Folkor positioned both hands on one sword and lodged it vertically in the serpent's mouth as it tried to clamp down on him, jamming its mouth open. His sword began to bend beneath the strain of the powerful jaws, but held long enough for the Vikings to attack from different angles like the points of a star.

Hallvardr plunged forward, slicing open a deep gash just below the back fin. The serpent curled around, giving his full attention to his attacker.

The red and yellow spikes from the crest of the serpents head, now visible, ran down his back like an armor of flames, while the thorn tipped scales puffed out protecting its flesh.

The overgrown snake coiled like a cobra ready to strike; and time stopped. In those moments Hallvardr looked into the beast's yellowed eyes and the beast looked at him. The serpent snapped the sword in half, uncoiling its snake like body and struck out at Hallvardr.

Like a dance of death, the Vikings simultaneously ran their swords into the serpents head.

Sigurdr left one of his swords lodged through its eye, piercing the beast's small brain. The serpent high pitched scream pierced through its enemy's heads, as it began to wither. The serpent thrashed its powerful tail as it blindly struggled to make its way back to the safety of the rift; even if it was to die. With one mighty swing, Gunnarr cut the serpent in half and the waters clouded with blood.

Justice was served.

Within moments of killing the serpent, the Vikings found themselves surrounded by the aggressive giant lamprey, as they tried to latch onto the warriors. This was the cue for Zane and his pod to join in the battle. They came out in a blaze, harpooning and slicing the toxic lampreys into pieces.

The water became thick with fragments of the parasites, and as pieces of the serpent descended slowly to the bottom of the lake; the lamprey joined their leader.

The war was over.

The revenging mermen started back to the compound feeling satisfied that Salmonia and the lost comrades had been vindicated. Pete swam alongside his brother, giving him a pat on the back that all had been righted. All Zane could do at that moment was feel a sense of relief for the mother of his child and his fellow soldiers. He smiled back and nodded.

As they returned to the cave, the Vikings went to the deeper entryway that allowed for their size and to report to the Father of the Lake.

Pete and Zane popped up knowing the women would be in the lab waiting to be of service. The three women breathed a sigh of relief when they saw that the men had returned unharmed. Zane slipped up alongside Salmonia and Roselyn hugging them both as he whispered, "They are gone Nia."

Meranda had been so worried, that when Pete came partially out of the water, she ran to him throwing her arms around his neck. Tears running down her face, and kissed him on those soft sensual lips, and it felt right.

20

The Father of the Lake called for a celebration, "We will have a victory feast and farewell to our Norse warriors. Without the warriors, the casualties would have been many, and their aid in the rescue of our huntress goes without saying." Pete's father had left the festivity arrangements to Salmonia.

The death of the serpent spread a much needed lightheartedness throughout the clan. Sadly, it also meant that the warriors would be going back home. Most of the pod had become very fond of the Vikings, except Zane. He appreciated their help, but was more than ready to resume being top commander of this pod.

In the meantime, the cavern was buzzing and everyone seemed to be doing something, including Salmonia, despite her forced human state. She was glad that she had previously filled all the holding tanks with fish. The twins, Eira and Einar, were bustling in the kitchen and had trays of fish lined up ready to be served.

In Salmonia's absence Eira had stepped into the role as kitchen manager; and would someday make some merman a very good wife, if that is what she chose. With her being a natural born mermaid, her bloodline was crucial to the next generation, being most natural born mer were male.

The Viking warriors enjoyed themselves and shared stories of when they were young, of a time when the population of the mer was large and they owned the seas and oceans.

A time when the number of serpents peaked in the thousands and territories were respected. When there was an hierarchy between species and the mer were at the top of that chain ruling the waterways. The warriors, had faraway looks of sadness in their eyes, remembering the old days.

The music played on late into the night before the gala came to an end. Everyone's bellies were full and skins of wine had been passed around as they had toasted the motherlands and anything else anyone could think of.

Roselyn had hung on every word until her mother motioned for her to head back to their quarters. Salmonia had had enough socializing for one night; she too could not wait until things returned to normal.

Sal smiled as her daughter babbled all the way back to their quarters, her eyes glossy with all she had heard. It had been a lengthy day and it didn't take long for Roselyn to fall asleep with a smile on her face. Sal no sooner let out a long exhausted breath when Roselyn woke up screaming, "Momma save the girl, she's drowning."

Sal rushed over to her daughter and smoothed back the sweat drench curls from her face, stroking her head until she fell back to sleep. Puzzled, Salmonia passed it off as too much stimulation this evening with all the festivities, and curled up next to her baby girl.

By the time everyone woke the next morning, the warriors were gone. Everything seemed as it should be; until Roselyn woke up, "Mom?"

"Hey baby, I'm right here." Salmonia had been up for a couple of hours already and came to sit by her daughter. She had been through so much lately. Roselyn blinked the sleepiness from her eyes and looked at her mother, "Did you save her?"

Salmonia's eyebrows pinched together and she poked out her chin, "Save who, baby?"

"The girl and her mother--they were drowning. Did daddy *save* them?" Roselyn's eyes opened bigger as she waited for her mother's response.

"Honey, it was a dream, no one was drowning." Salmonia tried to sound reassuring.

"No mama it wasn't a dream--I saw it. I saw the ship sink. The girl was with her mother and they went down with the ship. All the sailors went down too. It wasn't a dream!" Roselyn clenched her fists and pressed them at her sides.

"I'll tell you what, I will talk with your dad and Pete to see if they know of anything--now please calm down." Salmonia was concerned about what affect the recent events had had on her daughter and how that would play out.

She tried to change the subject, "Do you want to come to the lab with me; Meranda has more tests to run?"

"Yes, and I'm sure Meranda needs me to do stuff." Roselyn had a hard time letting go of things, especially if she believed it to be true.

Sal walked to the lab and Roselyn took the waterways, no one was there. So they proceeded to Meranda's room hoping she would be awake by now. "Knock—knock," Sal popped her head in the entrance.

"Come on in…how are you feeling?" Meranda inquired immediately.

"Good, Roselyn and I stopped by the lab, but you weren't there yet. I hope I'm not disturbing you. I can come by the lab later." Salmonia was anxious to get the results as it had been a week.

"No—your fine, just give me a minute we can walk down together?" Meranda felt rested and as eager as Sal to see the blood work.

"I'll meet you there." Roselyn voice still echoed her frustrations.

The caves had a quiet normal hum to them. Everyone was lounging around after all the visitors had left; a day of relaxation was well deserved.

The warriors had left early that morning not sticking around to say goodbye. Meranda had grown fond of them and hated to see them leave. "I don't think they liked sappy goodbyes." Meranda stated the obvious causing Salmonia to toss her head back and laugh. Her red wavy hair cascaded down her back and came to a point below her waist. She really was enchanting in either form.

When they entered the lab Meranda noticed Roselyn's quiet mood. "Hi Rosie, how are you today?" Meranda asked.

"Tired, I keep having bad dreams." Roselyn could really have a sad face when she wanted to.

"Well you've had a lot to deal with lately. I'm sure it's your mind's way of letting go. I hope they leave you alone though, bad dreams are no fun." Meranda tried being sympathetic.

"Meranda after we draw the blood--can Roselyn hang with you for a bit, I won't be long--I have few things to see to?" Salmonia had that look on her face which Meranda had grown to know that whatever it was; she needed to do it alone.

"I actually need my assistant to do some things for me." Meranda had to come up with a project quickly; they had made a mess converting the lab into a triage center. "To start with, I need you to restock the test tubes and beakers. Then file the notes we took during our exploration of helping your mom." Sal smiled at Meranda and left.

"Is my mom's tail going to grow back?" Roselyn asked.

"I don't know honey, at least the toxic levels in her body are almost gone. Pete said it would take time for it to grow back. I promise, she is going to be fine." Meranda hated see Rosie so worried and remembered how it was after she lost her mother; tragedy breeds uncertainty.

Meranda turned up the music and the two girls got busy cleaning the lab.

"The two men I am looking for. Do you have a minute?" Salmonia was glad she found Pete and Zane together. "Have there been any shipwrecks or drownings of late?

"Not that we know of ...why?" Pete spoke for both him and Zane who just shook his head in agreement.

"Roselyn keeps dreaming about a shipwreck and a mother and daughter that are drowning. I keep dismissing it as stress, but I have had suspicions that her dreams mean something." Sal stopped a moment to let the men wrap their heads around what she was saying.

Pete tilted his head, "Like premonitions?" Zane mirrored his look of concern.

"I think so. Many of her "dreams" have come true. Not exactly how she dreamt it…but they do come true." Sal was fidgeting and twisting her hands. When it came to her daughter she was not the brave huntress, but a scared mother.

"I could talk to my father and see what he thinks." Pete would find out as much information as he could.

"Can we keep this amongst us for now? I have this feeling…" Sal couldn't explain it, but she was reasonably sure that Roselyn was having premonitions.

"Can you tell me more details about the dreams, like are they in the past, present, or future?" Zane approached a situation differently than Pete, he was more apt to put something to a test and see if it held up.

"It seems like this one hasn't happened yet. There have been no reports of ships going down, at least in our territory. I definitely got the feeling it *was* going to happen. Are there any disturbances developing in the atmosphere?" Sal felt relieved to come clean and share her concerns, especially with Rosie's father. She subconsciously suspected that something was amiss for the past year and could no longer shake it off as coincidence.

Pete and Zane knew that disturbances were brewing later that evening. Unfortunately, the gales of November were coming in October which is always troublesome. With the water temperature still warm and the strong cold winds, it made prime conditions for brewing trouble, and the shipping lanes were in full swing.

"Actually, Zane and I were just discussing a plan that would allow patrols to go out and monitor the shipping lanes; this is their busiest time of the year before wrapping up for the season. Most of the danger with the lampreys is behind us and the serpent is gone. However, I still want armed troops whenever anybody goes out of the compound." Pete reiterated.

"No worries here, I couldn't swim if I wanted to," Sal looked down at her feet. She hadn't come to terms with the possibility that she may never hunt again. Both men's eyes darted around not wanting to look Sal in the eyes and see her pain. So, they just stood there looking at the floor.

"It won't be forever Sal," Pete found the courage to look at her and give her hope, even if it was false hope.

"I'm going back to the lab and see if I can be of some use there. I left Rosie with Meranda so that I could discuss her nightmares freely."

"We will keep an eye open for possible ships in trouble, so you can reassure her of that Nia." Zane stepped closer to Sal and rested his hand on her shoulder. He loved his beautiful daughter, but Sal was the one who nurtured her.

Pete and Zane focused on constructing a schedule for the security patrols. Sal slowly headed back to the lab to tell her daughter that her dad is going to watch for any trouble in the lake.

Before Sal could get to the lab, the emergency horns began to blow, signaling that trouble had arrived. The winds had picked up to 30 miles an hour gusting to 40, and the shipping lanes were full of ships as expected.

Pete, Zane, and the armed patrols were the first onto the lake. As they neared the surface they could feel the power in the waves swirling and coiling. The winds were coming from different directions resulting in the formation of large waves crested with white caps.

Everyone knew that it was going to be a long night. Pete and Zane both looked at each other confirming that Roselyn's dreams were in fact premonitions.

Whenever possible, the mermen would lend aid to a ship by keeping it afloat and away from the jagged edges of the northern shores. The treacherous islands and sand bars of the southern shores were equally as dangerous. If a ship became lodged on a sand bar it didn't take long for the waves to pummel the ore boat in half, causing them to sink within minutes.

If the sailors were able to get into a life raft, the icy waters and cutting winds would cause hypothermia and they would die before they were rescued. A stiff nor 'eastern wind shooting down the lake would translate into many casualties, but with all tails in the water below, the numbers would be less.

The storm strengthened in velocity, and it wasn't long before the weather stations named it, "Loretta," and she was creating havoc. The waves would build into rollers and toss the ships around like toy boats in a bathtub.

Pete saw that one ship was too close to the bay putting her in a dangerous position. There wasn't much he could do to help and knew the ship would've been better off if it had been positioned in the middle of the lake. It made for a rough ride, but chances of staying in one piece greatly increased in open waters.

A monstrous wave blasted across the deck sweeping a seaman overboard. The ship was then hit back to back by two twelve foot rollers washing the captain out of the control tower. Some of the crew ran for the life boats and some stayed behind to drop the anchor hoping it would catch some structure securing that they stayed in deeper waters.

When the storm hit, chicken dinner was just coming out of the galley. The ship made the most eerie moaned as the crew stood silent, some on their knees praying, and others throwing up from seasickness.

The steel walls twisted and sent bolts firing through the air like bullets. Then, came the awful ripping sound as the ship broke into two. The cook and her daughter were sucked through the bottom of the boat where the galley was located before the huge ore boat folded in on itself.

Pete and Zane were nearby trying to keep as many of the crew alive as possible. Zane looked over his shoulder and saw the young girl and her mother in perils, sinking to depths in which there was no return. He knew he didn't have much time.

He abandoned the men that were hanging onto a door hatch to get to the females. Pete followed Zane instructing the patrols to continue helping the sailors. When they reached the woman and her daughter they realized they were too far down to make it back to the surface alive.

Pete shook his head, the mother was already gone. Zane's fatherly instinct kicked in and he put a protective covering over the girl's face and torpedoed back to the caves.

When he got there Salmonia, Roselyn, and Meranda were ready to assist knowing that when the alarms went off they better get ready. Sal saw the young girl who was only a few years older than Roselyn. She doubled over unable to breathe, as the realization hit her, that her daughter was capable of premonitions.

Roselyn helped pull the girl out of the icy waters covering her with a wool blanket to preserve any body heat she might have left, "See mama I told you." Roselyn looked smugly at her mother, knowing her mother hadn't believed her.

Meranda immediately started pumping water out of her lungs after removing the coating Zane had put on her face. She kept doing compressions on her chest and blowing air into her mouth until the girl started to cough and puked the rest of the water from her lungs. She opened her eyes briefly and looked around, before slipping into unconsciousness.

Meranda stabilized the girl and then sat by her bed waiting for her to wake up, and her first question was, "Where's my mom?" Meranda looked up startled, she must have dozed off.

Meranda didn't want to lie to her, but she didn't want to tell her the truth right off either. "I don't know right now, honey. We are going to take you to a room and get you checked out. Your mother would want us to care for you." Meranda said in a soft voice.

"I want my mom." The girl kept asking over and over until she started to cry.

Roselyn hated hearing her cry for her mother and poked her head inside, "I will go look for her and see if she came in with the others," She knew there were no women brought in, She just didn't want the girl to be scared.

Many ships went down in that king of storms considering the time of year it was. There were some crewmen saved by the coast guard, but most went to their watery graves at the bottom of the lake.

Some longshoremen who would have otherwise died, were saved by the mermen and would be given a second chance to serve the lake beneath the surface. Most would be thankful for a second chance and willingly join the guardians, others would die trying to get back to the surface.

As quickly as Lake Superior had turn deadly, it calmed down. The blue skies returned and the water settled into non-threatening rhythm.

For now, the storm was over. The lake sported a red hue, as if it was a tribute to the lives lost. The reality of the red coloring was from the lake getting stirred up. Mother Nature was the victor today, and when she spoke, you listened.

Over the next months, a few bodies would wash up on shore barely recognizable. Sometimes, a bottle with a farewell note written by a sailor to his family would appear on the beach sometimes years after a monstrous storm.

Meanwhile, in the part of the cave that is considered the care unit, Roselyn took over sitting by the girl, as much as Sal would allow. She looked a few years older than Rosie by her physical development.

Rosie had never seen someone her own age, nor had she had a friend until Meranda. She felt sad that her new friend had lost her mother, knowing just how close she had come to losing hers.

For three days Roselyn sat waiting for her new friend to wake up. Salmonia brought her daughter something to eat and to see how things were going when she noticed something very different about her. "Rosie, when did you learn to transform?" Sal couldn't believe her eyes.

"I've been able to do it for almost a year now. I was afraid you'd get mad and forbid me, but I didn't want my friend to wake up and be scared. Are you mad mommy?" Roselyn gave her mother the sweetest face she could come up with.

"No, I'm a bit taken back, and I wish you would've talked to me about it. However, I agree, it would not be good to overwhelm the girl." Salmonia saw her daughter in a new light. Roselyn could transform much earlier than Sal had, but then again Roselyn was special in many ways. "Does your father know?"

"Nope you're the first, well besides Meranda and oh-Pete. Don't get mad at her mom I made her pinky swear not to tell you or dad, and if you break your promise…well you just don't do it." Roselyn knew her mother's temper and did not want her to be mad at Meranda or Pete, but Pete was the Prince, so she couldn't get that mad at him.

Rosie put out her pinky for her mother to seal the deal that she wouldn't be mad at Meranda. Sal got a smile on her face not knowing what to do exactly as Rosie hooked her finger around her mother's to make the deal. Roselyn broke out in the most dazzling smile melting Salmonia's heart. She loved her daughter more than anything, and it was hard to stay angry with her at times.

Salmonia went to find her friend and let her know she knew about her and Roselyn's secret, and had taken the pinky oath too. Sal didn't get too far when she heard Roselyn yell, "She's awake! Mom! Meranda, come quick she's waking up." The girl laid there and looked around until her eyes settled on Roselyn's smiling face.

Roselyn spoke first, "Hi, my name is Roselyn, but everyone calls me Rosie. What is your name?"

"Where am I?" The girl demanded. "Where is my mom?"

"You are in a cave and are safe." Roselyn knew it was not her place to tell her about her mom.

"I want my mom." The girl kept saying.

Roselyn sighed a long breath when Sal and Meranda showed up to take over. Sal looked at her distraught daughter and asked her to go get some broth from the kitchen. Rosie got up and left as her mother had asked. It felt good not to hide that she could transform. Salmonia watched her daughter's long brown legs gracefully exit the room, and shook her head in disbelief.

"Hi honey, I am Meranda, and I will be taking care of you. This is Salmonia, Rosie's mom." Meranda was nervous about telling her too much and better understood why Pete was so evasive in how he handled Meranda's introduction into this secret world.

"Where is my mom?" The girl remained insistent.

"First, can I ask you your name and how old you are?" Meranda looked like a doctor in her white lab coat and that was enough to convince the girl to open up.

"My name is LaTrice, and I am 12 years old. Where is my mother?" LaTrice had tears welling up in her beautiful brown eyes, even though she was trying to be strong.

"I'm sorry honey, but your mom didn't survive." Meranda hated breaking the news, but the sooner LaTrice knew the truth, the sooner she could start the grieving process. The tears slipped out of the corners of her eyes in a steady stream onto the pillow. She turned and faced the wall.

"I'll give you a moment?" Meranda knew it was best to give her some time to process the loss of her mother. She knew firsthand what it felt like to lose your mother and more recent her father too.

LaTrice turned her face into her pillow to stifle her cries. "I'll be right outside of the door if you need anything, or want to talk."

Roselyn had rushed to the kitchen to get LaTrice some broth, and when she came back her mother met her at the entryway, "We'll let Meranda take the broth in to her, honey. Let's give LaTrice some time to adjust to the fact that she lost her mother, okay?"

"Okay mom, but will you tell her I am sorry that she her mom didn't make it?" Roselyn asked.

"I'll give Meranda your message, sweetie." Having to stand on her tiptoes, Salmonia gave her daughter a kiss on the head and turned to give the soup to Meranda.

21

The next day Roselyn hoped she would be able to talk with the girl and rushed down to her room as her mom would allow. When she got there Meranda was just coming out of the girls room, "Hi Roselyn, are you here to visit LaTrice?"

"Can I?" Roselyn asked hoping desperately that the answer was yes.

"I don't know how talkative she will be, but it won't hurt you to try. Just be aware if she looks tired or doesn't want to talk, don't force it, she will talk when she is ready." Meranda didn't want to discourage Rosie, but knew how shocking this all was to take in at first; just the caves alone were mind blowing.

It had taken Meranda a few weeks to adjust when she had first arrived, and the no sunlight was hard to deal with. And, that was before the whole Merfolk thing exploded into living color.

Meranda knew how excited Roselyn was to have a someone her age, so she gave Rosie a squeeze on the shoulder and nodded a go ahead toward the room. Not only was LaTrice around Roselyn's age, but she was caramel color like her too. They could've been sisters.

Roselyn entered LaTrice's room and suddenly couldn't think of anything to say, "Hello. How are you feeling?"

"Okay." LaTrice's eyes instantly welled up with tears.

"Do you want to be alone?" Roselyn was still of an age that she spoke the simple truth.

"I don't care…you can stay if you want to." LaTrice shifted so that she was sitting up more. "I want to go home."

"You will have to talk to Meranda about that." Rosie was being so sweet and careful not to upset the girl.

"Where's the television? Roselyn looked at her blankly and didn't understand what she was asking, so she kept quiet. LaTrice wondered what there was to do, "So what do you do here?"

"I help Meranda in the lab mostly," Roselyn acted like it had always been her job.

"I brought a book if you would like to read it or want me to read it to you?" Roselyn was trying so hard to befriend this girl. "It's called 'Night Flying Woman' by, Ignatia Brooker, it's a classic."

"I guess you could read if you want to." LaTrice didn't really care; it was something to do other than stare at the wall. Roselyn open the book and began to read.

There were meetings going on all over the compound. Zane was reorganizing his patrols and Pete was in a meeting with his father. Salmonia was in the lab with Meranda who had her test results.

Sal braced herself for whatever the verdict was, "Am I cured?"

"There is only a hint of green left in your cells, and I hate to say it again, but time will tell." Meranda had hoped that the healthy cells would kill the unhealthy cells off completely. "If you feel okay---I would rather wait before taking any further action."

"I feel good, except the fact that I can't hunt. I'm going stir crazy." Sal was not use to endless days. It gave her a better idea of how her daughter and Meranda felt. "I'm going to go find Pete and go over a few things with him." Sal stocked out of the lab.

"Okay, I have more testing to do on the lamprey." Meranda wasn't sure if Sal even heard her.

Salmonia had to take the long way, and headed toward Pete's new quarters; he was seldom there and today was no exception. She decided to head back to her own quarters and freshen up, when she saw Pete coming from his father's tunnel. He looked like he was miles away.

"Hey brother," Sal tried to sound lighthearted.

"Hello, how is the patient doing?" Pete hated when the newbie's were children, even though that was fairly uncommon.

"Physically she is doing well; mentally she is confused as to be expected. Roselyn is in with her now."

"That's good." Pete replied.

"What's up? You look like you found out, that the end of the earth is on the horizon, so spill it." Salmonia knew something was eating at him.

"I was just talking with my father who made a point about Meranda needing to make a decision on whether or not she will be joining the family. I don't want her to leave, yet I don't want to rob her of her human choices either." Pete flopped down on the couch in the commons.

"I don't think it is your decision to make. It's Meranda's." Salmonia did not want Meranda to leave either, but it wasn't her choice either.

Suddenly, the warning bells went off and within moments, the once empty commons filled with mermen exiting to the lake. Pete transformed as he joined the troops to deal with the current crisis.

Pete's pod ran into the Isle Royale pod from Canada, along with the pods from Michigan, and the Native American bands from the Wisconsin. Pete was relieved that all relations were good between them as they worked together keeping the waterways safe.

The winds were blowing 30 miles an hour and were north northeast. This made for high seas, and even an experienced captain would have trouble maneuvering through these rogue waves. Inexperience boaters would have a far less of a chance of surviving the sudden onset of a storm blowing across Lake Superior.

In this particular case, it was a small vessel only 400 feet from stern to bow. The white capped waves picked the boat up and slammed it back down on its side, another roller hit right behind it and pushed the boat in the opposite direction before climbing the next swell. This boat was in danger of being swallowed.

The pod's worked together as they aligned themselves on each side of the boat keeping it afloat. They maneuvered the vessel away from a sand bar, thus preventing the waves from slamming it until it came apart at the seams.

The boat was now out in open waters and away from immediate danger. It was caught by a fifteen foot wave that carried the boat to the crest before flipping it on its side, and dumping five sailors overboard.

Luckily, the mermen were already on the scene and grabbed the men under the arms to keep their heads above the water while herding them toward shore.

It was always amusing to see the look on these brawny men's weathered faces when they realized they were being helped by a merman. Later, when asked, they would tell the story of how they were saved by a beautiful mermaid, and the story would forever be a part of that storm.

The mermen were busy and continued helping boats by redirecting them behind islands where the waters were calmer. The captain feared the five men they lost at sea were all but gone, not knowing they were already on shore.

Meanwhile, Sal had wandered back to the lab lost at what to do with all her free time. Meranda was sitting there having some tea. "Hey girlfriend, come have a seat and some tea."

"Sure why not." Salmonia looked really down.

Since things were relatively quiet Meranda felt this was a good time for some girl talk, "I've been meaning to ask you--what's the deal with you and Zane?"

This took Sal by surprise and having never voiced any personal information with well--anybody, it made her uncomfortable. "What do you mean?"

"Hum--you did have a child together, so there must be history between you two." Meranda felt awfully pushy at that moment. "I mean you don't have to tell me, but do know girlfriends talk."

Salmonia cracked a smile and started to explain that yes she and Zane had something between them a long time ago, but it didn't work out very well. Relationships were work and Salmonia didn't have time for all that...that togetherness.

"Is that when Roselyn was conceived?" Meranda surprised herself on how bold she was being.

"No. The feelings never completely diminished between Zane and me, so when I came into season ten years ago, well Zane was there--and that's all there is to it." Sal never said it out loud before and for good reason, because it didn't sound very good.

Seeing how uncomfortable Sal had become Meranda felt she had come on too strong. "I'm sorry that was awfully bold of me, and probably none of my business. I was just curious. When either one of you was hurt, the other seemed very distraught." Meranda had observed on several occasions that their emotions for one another were more than just *friends,* and not just ten years ago or casual.

Meranda was hoping the conversation would come around to include a little insight into Pete's past, but instead Salmonia turn the conversation on Meranda, "So girlfriend--how about you? Do you have a fellow you left broken hearted?" Immediately Salmonia knew she had said the wrong thing by the look on Meranda's face. "I'm sorry Meranda, I was just...."

"It's okay," Meranda waved off her apology as a tear slid down her face. "Actually he left me--the night we graduated from high school. We were in an accident and he...he died." Meranda swiped at the tears that were now streaming down her face.

"I don't do girlfriend very well." Salmonia was at a loss.

"You couldn't have known—and besides, I started this getting acquainted session. He's been gone for 8 years now, but sometimes it feels like yesterday. Don't worry about it. I don't know why the flood gates opened."

Both Meranda and Sal sat there in silence for a moment.

"What about Pete? I mean, what's his story?" Meranda was trying to shake off the pain in her heart and stuff it back down where it lived.

"Well, what do you want to know?" Sal was more than happy to change the subject.

"Does he have someone special? Is he or has he ever been married, or have children?" Meranda could feel the color of her face deepening.

"No. He has never found that special someone, but he is still pretty young." Sal cocked her eyebrow to see if Meranda caught the humor.

She did. She started laughing so hard squeals were coming out of her, which turned contagious as Sal started to laugh too. They laughed until it hurt making them clutch their stomachs.

They hadn't noticed that Pete had come in, "What's so funny?"

Both Sal and Meranda clammed up, but one look at each other started them laughing all over again. Sal got up chuckling all the way to the door as she bid her friend goodbye.

"Are you going to let me in on the joke?" Pete felt he could use a good laugh.

"It was nothing just some girl humor. Did everything go okay out there? Were there any casualties?" Meranda wanted to make sure she wasn't needed.

"Everything went fine. Have you eaten yet?" Pete was ravenous as a bear who just woke from his long winter's nap.

"No, I was waiting for you." Meranda liked ending the day having dinner with Pete and their ritual glass of wine.

They left the lab and headed to Meranda's quarters. She was hoping he would share some of what took place out in the lake, but decided not to ask any questions. Every time Meranda thought about her and Sal's discussion, a smile broke out on her face. It had been so long since she had belly laughed, it felt good. Pete seemed quiet tonight or preoccupied. Meranda just figured it had to do with merman stuff.

"Have there been any more sightings of giant lamprey?" Meranda couldn't hold her questions in any longer.

"No." Pete replied. "Why?"

"Just curious, I was hoping we could have an outing again. That is--if you think it is safe enough out there."

Pete remained quiet and then casualty answered, "Sure," and poured himself a second glass of wine. "Meranda, I don't think I have ever thanked you for all you have done down here. I mean with the research and saving Sal. There just aren't words to express my gratitude. We would have lost our huntress and many others without your unwavering efforts."

"Well I could say the same in return, you saved me. I would have drowned, so on that account I would have to say, we saved each other. Is that what's bothering you tonight?"

"No. Now that things have calmed down, I have been reflecting on the past few months, and it dawned on me that without you everything would have been so much worst." Pete looked up at her with pained eyes, which took Meranda by surprise. Pete was always the beacon in the storm.

"An outing huh. I do have to go up the shore to collect information and samples from the North Shore pods. If you wanted to join me you would be more than welcome. We would be gone for a week and I would insist that you get out of the water every fifty miles. Plus, it's important to accept the hospitality of the pods along the way."

"Say no more, I'm in. I would love to see more of the oldest molten rock that is unique to this area. I find that stuff super cool." Meranda was getting very excited. "Would Sal get to come?"

Pete instantly gritted his teeth, "I don't think she can swim with a half a tail."

"I hate to state the obvious, but I realize that. Can't Zane help her? I know it would do her a world of good to get out in the lake. Ya know, her 'state of mind.' Maybe if she was in her mermaid form with Zane supporting her like you do me...I don't know. Maybe it would tell her body to grow a new tail."

This was one of the things Pete loved about Meranda, her unselfish nature and ability to dream the impossible and make it happen. "I will talk to Sal. I guess it wouldn't hurt and I agree, I think it would be good for her "state of mind" as you call it."

"When are you thinking of going? I want to make sure LaTrice is stable and doing okay before leaving." Meranda was not so much worried about her health issues as she was her emotional stability so soon after the loss her mother.

"It will take me a few days to get things worked out. Is that enough time for you to wrap things up?" Pete was careful not to disclose his whole plan.

"Can I get back to you tomorrow after my re-evaluation of LaTrice?" Meranda was at ease asking for what she needed from the Prince. She had grown up a lot in the past three months.

"Absolutely, Doc," Pete was repressing a smile once again, what was it about her that brought him such joy. "I will talk to Sal and Zane about your tail theory. Goodnight Meranda, sleep well."

"Goodnight Pete." Meranda was tired from the long hours in the lab and caring for her young patient.

Pete went to find Salmonia and run it past her about tagging along. He hoped she would take it as it was meant, and that it would be therapeutic for her to join them. He headed to the recovery room to see how the patient was doing when he ran into Sal who was just leaving there.

"Just the person I wanted to talk to." Pete was trying to make it sound like an opportunity.

"Oh really," Salmonia was in a good mood which was promising, "How can I be of service to you Prince?

Pete felt it would come out better if he mentioned that it was Meranda's suggestion, "Meranda felt that you should join us as we tour the northern shores and check in with the other pods."

"Meranda huh, does Meranda know how this is going to happen without my tail?" Salmonia's mood and facial expressions turned slightly darker.

"She felt that since she needed assistance that Zane could assist you, and that maybe it would be therapeutic too." Pete was stumbling over his words.

"Hmm--Meranda's idea...well I can't say that it wouldn't be nice to get out into the lake. I will talk to Zane and see if he would mind letting me piggy back. When are you going?" Sal knew she would love to get out of the cave for a bit.

"It wouldn't be for a couple of days. I need to get supplies gathered and send word that we will be making our rounds up the shore to collect data from the other pods."

"I'll speak with Zane and get back to you." Both Salmonia and Pete knew the answer to that question, "yes". Zane would do anything for Sal.

"How is the girl doing?" Pete figured he wouldn't stop by since Roselyn was sitting with her.

"She is doing well overall, but keeps asking when she gets to go home. She will have to be told soon that her life will be changing. I will leave that up to you. Her and Roselyn seem to be hitting it off nicely though."

"Excellent and we will deal with that conversation after we return. I am glad Roselyn has a companion. It must be hard for her being the only youngster in this compound." Pete understood just how hard it was being the youngest mer, because his whole childhood was the same way.

"I will bid you goodnight then." Pete set out to find Zane, his confidant and commander. He sent a telepathic message out to him and headed back to his quarters.

It didn't take Zane long to surface, "*Good evening brother, how may I be of service?*"

"*Good evening. In a few days we are going to travel up the north shore to collect samples and information other pods might have. I figure we will be gone about a week. Salmonia may be joining us, but that is something she wants to discuss with you personally.*"

Zane could tell something was weighing heavy on Pete's mind, but thought better of asking him. Pete switch to a vocal conversation to keep it private, because telepathic dialog could be picked up by anyone wanting to listen. "Zane before you go I would like to discuss something with you, but you must keep it between us."

Pete and Zane discussed the concerns Pete had and what his father had presented to him about Meranda. "My father will be making his journey back to the Norwegian Sea to complete his life's cycle. I will need him to be escorted to the entrance of the ocean where the Vikings will meet us and accompany him the rest of the way home."

"Just tell me when brother and I will prepare for that epic event." Zane tried to make it sound respectful, but he knew that meant Pete's father was going back to die.

22

A couple of days had past as they gathered for the outing. Seeing everyone together gave Meranda a sense that they were a real family going on vacation. They were packed and had enough supplies to last them a week or more. Salmonia agreed to let Zane assist her and surrendered herself to him. Her pride wouldn't have allowed for anyone but Zane, to shadow her.

Sal smiled to herself privately acknowledging the feelings she still had for Zane, knowing she would be coming into season during the next blue moon. Maybe another child would be a blessing, especially if she never grew her tail back.

She inhaled deeply remembering Zane's musky scent making something deep inside her belly tighten. She felt strangely content for the moment in his arms. She knew her hormone levels must be revving up. The only thought she wanted to entertain at this moment was her tail growing back. Looking farther into the future right now saddened her.

Meranda was excited and nervous at the same time. Her first sightseeing adventure didn't go well and ended in them being attacked, but if Pete and Zane said it was safe, then it must be.

Needless to say, it was not any easier getting into the wetsuit the second time, but her shoulder was completely healed giving her the much needed strength to inch the suit over her shoulders.

Salmonia came by to see if Meranda needed help, "Hello...Meranda?" She entered her alcove and heard a lot of noise coming from the back room.

"I'm in here squeezing into my second skin," as she let out a few grunts.

"Do you need help?" Sal asked with a chuckle in her voice. While waiting she looked around and noticed the changes that Meranda had done to the place. It was nice. It had a female's touch to it.

"No I almost got it..." she zipped it up with a few more grunts.

"Everyone is ready to go, but there's no hurry." Salmonia couldn't imagine what it was like to get into a second skin, but then again she couldn't imagine not having a tail either until it happened. "I wanted to thank you for the suggestion that I come with. I think it will do me good."

Meranda emerged from the bathroom and felt less embarrassed about the tight suit showing every curve. A diet of mainly fish had made her lean and Meranda felt more confident. Sal smiled at her and nodded toward the door and they went to join the rest of the party.

Pete had a strange mixture of emotions on his face, his mouth reflected a smile, but his eyes were sad. Meranda wondered what was up with him lately. Maybe he was upset about his father.

Zane came behind Salmonia placing his hands gently on her waist and together they jumped into the icy cold waters of Lake Superior, followed by four armed mermen. Then Pete and Meranda took the plunge followed by more security.

It took Meranda a few minutes to adjust to the mask that allowed her to extract the oxygen from the water. Giving the thumbs up, Pete moved into place behind her and the mer procession headed out.

The waters were clear and the sights were beautiful, even the shipwrecks had a peacefulness to them. They made their way up past Silver Bay which was about fifty five miles up the shore making this their first stop.

The mermen in this family were small in numbers, but they were very pleased that the Prince had come to their humble caverns. They didn't have the luxuries that Pete's compound had, but what they had they gave freely.

Salmonia and Meranda shared a space in a rock dugout; it was simply and comfortable and had soft pallets to lie on. There was no furniture or hearths, no wonderful smelling stews, but they had plenty of salted fish to eat.

It was apparent that these mermen had been fishermen. They were polite to the women, but Meranda could sense that women had their place and it wasn't sitting around sharing drink. Both Meranda and Salmonia were glad to be on their way when the sun came up.

The landscape became more rugged, and Meranda noticed that the rocks had taken on a sculpted look to them, probably from the pounding waves. The stacked layers exposed the dark gray coloring with veins of copper, silver, and gold that made inconsistent designs throughout the rocks.

Meranda giggled when they surprised a school of fish that scattered in a united pattern, it reminded her of the ballet. They would all dart to the right and then zigzag to the left in perfect synchronized movements.

She was absorbed in the beautiful underwater world she was fortunate to be a part of when Pete spoke, *"We are approaching Taconite Harbor. We will rest here for a bit and let you warm up before going on to Grand Marais."* No one made her feel bad for holding them up due to her humanness, but she still felt bad nonetheless.

She was enjoying herself and didn't realize how cold she was until she got out of the water. Pete built a fire and heated up some broth for her to drink, warming her from the inside out.

Soon they were off again and when they arrived at Grand Marais, she was surprised at how large this clan was. They were around the same size as Pete's pod and just as civilized.

They welcomed their Prince and his guests providing plenty varieties of fish and bread or stews. They had different levels of rooms in their cavern, but no furniture. It was a place to lay their heads and more important, a place for Meranda to warm her bones while Pete saw to clan business.

The mermen were extremely happy to have guests. They sat around drinking wine and ale and sharing stories. Many were of Scandinavian descent and would break out in their native language. They treated the women like they were delicate flowers which Salmonia was definitely having more trouble with than Meranda.

The women "folk" said goodnight and retired to their alcove. Sal was bursting at the seams, unable to hold her feelings in a single minute longer, "I have never felt so girly in my life. Do they not know I am a huntress? I, all of a sudden have legs and my hair is braided and I am woman." Salmonia was definitely blowing off some steam. "How do you stand it Meranda?"

"I have never appreciated being treated like a girl either, but sometimes you can catch more flies with honey. I try not to be too offended by their doting actions. They are men of an older generation and that is part of who they are."

"I could put a harpoon right between their eyes from fifty feet away in cloudy water." Sal was really worked up.

"I know, and they probably know it too. They really were trying to be on their best behavior Sal." Meranda was use to that type of manly man back home on the range.

"Okay, I think I am done ranting. I just couldn't sit there and smile one more second. I could feel Zane becoming uncomfortable as he felt the anger roll off me. I suppose he would have felt the need to defend my honor or something." Sal was beside herself and started turning her anger on poor Zane. Meranda just listened with a kind ear, because she knew this was more about Sal's disabled tail and relying on others, than about how the mermen were acting.

"Well, we are leaving tomorrow." Meranda hoped that the next stop would be more isolated.

Morning came quick enough; and they thanked their hosts and then headed for Pigeon River. Meranda had noticed they turned away from shore and were heading out into the lake. It seemed like the lake was getting shallower instead of deeper, but the water was magnifying glass clear.

It was amazing; the rocks that lined the bottom of the lake were spotted and varied in size and the agates look like they had been polished.

"Where are we, the structure looks different in this part of the region?" Meranda mouthed to Pete.

"We're in the Isle Royale area. It's has an ecosystem all of its own that has remained untouched by modernization." Pete messaged.

Meranda made a mental note that someday she would have to come and see what Isle Royale looked like from land. She was very impressed and felt privileged to see it from the serene world below the surface.

What Meranda didn't realize was that the floating lab she was supposed to visit that turbulent day was located a few miles off the northeast point of Copper Harbor. The lab was anchored in the middle of the lake where the United States and Canada share an invisible border.

The sun was setting and said goodnight by treating them to a pinkish-orange sunset. The group settled in for the night within the rock structure of Copper Harbor. Pete had that faraway look again, the same look he had the day their boat went down.

Even Meranda could feel the change in the atmosphere and the momentum of the lake waking up. Slowly the fingers of the waves began to slosh back and forth caressing the entrance of the cave. Pete's skin became prickly as the waves grew in force, now slapping at their safe haven.

"Are we in any danger Pete?" Meranda didn't feel all that confident of her read on Mother Nature's subtle signals. "Pete?"

"I'm sorry. I am not sure what's going on, but something is brewing." Pete was extra sensitive to changes in the weather patterns. "I think to be on the safe side, we should move around to Berte Grise Bay, and hold up there."

Meranda agreed and felt like they were sitting ducks in the small shallow caves they were currently in.

As they gathered their equipment the wind started to pick up and began whistling throughout the cave's sinuses and the waves grew larger, rolling in one after the other. Soon there were no breaks between the crest of one wave and the next. Meranda had never seen a storm actually form before her eyes.

The waves splashed higher and harder against the entryway and the pod quickened their pace. Mer were still susceptible to being smashed up against the jagged rocks risking injury or even death. The power of the water seemed more solid and organized; and had taken on a life of its own.

The higher ground they sought was around the tip of the island. Once they left the lower caves they'd be exposed to the elements, and Meranda was already getting pushed around like a rag doll. She couldn't stay in rhythm with Pete who reached around her waist pulling her snug against his body to keep a hold of her.

Meranda looked out onto the water and her eyes widened. A monstrous wave had split around a large protrusion of rocks before rejoining and becoming one giant wave, heading straight for them.

They were out in the open and vulnerable. The watery wall hit them hard pushing their party up against the razor sharp cliffs behind them. Meranda did not escape the assault. She smashed into the rocks knocking her unconscious.

Pete, informed Zane, *"I'm going for it brother. I'm bringing her back to her world. Take cover and I will let you know when I am there."* Salmonia tried to wiggle free in protest, not only was Pete was going it alone, he was taking her friend with. Sal's heart tightened as Zane pulled her out of the water. She didn't get to say goodbye.

Salmonia felt more helpless at that moment than she could ever recall, and being without a tail made her feel the full ramifications of her disability. Zane took one look into Sal's eyes and knew Meranda's departure was more than she could handle at the moment.

He grabbed her around the waist and reentered the water and brought her to a cave where they could be alone. Once in the cave she started to cry pounding on Zane chest releasing the anger she had choked down from all she had been through. Zane didn't move a muscle and when she stopped he held her tight and let her cry her heart out.

Pete and an unconscious Meranda disappeared into the storm. He kept her head above the water as often as he could, and pushed toward the lab knowing it was only a few kilometers away. His powerful arms held Meranda's limp body afloat, while he fought Mother Nature's building fury.

For a minute, Pete wondered if he made a mistake and was jeopardizing both their lives. He was blinded by the walls of water, but caught a glimpse of the lab. He knew his approach would have to be in sync with the momentum of the powerful waves, giving them the lift they would need to make it on deck.

If he misjudged the timing they would be smashed up against the barge. Pete went around to the back side of the lab where the deck was larger, giving them a bigger platform increased their chances of a successful landing.

With the next round of waves he pushed with his tail and rode above the crest bringing them even with the deck. Just before the wave broke--he launched Meranda forward holding her at arm's length, while propelling his tail in the water trying to keep her high enough to clear the pontoons. She was inches away from the safety of the barge, when the next wave hit, and washed her out of his arms.

He dove into the black churning waters grasping and searching for her, if he lost her to the undertow, she would be gone forever. He turned franticly searching behind him going in circles. Where was she? He dove deeper and caught a flash of her white arm.

He powered his tail pushing him deeper and grabbed her and pulled her into him. He locked his arm around her waist as she slumped forward. He shot straight up through a wave, only to find he was too far out to make a landing.

This operation had not gone as he had planned, and he knew time was running out for getting her out of the water, if it wasn't already. A wave started to build its momentum and carried them in the rise toward its peak pushing them closer to the lab.

Pete used all the power he had left and shot them up through the eye of the wave propelling them onto the deck. He was exhausted.

Dragging himself over to Meranda he leaned against the wall pulling her onto his lap and checked for a pulse. She had a pulse. Thank Odin.

He transformed before grabbing her under the arms lifting her out of the pelting rain and laid her on the couch. He found his stash of jogging pants in the closet along with a wool blanket.

He was no doctor, but lifted her eyelids making sure she didn't have blood behind her eyes before cocooning her in the blanket.

He was sure she had a concussion, but her pulse was steady. He sank back in relief and calmed himself for a moment wondering how exactly he was going to re-enter her into her world.

As promised he sent a telepathic message to his commander, "*We made it. I will see you back at the compound in a few weeks. Tell Sal I'm sorry. I saw the opportunity to give Meranda back her human life and had to take it.*"

Pete radioed ship to shore, requesting helicopter assistance. That there was a woman injured aboard the research lab. Her coloring was not right and her lips were blue. Her breathing was shallow, but regular. He tucked an electric blanket over the wool one to bring her body temperature up.

It seemed to take the medics forever to reach them in this storm. Realizing this was probably their last moments together, and his heart felt like it was breaking. He had to let her go, he had made the right choice, at least that's what he had to keep telling himself.

The helicopter hovered overhead and lowered a sled down and Pete grabbed it. Two paramedics descended onto the lab's deck and immediately put a neck brace on Meranda and an oxygen mask. Pete stood back and fear like he had never known coursed through his body.

"Are you injured sir?" One of the paramedics yelled out.

"No, I'm fine." Pete yelled back. All the while Pete was thinking she didn't deserve things to end this way. She had helped so many at the compound.

After they lifted Meranda into the helicopter they lowered a harness for Pete. It was slow going on the way back fighting the wind the whole way. He finally saw the red flashing beacon on top of the hospitals roof and breathed a sigh of relief.

Other medics were ready with a stretcher to transport her to the emergency room. Pete sank back against the hospital door praying that she had survived without suffering too much damage. He knew she was a fighter and that gave him some comfort.

He didn't have his cell phone to call—who? Who would he even call? He didn't know who her next of kin was. Hopefully they had her information in the system, and they did. They had her dad's number, but her dad had recently passed. Her brother was who knew where.

The nurse had found a second contact number, for a Jena Nelson. Pete thanked her and used the phone in the family room. While he waited for someone to answer Pete tried to figure out what he was going to say. What would even make sense? Everything happened so fast he never thought it through.

"Hello."

"Hello, my name is Pete Moss, from the Environmental Protection Agency. Is Jena Nelson available? I'm calling in regards to Meranda Michaels." Pete decided he would be as vague as he could get away with.

"Hold on sir, I will get my daughter-in-law. Jenaaaaa, telephone, it's about Meranda. Can you hold on sir Jena will be right with you?" Ma Poleski sat down so she could hear the conversation. Her stroke had only affected the left side of her body and not her speech, so she could still yell for Jena with no problem.

"Hello, this is Jena." Jena's stomach tightened as she braced for confirmation that they had found Meranda's body.

"Jena, I'm Meranda's boss, there was an accident at the lab. Meranda is fine, but she is in the hospital. She had you as her contact person." Pete ended it there not knowing what else to say.

"Oh thank God she's alive. What hospital is she in?" Jena asked.

"I think Saint Mary's...yes, Saint Mary's." Pete felt foolish that he didn't even know what hospital they were at.

"I will be down as soon as I can, but it will take me a few hours. Her brother is back in town and staying at the farm. I will call him. Is she going to be alright?" Jena eyes welled up with tears.

"I believe so; she may have a concussion, the doctors are with her now." All Pete knew was that she was alive. "Can you stay with her until someone can get there...please?" Jena couldn't stand to think of her being alone, what if she woke up and no one was there.

"Yes, absolutely--I will stay." Pete had no intention of going anywhere until he knew for sure that she was going to be okay.

Jena's hands were trembling so bad she had to make several attempts at dialing, "Hello Thor. It's Jena. Meranda's in the hospital."

"Hospital...? Why? Which hospital...?" Thor sputtered.

"Saint Mary's, can you go down there? It will take me a couple of hours before I can get there." Jena would have to wait until Logan got home because she couldn't leave the kids in Ma Poleski's care and Billy wasn't old enough to handle his baby sister and Grandma.

"I'm there." Thor hung up the phone. He jumped in his father's old truck and pushed the truck as fast as it would go, not caring if he was speeding. His sister needed him.

Pete was pacing the floors waiting for an update on Meranda's condition when Thor showed up all loud and demanding.

He stopped at the nurses' station, "I'm Meranda Michaels's brother? Which room is she in?"

"She will be in room 2068, down the hall to your left. You can wait there for her there or in the family room. She is down having an MRI. The gentleman in the family room came in with her," the nurse informed him.

Thor walked to the family room to see who this person was, and what information he had about his sister. "Hello, are you the guy that brought my sister in?" Thor looked accusingly at Pete.

Pete extended his hand, "Hi, I'm Pete Moss, Meranda's boss, and yes I came in with her."

"What the hell happened?" Thor did not shake Pete's hand.

Pete withdrew his hand, "She was not answering the radio out in the field, so I went to check if she was okay. A storm blew in and she must have hit her head." Pete thought that sounded reasonable.

"Well she has family here now, so feel free to take off." Thor didn't care for some guy hanging around his sister.

"If you don't mind I would like to make sure she's alright first." Pete said stiffly. Who did this punk think he was. Did he care what was going on with his sister while he was out running around the country side?

"Suit yourself, but keep your distance." Thor was hardened and suspicious of everyone, not the same boy who had left the farm years ago.

"Not a problem." Pete felt it would be best if he put some distance between him and her brother before he felt the need to put him in his place.

After sitting at opposite sides of the waiting room the doctor came in and looked at Pete, after all, he was the one who brought her in. "Miss Micheals is going to be fine, but she has a head injury. We won't know to what degree it has affected her until she wakes up, and we can do more tests.

Thor jumped up and stood in front of Pete, "I'm Meranda's brother."

"Are you Pete?" asked the doctor.

"No--I am Thor Michaels. Thor looked puzzled.

Pete stepped out from around her brother, "I'm Pete, sir."

"Pete was who she kept asking for." The doctor just looked at the two men and raised his bushy eyebrows up and down and shrugged his shoulders.

"Well I am her next of kin, so I would appreciate it if you talked to me." Thor rudely stated.

"She will be transported back up to her room shortly." The doctor turned and walked away. Whatever was going on between those two men was no concern of his.

Pete stayed in the waiting room and Thor went to sit in his sister's room. Despite his hard demeanor, his eyes welled up with tears when he saw his baby sister with her head bandaged up. He pulled up a chair and sat there feeling bad, especially about not staying in contact with her for the past few years.

It wasn't long before Jena showed up and sat with Thor, hoping her best friend would wake up and be okay. Pete kept his distance, but walked by her room a few times prompting Jena to get up and talk to him.

"Hi, are you Pete?" Jena had a feeling that that's who he was, from Meranda's description of him.

"Yes, and you must be Jena?" Pete broke into one of his dazzling smiles. He felt like he knew Jena through Meranda's stories.

"Thank goodness—we didn't think either of you survived the storm. The receptionist at your office had called the police after you and Meranda hadn't come back after that storm had hit. They gave up searching and said it was probable that no one survived."

Jena hadn't known the how's or what's of Meranda's job other than it was somewhere in the middle of the lake. She had tortured herself going over and over their last conversation. Jena's lip began to tremble and she looked up at Pete eyes brimming with tears pleading for an explanation of how her best friend in the world could let her think she was dead.

Pete put his hand on Jena's shoulder to comfort her telling her over and over that Meranda was going to be okay. Jena was so relieved that she wrapped her arms around Pete's waist and gave him a hug. She couldn't find the words for how thankful she was that he had saved her best friend, her sister.

"I'm so sorry the communication was incomplete." Pete didn't know what to say, but he had to come up with some explanation that made sense.

"Our boat did go down, but we were able to inflate the raft. We were pushed into a cove on one of the remote islands." Pete was surprise at himself on how the story just started to flow out of him. "It took us a week to get back to the lab, but we did radio the police department and talk to them. Meranda had radioed ship to shore to your house and left a message that she was fine and would see you in a few months."

Jena accepted the explanation and knew that if Ma Poleski had got to the message first, she very well may have forgotten to pass it along. "I guess all that matters is she is alive. Thank you for bringing her home."

"Again Jena, I'm so sorry for the failed communications. After Meranda was settled at the lab, I went on to Norway." Pete knew he should just end the story and leave it at that. He succeeded in merging Meranda back into her human life.

There was no improvement with Meranda that night, or the next day and Jena had to get home to the baby. Thor on the other hand, sat by his sister's side day after day for the next week. Pete had went back to work, but called the nurses desk daily for updates. The doctors said that when the swelling in her brain went down chances were good that she'd wake up. All her other vitals were normal and she had brain activity, so it was just going to take time.

Loretta Rose Didrikson

23

Meranda's eyes popped open, her eyes stretched wide with fear. Pain sliced through her head and she immediately covered her eyes. She blinked repeatedly allowing small amounts of light in before trying to open her eyes again and when she opened them it was only a crack and peeked out through her lashes. She was not use to bright lights, any natural light for that matter.

Meranda slowly took in the room. This isn't the cave. It's a hospital. There was a man sleeping in the chair by the window, "Dad?"

Thor jumped up from the chair he had occupied for the past week, "It's Thor, Rand." Meranda just looked at him as if she didn't know who he was. It had been so long since she had seen him that it took a minute for it to register that it was her brother. When he had left the farm, he was a boy with peach fuzz above his lip.

"Thor?" Meranda's head felt scrambled and not just from the concussion.

"I'm here sis; I've been here all week." The tears in Thor's eyes returned.

"Where am I? Where's Pete and Sal?" Meranda didn't know how she had gotten here, on land.

"I don't know where that Pete guy is, and I don't know who Sal is either. You had an accident on that lab you were on." Thor didn't understand anything about his sister's life.

"Where am I?" Meranda asked again.

"You're at St. Mary's hospital. You've been unconscious for a week. You have a head injury. I'm going to go get the doctor." Thor ran out of the room yelling for a nurse, or somebody.

Meranda realized that this was not the reoccurring dream she had about the night her and Mitch were in that fatal car accident. Pain gripped her heart as she remembered her dad was gone now too, and the tears started to roll down her face. She couldn't deal with this right now. She wanted to go back to the caves.

When the nurse came in, Meranda was curled up in a fetal position and had the covers over her head. "You're going to be okay honey. I do need to pull your arm out and get a blood pressure reading."

The doctor came soon after and he asked her to follow the light he was flashing in her eyes. He performed a few more tests and asked her a bunch of questions before they all left her alone. He said he would order her something to help with the headache.

Her nerves felt jumpy from all the noise, the television was loud, the nurses' station was beeping, and people were coming and going. She could hear the cars outside, and phones ringing, every sound echoed through her nervous system. Meranda sank back into the pillow and closed her eyes.

She was above the water. She did not want to be here. She liked the quiet life under the water. Meranda tried to remember how she got here and where everyone else was.

She asked the nurse to shut off the television and turn off the lights. Instantly, she felt more relaxed, "Is there anyone one else here?"

"No sweetie, the man that brought you in stayed here until your brother—'showed up.' He's been calling every day inquiring how you are." The nurse must be talking about Pete.

"I need to make a phone call, but I don't have the number…wait I know the number, 555-SAVE. Is there a phone I could use?" Meranda asked. The nurse pushed the table over to her bed with the phone on it. She fumbled, hitting the wrong numbers and it made she became frustrated and felt like throwing the phone across the room. The nurse asked if she would like her to dial the number, "Yes, please."

Everything sounded foreign to her as the phone rang, "Environmental Protection Agency, how may I direct your call?"

"Is Pete Moss there?" Meranda's words seemed hard pressed to find their way out of her mouth.

"May I ask whose calling?" Chloe's high pitched voice was unmistakable.

"Meranda Michaels." She replied.

"Just one moment," Chloe had specific instructions from Pete that if anyone from the hospital called she was to put them through immediately.

"Meranda, how are you? You're awake." Pete was at a loss for words and stated the obvious. He knew he would have some explaining to do to help her integrate back into her life.

Meranda's mind flashed with everything and everyone who had been a part of her life for the last three months. She asked where Sal and Zane were and wondered if they were here at the hospital too.

"I'm sorry Meranda; I don't know who you are talking about." Pete became quiet. He hated this. Every lie assaulted his heart. He was doing this for her, because he loved her.

"Pete, you know who I mean. Where is everyone? Is everyone okay? Did they survive the storm?" Meranda's brother went to find the doctor again, she wasn't talking right.

Pete continued to reassure Meranda of the events that happened and kept insisting he didn't know who Zane and Sal were. "You hit your head, Meranda, I'm sure things are confusing right now. Is your brother still there?" Pete tried to change the subject because he didn't know what else to say to her.

"Pete, you know---the pod, the guardians of the lake, your father, and Roselyn?" Meranda's whispered her frustration into the receiver. Her emotions were all over the place and she felt a flood of tears welling up behind her closed eyelids. Why was Pete acting like he didn't know who she was talking about. She would never tell anyone about the Merfolks. Didn't he know that?

Thor walked in the room and seeing how upset his sister was getting took the phone from her, "Look boss man or whoever you are, you're upsetting my sister so this conversation is over." Thor slammed the phone down.

Meranda squeezed her eyes shut forcing the rest of the tears streaming down her face. "Dad's gone." The pain stabbed through her heart.

"I know, sis. Andy got a hold of me. I came as soon as I could get some money together." Thor looked down at his feet feeling the weight of not righting things with his father. "I'm sorry I wasn't here for you and that I missed his funeral. I'm staying at the farm and don't plan on leaving."

Meranda couldn't do this right now; listen to her brother's excuses. "Please stop."

"I'll let you get some rest, but I will be down the hall if you need me. I'm not going anywhere. I love you sis." Thor went to sit in the family room hoping his sister would calm down.

Pete had to go see her in person, she sounded so distraught. Maybe if she saw him she would…what, be all better. Pete wasn't sure how he thought he could help her. He had to see her awake to remove the last image he had of her lifeless body.

Meranda laid on her side facing the window as her eyes began to adjust to the light. She was now able to stare out the window. She had asked for sunglasses to help with the horrible headache she had and they offered to shut the window shades, but she declined. She wanted to see the beautiful blue sky…and the sun. She had missed the sun.

She began doubting herself. Had she dreamt all those people up? The whole mermaid world…it seemed so real. She knew these people. She pulled lamprey off of Zane, and helped cure Salmonia. It did seem farfetched.

Thor peered into her room and could see the torment on his sister's face. He slowly approached her bed, "Blue will be so happy to see you. Rand…he misses you. I miss you." Thor's hardened face had softened, making him look more like the brother she remembered and not the hardened man she first saw when she had first opened her eyes.

"I missed you too," was all Meranda could say before her head started spinning and she felt like she was going to puke. She just wanted to go back to sleep and see everybody, if this had truly been a dream. Whenever she wanted to see Mitch she would find him in her dreams.

Pete had stopped by, but she had been sleeping. He had kissed her lightly on her forehead and left leaving her a note for her to call him when she felt better.

After a few more days of observations they released Meranda from the hospital. She stopped trying to make sense of her apparent dream about the guardians of the lake and tried to stay in the present. A smile crossed her face as her and her brother turned up the driveway and she saluted the pine soldiers that lined each side of the road, welcoming her home.

She could hear her dog, Blue, barking up a storm when he heard dad's truck. It felt good to be home, her world made more sense here. She still felt confused, but was starting to accept the fact that Zane, Sal, Roselyn, and Prince Pete were the guardians of her beloved Lake Superior, was all a dream. Merfolks—really, Meranda.

She still felt the urgency to check on the progress of the removal of the barrels that were dumped in the lake. It was first on her list of things she felt she needed to do.

24

Meranda felt unsettled and her head felt thick like fog, fluorescent green fog like her dream. At night her dreams were filled with giant red eyed lamprey, serpents and toxic barrels. During the next few days she called the Environmental Agency and left numerous messages.

Tired of hearing Chloe's voice, she decided no more phone calls. Either Chloe wasn't giving Pete the messages or he wasn't in the office.

Meranda had made up her mind, she was going to town and talk to Pete face to face. To find out if she still had a job or not, last she knew she was still an employee of the Environmental Protection Agency.

That night she sat down to dinner with her brother and they were getting to know each other as adults. Things still seemed different at the farm without dad there, and she knew it would never be the same. Time would win and she would come to terms with yet another loss in her young life.

She and Thor sat watching American Ninja Warrior when Meranda announce that she was going into town tomorrow, because she needed to see if she still had a job. She wasn't asking her brothers permission, but she still had driving restrictions.

"I'd be happy to take you." Thor frowned looking more like their father as he got older. "What time are we leaving sis?"

"I would like to be there at eight, so be ready to leave by seven." Meranda didn't care about anything at that moment; she just wanted to talk to Pete face to face and straighten out her future.

"Not a problem, I'm going stir crazy around here anyways. I'm not use to all this quiet time. Frankly, I am bored senseless." Thor tried to suck the words back hoping Meranda wouldn't take it wrong. She still seemed so sensitive. Meranda looked over at him and smiled at his discomfort. "I want you to know sis--that I don't care for your boss."

"You don't have to like him, but he is my boss, so you need to mind your manners. If you can't control yourself then you need to wait in the car. Are we clear?" Meranda's tone was loud and clear.

"Yeah, we're clear." Thor didn't like his baby sister calling the shots.

The morning couldn't come fast enough. Meranda had laid awake most of the night thinking about her imaginary family. She finally had fallen asleep just as the alarm went off, at least that's what it felt like. She looked in the mirror and her eyes looked like they were bleeding they were so red.

She woke to the smell of coffee brewing and that always put her in a good mood. Climbing out of her loft she stumbled into the kitchen and there was her big brother cooking breakfast for his little sister. She smiled realizing how much she had really missed him. How lonely she had been and how abandoned she really had felt.

"Yum smells good." Meranda gave him his kudos and decided she had to let the past go.

"Well, I figured we might want to start this day out on the right foot. I'm ready to go when you are." He was excited to go to go to town. He looked quite handsome, clean shaven, shined cowboy boots and a clean shirt. If Meranda didn't know better she would think he was going on a date.

They got to town early and Meranda asked Thor to drop her off at the Lakewalk, she wanted to go for a walk to clear her head. Her brother just shrugged nodding his head yes. He had a few errands to run and would meet her back at the EPA in a couple of hours.

The Lakewalk was a paved path which followed the northern shores of Lake Superior. She was surprised that it was bustling with so many people this early in the morning. People were setting up booths and stands for some event and she wondered what was going on, until she saw a sign, Fall Fest.

It smelled like it was going to be a beautiful day. The lake was shimmering and calm and heavy dew hung on the vibrant colored leaves. She looked up at the hillside and fall had painted the backdrop of this port city with yellows and oranges, and splashes of red. It was breathtaking.

Meranda had walked quite a ways smiling at and wishing people good morning. Her eyes scanned ahead at all the people when she saw a head of bouncing brown ringlets amongst the onslaught of bobbing heads. Her heart quickened, and before she could stop herself she yelled, "Roselyn!"

In surprise, the girl turned and frightfully looked over her shoulder before she was whisked further down the lake walk by the crowd of people behind her. Meranda sucked in her breath, as a flood of memories poured into her head.

Her heart knew this young mermaid and she had befriended her whether it was in a "manifested dream world" or not. Meranda tried to plow forward toward the girl, but she could no longer see her in a sea of humans.

She stormed back to the EPA to question Mr. Moss again. Breathless she pushed the heavy doors opened so hard they slammed against the wall making quite an entrance. She marched down the hall, despite Chloe's protests to Pete's office.

His office doors were already open saving her the effort of bursting through another set of doors. As she entered his office, there sitting in a chair opposite of Pete was a flaming red head. "Salmonia" Meranda gasped.

The woman turned around and looked at Meranda, but the moment she had started to turn her head, Meranda knew she had mistaken her for her" imaginary" friend. The woman was commonly and older, nor did she posse that almost translucent coloring that Sal had. "I'm sorry—I didn't mean to interrupt."

"I will be with you in a moment Miss Michaels." Pete replied looking pained.

Meranda pushed past Chloe as they passed in the hallway. She felt she was losing her mind, but her heart was telling her different. Her heart wouldn't lie to her. It couldn't have all been a dream, it was all too real, too vivid.

Meranda decided not to wait for Pete, so that he could continue telling her that he didn't know what she was talking about. She walked out the door and toward the lake. She felt the warm southern winds blowing on her face and mindlessly walked to a place where she could find some solitude, on the shores of her beloved lake.

She settled down amongst the rocks listening to the waves gently tap at the shores, then buried her head in her knees and cried. Her dream world seemed so real. It felt real. Mermaids were only a legend, they aren't real. Meranda would keep telling herself that over and over until her heart believed it.

Pete rushed to the lobby where he thought Meranda was waiting. He didn't see her anywhere, but knew where she most likely had headed for, the lake. He all but ran out the door.

"Meranda, there you are. Why didn't you wait?" Pete jockeyed his way down to her jumping from rock to rock.

"Why—so you could tell me how my concussion made me dream a dream so real that I don't know what reality is anymore. No thank you Mr. Moss." Meranda wiped the remaining tears away with the back of her hand, not caring if Pete saw that she had been crying.

"Meranda--I wish I could help you come to terms with your feelings, but I don't know how to help you." Pete came and sat by her side.

"I saw a girl on the lake walk that fit the description of Roselyn, and when I yelled her name, I could have sworn she turned around." Meranda buried her head again. "Then when I went into your office and saw the woman with red hair, the same color as Sal's. You know the mermaid in my dream world, my friend." Meranda voice was breaking up with hiccups of anger bursting through.

Pete just looked out over the lake not knowing what to say.

The lake worked its magic and she became calmer as the waves lightly pushed ashore wetting the tips of her shoes. Meranda stood up having nothing left to say to Pete and started to walk back to the EPA where she was to meet her brother. Pete quietly followed.

When she walked into the building, there was her brother leaned up against the information desk talking with Chloe, who was blushing and making giggling sounds. Meranda rolled her eyes and told her brother she would be ready in a few minutes. He nodded at his sister grabbing a piece of paper and asked Chloe for her number.

Meranda was more in control of her emotions and she turned to Pete, "There is something you could do for me."

"Anything," Pete was more than eager to finally fulfill one of her requests.

"Could you drive me up the shore? I could really use the ride." Meranda's eyes pleaded for a yes.

"Not a problem. Give me a minute to clear my schedule and I will be ready to go." Pete headed to his office. Meranda informed her brother that she would be back later.

Of course, he protested that she should not go anywhere with Mr. Boss man, but he didn't mind hanging around until she got back and that he had his phone if she needed him.

Silently, they got into Pete's hummer, only this time Meranda took control of the music and put on some Bruce Springsteen, turning it up to drowned out her thoughts. She was in no mood to talk and stared out the window.

Pete tried to break the silence, "Are we driving anywhere in particular or just heading to the Canadian border?"

Meranda looked over at him letting him know that his comment was not well received. "If you wouldn't mind I'd like to go to Split Rock." It was one of her favorite places to go to. She had gone up there for picnics when she was little when both her parents were still alive.

From the steep cliff that the lighthouse sat on you couldn't see land, only the horizon where blue sky met the darker blue lake. "That is…" Meranda eyes had darkened, "…if you don't mind." Pete got the message that she was not asking a question.

"Nope, that's fine with me. It's a great place. I haven't been there in a long time myself. If you're hungry we could stop at that café?" Pete was trying hard to get back to a place where there wasn't so much pain and tension.

"No thanks, maybe later." Meranda turned and stared out the window again.

When they pulled into the parking lot they both got out of the truck; they hadn't spoken a single word during the last five miles. Pete followed Meranda's lead which led them to the light house.

She ducked around the orange construction fence and proceeding toward the cliff. Pete was beginning to get nervous, because she walked like she was on a mission, and she wasn't in the best frame of mind. It was a rugged mountain of rocks.

She finally came to a stop and sat down with her legs crossed dangerously close to the edge of the cliff. Pete released his breath and sat next to her and remained quiet. They sat there for a long time and when the sun departed behind the trees, she could feel the last rays of the day hitting her back.

The wind off the lake kicked up and Meranda felt a shiver climb up her spine. She stood up---and jumped off the cliff.

Pete could not believe what just happened as he watched Meranda's body quickly disappear. He franticly looked around as if someone should come running up to help. No one came.

Pete dove over the cliff after her, praying she would survive hitting the water from that height.

Meranda positioned her arms above her head to part the water and on impact felt the icy waters embrace her. She didn't know how deep she would go down, but took the biggest breath of air her lungs would hold.

The cold fresh water seemed to offer peace and clear her mind. She didn't care if her thoughts were a dream or reality or whether she was going insane from all the losses she had suffered. She would be alright in the afterlife with her Mom and Dad, and Mitch, if that was her destiny.

For a moment she felt bad about leaving her brother, but it was too late to change her mind; her fate was sealed.

The bubbles began to escape from her mouth---then she felt something grab her from behind, and before she could protest something sticky was clinging to her face.

It was Pete. He was here in the water. Her hands reached down and she felt scales, he had a tail. In the next moment she was being torpedoed toward the surface as she buried her head into Pete's bare muscled chest. She smiled. She knew it. Her heart would never lie to her.

With a flick of Pete's tail he landed them on the large boulders that formed this part of the shoreline. Before Meranda could catch her breath, he was yelling at her, "Have you lost your mind? Were you trying to kill yourself?" Pete's eyes were stormier than Meranda had ever thought possible, but she couldn't wipe the smile off her face.

She reached up trying to take the film from her face and Pete leaned over and helped her. "I knew it wasn't a dream. Why did you lie to me? I would never have told anyone! I thought you knew me. I thought you trusted me." Meranda's smile was replaced by eyes filled with anger and pain.

"I did. I mean--I do. I just wanted you to have the chance you deserve at a normal life. I saw the opportunity to give that to you--for everything you have done for us." Pete looked away because he could not stand the way she was looking at him, like he had squeezed the last bit of life from her heart.

Meranda looked up at the steep cliff and wondered how they were going to climb up it. It was getting dark. She hadn't thought her plan through, at least past the part of forcing her hand and making Pete man up and tell her the truth.

"If we are going to get out of here, I'm going to have to transform and I didn't *dress* for the occasion." Pete was past the point of remaining calm with this new complication. "Another words, I don't have any clothes to put on."

"Well it seems like you need me again." Meranda said feeling empowered.

"It seems I do need you again." Pete transformed right then and there and stood before her in all his nakedness. His eyes daring her to look away, but she didn't. He pulled himself up onto the large rock they needed to climb over just to get to the cliff. He reached down to grab her hand as she walked up to his level.

It was now dark enough that Meranda could only see his outline. The sliver of moon that rose in the sky, stood alone, with only a few stars to light the way.

In truth, she needed him. His night vision and strength was what would get them out of the predicament she had got them into. Once they had reached the top of the cliff, Pete stayed in the tree line while Meranda went to the hummer for his clothes. The smile returned to her face.

The visual of Pete's beautifully sculpted body streamed through her mind stirring a part of her she thought she had buried with Mitch. She watched the moon glimmer off the contours of his muscles as they moved in unison pulling her up the cliff.

The lighthouse had been constructed in 1905 after 29 ships had been lost to one of the worst storms recorded on Lake Superior. It was not made for rock climbing and had it not been for Pete's superhuman strength they would have never made it up the 130 foot cliff that the lighthouse was perched on.

Pete waited in the darkened shadows thankful for the moonless night. Meranda stumbled her way back with his clothes and a flashlight. She couldn't remember exactly where she had left him and quietly whispered, "Pete. Pete—where are you?"

Pete purposely remained quiet until Meranda had past him before stepping out behind her. "I'm right here."

Every muscle in Meranda's body reacted as she almost flung herself off the cliff again. Startled she eyed him from head to toe. He was beautiful. "You scared me have to death, Pete." She was glad it was dark and hoped he couldn't see the many shades of red she knew she was sporting. She handed him his clothes. "I'll wait over there.

"Why, it's nothing you haven't seen before." Now it was Pete's turn to wear a smile.

Meranda didn't reply, and fought to keep her eyes above his waist. She stomped off in the direction of the hummer with flashlight in hand and climbed in the passenger's seat. Her mind was full of all the things she had been told was a dream, her life amongst the guardian's. The questions started to pour into her mind.

By the time Pete reached the truck, she barely waited for him to get in before firing off the first round of questions. "How is Sal doing? How are Roselyn and LaTrice? Did Sal's tail grow back? Has your father left for the homeland? Why did you lie to me?" With that last question she became quiet.

"Sal is doing okay, and no her tail has not grown back. She is furious with me that she never got to say goodbye. Roselyn is still very upset you are gone and that she never got to say goodbye either.

However, she and LaTrice have become best friends. The girl is recovering both physically and mentally. She is rather fascinated with the whole Merfolk thing.

Apparently her life on land wasn't so great which was the reason she was out on the ship with her mom in the first place. She has no other family...and no, my father has not yet departed." Pete hoped that was enough information for her, but he knew he wasn't going to get off that easy.

"Why did you lie to me? You made me feel like I was going crazy. My heart ached for my new family." Meranda's voice dropped off.

"I thought that you would want a second chance at your human life on land. I wanted you to have that chance. It was not an easy decision Meranda." Pete still believed he made the right choice and it almost worked until she pulled that sky diving stunt without a parachute or a life jacket.

"You should have asked me. It was my decision, not yours. That's why you were so distracted before we left for Isle Royale that day wasn't it?" Meranda emotions were raw.

"No, only Zane, and he didn't agree. He just respected my decision." Pete took full responsibility for his choices. They rode the rest of the way back in silence. This surprised Pete somewhat and would have liked it better if she talked, at least he would know what she was thinking.

"Are you hungry?" Pete tried to engage her in superficial conversation.

"No, I want to get back; my brother is probably worried about me." Meranda's voice was soft.

"Look Meranda---I'm sorry. I thought I was doing the right thing by you. Please forgive me." Pete pleaded.

"I get it. I understand what you're saying, but it is going to take some time for my heart to forgive you. I have lost almost everyone I have ever cared about and you made me lose the family I had grown to love." Meranda was trying to process the truth she had unveiled, but she was drained.

"So--am I ever going to see anyone again—Sal or Roselyn? Meranda looked over at Pete pleadingly, but he had no answer for her.

"Why don't we talk about everything in the morning? I never imagined things turning out this way and I don't know what to say or do." Pete had never felt so confused.

Between his heart breaking over the painful decision to let her go to now realizing how badly he had broken her heart. "Meranda, I'm sorry. I made a bad call. You don't deserve this. I just thought...." He didn't even want to hear himself say the meaningless words again, that it was for her wellbeing and happiness. "Here we are and there is your brother not looking very happy. Can I call you tomorrow?"

"I will call you. I need some time." Meranda got out of the hummer and without another word got in her dad's truck.

Immediately her brother was lecturing her about how worried he was and why didn't she answer her phone. Meranda just quietly reminded him of all the years she didn't know if he was dead or alive. Not that worrying him was a payback or her intent, but she wasn't in the mood to listen to him scold her either.

Pete watched as they drove away and his heart ached at the pain he had caused her. It was never his intention. He got in his hummer and headed home to the Knife River marina. He had lost Freya, his boat in the storm, but had replaced her with another boat. He had not named this one yet, but she still offered him comfort.

He parked and headed toward his boat. His posture slumped with exhaustion and defeat when he received a telepathic message from Sal. *"Brother, Roselyn is missing. LaTrice says she went to find Meranda. It appears that LaTrice has been drawing her pictures of the world above. I'm coming ashore--meet me at the marina."*

Pete thought back to what Meranda had said this morning, and that she thought she had seen Roselyn. *"I'm at the marina now."* He wondered where Roselyn could be, and how she must be terrified. Pete immediately started sending out signals for Roselyn to respond to.

He knew he owed Meranda an apology and even thou she had asked for time, he had to let her know, she had seen Roselyn.

"Hello?" Meranda sounded sleepy.

"Meranda—it's me Pete."

"Pete I told you I would call you." Meranda voice immediately amped up with anger.

"I know, but Roselyn is missing. LaTrice told Sal that she came to find you. I think it was her you saw yesterday." Pete sounded frantic.

Meranda snapped awake, "I'll be down in an hour I'm leaving right now." Meranda hung up the phone before Pete could say anything else; she was not going to sit there.

Luckily, her brother wasn't home yet, because she wasn't in the mood to try to explain why she was leaving in the middle of the night, not that she could anyhow. The doctor hadn't released her to drive, but she felt fine. "Come on Blue let's go for a ride." Blue was old and couldn't hear or see anymore, but he could smell.

Meranda wrote her brother a note and left.

The fifty miles to Duluth seemed to take forever. As she neared the lake she realized she hadn't asked Pete where he would be. So she pulled into the EPA's parking lot under the street light. She got out to stretch her legs and helped Blue out of the car so he could take care of his business when he started to growl.

Meranda looked up to see Pete and Sal stepping out of the shadows. Meranda's eyes filled with tears and her heart felt like the death grip released as she ran toward Salmonia.

Sal usually reserved, opened her arms to receive her friend. Pete knew at that moment, the decision he made for Meranda was wrong. "Look at you—you're on land."

As she released Sal from her bear hug, she saw the fear for her daughter in her eyes. "We will find her Sal." Meranda said so confidently, that Salmonia believed her. She was too afraid not to. "I brought Blue; he is a good hunting dog and can help." Blue started to relax and wagged his tail. Any friend of Meranda's was a friend of his. Pete reached down and gave Blue a few scratches behind the ears.

"Do you have anything of Rosie's with you?" Meranda hoped Sal had something to help Blue take in her scent.

"I do. I brought some clothes in case she didn't dress warm enough." Sal handed the backpack to Meranda with trembling hands.

Meranda opened the pack and let Blue smell the contents. When he seemed satisfied he laid down. This had been quite a journey for the old boy. "Blue, find our Rosie."

"I thought I saw her yesterday down on the lakewalk, so I suggest we start there." The three of them jumped in the hummer helping Blue in, and headed to the lakewalk.

Pete and Sal sent telepathic messages out and Meranda quietly yelled for Roselyn. They had walked approximately a mile when they came to the Rose Garden. Blue began barking his hoarse old dog bark and took off toward Leif Erickson Park on the far side of the garden.

At the edge of the park was a statue of Leif Erickson himself, and down below was an old Viking ship that had been in restoration for the past forty years. Sadly, the city never came up with the funds to finish the relic.

Blue was going wild jumping up and down as if he was trying to get in the boat. Meranda quietly said, "Rosie, honey. It's me Meranda. If you're in there please come out." She heard a stirring, but no reply.

Sal jumped in, "Baby its mom. Please say something that you're okay. You're not in any trouble---I just want you safe." Sal could not hold her tears in any longer and sank to her knees letting out a gut retching cry. One Meranda will remember forever.

"I'm okay momma. Please don't cry." Roselyn's voice was shaky, but music to their ears.

Pete had already jumped up onto the unstable boat and saw Roselyn through some cracked boards. "Grab my hand, but be careful the boards are jagged."

Roselyn reached up and Pete lifted her out of the rotting Viking ship. When he got her close, his emotions let loose and he hugged her tightly before lifting her down to her mother's waiting embrace.

Pete then went over to Meranda and quietly spoke in her ear, "Thank you again, and please forgive me. I was wrong not to trust your judgement on whether you should stay above or below the surface."

Meranda turned and gave him a hug. There is nothing like a happy ending to put things in perspective. And she whispered back, "I forgive you."

Once Sal and Rosie started to stand up from the grass, Meranda barreled over to them both and went in for a group hug. Then turning to Roselyn she wiped away the tears on her face while pulling her hair in a make shift pony tail, so she could gaze at her beautiful face. A face she thought she would never see again.

Roselyn started to apologize with explanation, "I'm sorry I worried all of you, I just had to find Meranda. I never got to say goodbye." Roselyn barely got the words out before the mermaid tears welled up in her eyes and she cried her young heart out.

Salmonia had felt the same way as she looked at Pete with an accusing look, as if this was his entirely his fault. With the truth out everyone was more relaxed. Salmonia started a tearful apology to Meranda in that she didn't know what Pete's plan was, and she too never got to say goodbye.

Pete stood in the background looking guilty. Meranda deserved better than being deceived like that and he knew now it was never his choice to make, but hers. Pete still felt confused on how wanting her to live a normal life was so wrong.

"Is anyone hungry? There's a restaurant down the road?" Pete was desperate to change the scenery of dirty looks that were being sent in his direction.

The three women all nodded *yes* in unison. "Then Roselyn and I will be heading back home."

"But Mama, can't Meranda show me around since we are up here?" Roselyn tried to plead her case with her mom.

"No."

"Mama, please."

"No. I will not reward you for endangering yourself and the pod. We will be going back tonight. Your father is waiting for us." Sal had already sent Zane a message that they had found her.

Roselyn was extremely disappointed, but knew better to push the issue any farther. They headed to an all-night diner to have something to eat. Roselyn's eyes glistened as she scanned everything she saw recording it to memory. Some day when she was grown she would come back up here like Pete.

After dinner, Sal and Roselyn headed toward the lake leaving Pete and Meranda in awkward silence, neither of them had spoken to each other over dinner. "I don't know what to say, except that I'm sorry. I now know that I made a huge mistake." Pete couldn't take the silence any longer.

"I wouldn't have ever said anything, not that anyone would've believe me. You didn't have to lie." She looked at him like he had broken her heart.

"I knew that Meranda, I just didn't want you to be torn between two worlds." Pete's eyes focused on the ground at her feet.

"I forgave you, Pete." Meranda knew he thought that in his heart he had made the right decision. "It's going to take me a little while to let it go."

"I understand the damage I did, and I promise I will never lie to you again." With that being said, Pete asked, "So what's next?" Pete had no clue where things should go from here.

"I don't know. I do know that I need to be up here to push for the removal of the barrels. Do I still have a job at the EPA? I mean has anything changed with the grant and data needing to be collected?" Meranda didn't know where things would go from here either. She just felt whole again. Her mind and her heart were on the same page.

"No, nothing has changed and the grant is still available. If you still want the job?" In a way, her knowing the truth made things a lot easier.

"I do, and maybe I can work my findings on the lab into getting the barrels removed faster. I also want you to come and get me and bring me to visit my mer family?" Meranda face was stern, she felt Pete owed her that much for the turmoil he had put her through the past month.

He smiled his million dollar smile and agreed.

"Actually, working on the lab will account for my absence when I come to visit. By the way, what happens with LaTrice going forward?" Meranda asked.

"LaTrice has accepted her new life. In fact, her ceremony into the family will begin in a few days."

"I would like to be there for that." Meranda jumped at a definite date to return to her underwater family.

Pete nodded with resignation. "We will talk about the details tomorrow."

"Oh wait…what do you get a mermaid-to-be for a present?"

Pete laughed endearingly at Meranda's first thought being not of how the process of her inauguration was going to happen, but only that she needed to get her a gift.

"Never mind, I will think of something. I'll have to let my brother know that I will be heading out to the lab for a few weeks."

Meranda's cell phone rang and she knew it was Thor before she answered it. "Hello brother. I'm fine. I just needed some air. I will be home in an hour or so. Bye." He was mad, but Thor also knew Meranda could take care of herself.

"Okay then. I will see you in a couple of days to work out the details."

Pete grabbed Meranda and pulled her in close, and kiss her softly. Meranda wrapped her arms around his neck and kissed him, demanding more.

ABOUT THE AUTHOR

My childhood home sat on the top of Duluth, Minnesota's mountainous terrain. Every thing was downhill leading to Lake Superior. To go down, meant climbing back up, despite the severity of the weather.

The best thing, I looked over the big lake every morning and night, except when it was fogged in. It allowed my imagination to dream and create what could not be seen, below the waters surface.

Mystic Waters was born, from that in which, I could only imagine.

CPSIA information can be obtained at www.ICGtesting.com
Printed in the USA
LVOW07s0257160916

504831LV00007B/221/P